Murder on the Mary Celeste

ISBN 978-0-6480789-4-4

Aenghus Chisholme

Connect with Aenghus Chisholme: www.aenghuschisholme.com

Original Author's version 1.2

Cover by Susan Krupp

Also by Aenghus Chisholme

Merlin the Sorcerer AD 491

Guinevere the Queen AD 494

Sir Gawain and the Green Knight AD499

Arthur the King AD 517

Murder on the Mary Celeste

Jack the Ripper: The Murder of Madam Athalia

The Best Things in Life Begin with the Letter B

This book is dedicated to all those that love a good mystery.

Contents

Chapter 1: New York City 1871

It was a cold day on November the seventh, Captain Benjamin Brigges and his wife Sandra were walking arm in arm through the busy streets of New York City. They had just come from the office of the insurance company that had underwritten the cargo for the latest voyage of Captain Brigges' merchant ship, a brigantine class sail boat named the Mary Celeste. They had been talking about the many tasks still required to be undertaken prior to their voyage when somebody called the Captain's name.

"As I live and breathe if it isn't Captain Benjamin Brigges and his lovely wife Sandra!"

Both of them looked up. It was not uncommon to run across people that they knew here in New York. After all they had been living here for some years now and had made lots of friends and acquaintances. They beheld the person that had claimed them, or rather people. It was as if they were looking in a mirror. Before them stood a man clearly dressed as the Captain of a ship with his wife locked upon his arm. Just as is the case when you see somebody that you know, but outside of the environment that you are accustomed to seeing them in; it took a moment for Benjamin and Sandra to identify the couple. Nevertheless they did; Benjamin putting into words their surprise.

"Captain David Moorebank and *hi*s lovely wife Penelope" he said mimicking his friend's earlier words. Benjamin offered his hand to his old friend. They shook vigorously not believing their luck in finding each other in such a large and crowded city. Penelope and Sandra kissed each other on the cheek affectionately and then in a truly gentlemanly way both Captains took the gloved hands of each other's wives and kissed them respectfully.

"What brings the both of you to New York?" asked Sandra "Have the allures of Boston begun to wane?" It was a question filled with hope that their friends may have tired of life in Boston and were contemplating a move to New York. Penelope answered.

"David is Captaining a vessel from New York harbour mid-month and I have come down to spend time with him whilst the preparations are made. You know what it is like being the wife of a sea-faring Captain Sandra; we must take every opportunity to be with our beloved husbands whilst they are still upon dry land".

"That is splendid news David" exclaimed Benjamin. "I too am Captaining a vessel from the harbour only a few days from now. I want to hear all about yours and tell you all about my fine ship" Benjamin was clearly excited about the news and wanted to hear more.

"She is a Brigantine called the Dei Gratias and we are bound for Genoa carrying petroleum and we set sail on the sixteenth of this month" summarised David. He gave his friend a look as if asking him to give the same one sentence brief.

"She is a Brigantine called the Mary Celeste and we are bound for Venice carrying alcohol; we set sail tomorrow morning" responded Benjamin.

"Splendid!" laughed David. It looked as if he were about to launch into a new tirade of questions when his wife politely interrupted.

"My Dear, we have and appointment to keep and we may already arrive late" Penelope indicated to a clock on the façade of the nearest building to them.

"Indeed" he said now more sombre than before. Sandra offered them all an opportunity to continue their conversations and queries at a later time.

"Dine with us this evening Penelope, David; we shall make a reservation at Claudes for 8pm" It was a timely offer. It would allow their friends to extract themselves politely from the reunion and forestall it for a more convenient time.

"Excellent suggestion darling" complimented Benjamin. Then turning to the invitees, he offered his encouragement.

"Yes, please say that you both dine with us this evening. Do you have any other plans?" David and Penelope looked at each other and shook their heads indicating that they did not have any prior engagements.

"Thank you Sandra" accepted Penelope on behalf of them both. "That would be lovely. I have not seen you since my wedding and we have much catching up to do. And our two Captains clearly have notes to compare on their new mistresses." Penelope almost winked with glee at her jibe that their husbands think of their ships as their other wives.

"Then it is settled. Claudes at eight pm tonight. You know the restaurant? The one on Judith Street facing Stuyvesant Square"

Benjamin wanted to be sure that they were talking about the same place.

"Yes we know it, a fine reputation, fit for ship's Captain and his wife" said David.

"Very droll my good man; on your way then we shall not hold you up any longer. The usual handshakes between the men and hugs between the women followed before they parted company. Looking back Sandra soon lost them in the hustle and bustle of the crowd.

"That was a pleasant surprise" she said.

"Indeed. I am looking forward to dinner already. Now, next I must go and oversee the loading of the cargo." He stated.

"Yes, I will take little Sara to the park to play. She loves to run after the squirrels" said Sandra. There was a look of happiness on her face as she remembered their last visit to the park near to their home. They moved through the crowd with renewed purpose.

***

The docks were a noisy place to be. There was always the sound of shouting as orders were barked to crewmen carrying out various shore-bound duties. Cranes filled the air as did the tall masts of the various ships that were docked. Cargo was strewn around in all shapes and sizes. But it was just the one cargo that Captain Benjamin Brigges had his eyes set upon; the one thousand and seven hundred barrels of alcohol that would be nestled in the lowest area of the ship. He had various papers in his hands. One was the receipt that he had just been given taking ownership of the barrels. He scowled a little and then resumed counting the barrels again. They were stacked in neat cube-like piles of five across and five down and five high. Each grouping of barrels would therefore total one hundred and twenty-five. That would make thirteen full stacks of barrels and one with seventy-five barrels.

It was the smaller pile that he was counting one more time just to make certain that every single one of the barrels was present. Satisfied that he had indeed taken delivery of the correct amount he motioned for his first mate to have the crew begin to load them. This would have to be done one by one as the ships masts and rigging prevented the large crane from loading the cargo to the deck area. Also, the Mary Celeste's deck would not be able to take the weight of the large mound of liquid-filled barrels. It would be safer for them to be done individually. Each barrel was small enough to be lifted by one man. Working together the crew should be able to load them all aboard before the end of the day.

"Be sure to stack and tie-off each group before beginning the next" ordered the Captain. His first mate gave a customary *Aye Aye Sir* and went about ordering the seamen to work. The barrels would fit nicely in the lowest deck of the ship between what was effectively the rib-cage of the hull. That alone would stop them from rolling about, but he was a cautious man which is why he had ordered them tied down as well. The weight would also serve as ballast for the Mary Celeste. Captain Brigges now had time to study the crew and passenger manifest. He held it up. There would only be his wife and two-year-old daughter as passengers aboard, the rest were his crew.

Captain	**Benjamin S. Brigges**	**37**	**American**
First Mate	**Albert G. Richards**	**29**	**American**
Second Mate	**Andrew Gill**	**25**	**Danish**
Steward	**Edward W. Heed**	**22**	**American**
Seaman	**Vaughn Lorensen**	**29**	**German**
Seaman	**Bill Lorensen**	**26**	**German**
Seaman	**Hans Gondeschall**	**23**	**German**
Seaman	**Adrian Martins**	**30**	**German**
Passenger	**Sandra Brigges**	**32**	**American**
Passenger	**Sara Brigges**	**2**	**American**

Captain Brigges noted that two of the men serving were brothers; they were both German, as were Martins and Gondeschall. Gill, the second mate was Danish and the rest were all Americans. He had only served with Albert Richards before. All the other crewmen were unknown to him. No matter, he thought, the Danish and Germans have a good reputation for producing fine seamen. He had been recommended all of the crew by his co-owners in the Mary Celeste. Although he did not have to take any of them on, after all he was the Captain and the decision was his. But the convenience of having a ready-made crew handy just as the paperwork was finalised for the first merchant voyage under his command was too good to pass up.

All going well they would make their maiden voyage, deliver the cargo to the owners in Venice and find a cargo in Italy to carry back to America. This would mean that the two trips would net two very healthy pay-cheques. He looked up at his crew; all had a barrel under arm and were moving in line to the gang-plank leading up to the Mary

Celeste. Producing his pocket watch he opened it just to assure himself that he had plenty of time to finish loading the ship, return home and ready himself for dinner tonight. He nodded with satisfaction that all was going to plan.

Chapter 2: Claude's Restaurant

Both couples had arrived simultaneously at the entrance to the restaurant. They exchanged greetings once again. Ascending the external stairs all entered together as one group. The Maitre d'hotel stood imposingly behind a small desk and smiled when they arrived.

"Good evening ladies and gentlemen. Do you have a reservation?" he said looking expectantly at either of the gentlemen.

"Brigges" replied Benjamin. The head waiter looked at his list finding the entry made earlier that day.

"Yes, here it is. Four people" he confirmed. He clapped his hands and two attendants hurried forward to relieve the foursome of their overcoats, and the men of their hats. Satisfied that the party was now ready to be seated the Maitre d'hotel said

"Please follow me."

The restaurant was very elegant, full of tastefully sized and placed chandeliers hanging from the high ornate ceiling. The large room was full of evenly placed tables and chairs. The chairs were finely crafted and tables sat beneath thick white perfectly pressed tablecloths. Candles were placed at the centre of each table, making the silver wear glimmer in the flickering light. The head waiter led them to a table near a large window laden with heavy looking curtains. It offered a view over the small green square to the front of the brownstone building.

Settling into place the group resumed their conversation from the morning. David spoke first.

"Tell me everything about this ship of yours, what was it? The Mary Celeste?" It was an invitation to good to refuse; a captive audience to tell his story too. Benjamin breathed in and out and put his thoughts together. Penelope and David leant forward in anticipation.

"I contemplated giving up life on the sea for a time" he began. This raised eyebrows. "There was a plan to open up a hardware store with my brother. But seeing how hard such a life can be, my father was a retailer with a small store; put an end to that idea. Instead I found a way to be with my beloved and still Captain a ship. I searched for a ship to take an interest in and found a group of astute business men that needed a captain for their latest purchase and were amenable to allowing me to buy a share of it. I own ten percent of the Mary Celeste. It has been extensively reworked since the new owners took possession. I was able to offer input and have the Captain's cabin enlarged so as to offer more space and comfort for myself and my beautiful wife and daughter." He allowed the news to sink in. Both David and Penelope were astounded.

"You will be taking Sandra and Sara with you on your voyages!?" Penelope was amazed.

"Yes, isn't it wonderful" exclaimed Sandra "I no longer have to feel abandoned for months at a time whilst Benjamin is at sea. We can remain together as a family whilst Benjamin indulges his love of the sea and earns our living." Sandra knew that the news may be hard to take for a stoically traditional couple like their friends. She watched them carefully hoping that the idea was not too radical for them to accept.

David and Penelope looked at each other to try and ascertain what the other thought of the progressive lifestyle that their friends were implementing. Turning back to their friends David spoke on behalf of the both of them.

"We think that is a brilliant idea Benjamin, Sandra. Good luck to you both." He smiled broadly. There was absolutely no sign that this was a polite masquerade of disapproval. Sandra was relieved.

"I knew that the two of you would understand. When, in time, you have children of your own Penelope, you will want to have your husband by your side and not an ocean away." This made Penelope blush slightly. It had only been a year since their wedding but thoughts of starting a family were high on David and Penelope's agenda.

Conversation was interrupted by the waiter that would serve them for the evening introducing himself and handing out the menus. Whilst he did so he spoke of how their wine-list was the envy of all of the other restaurants in the area and that if they were to choose a red wine then it would simply have to be the Bordeaux that had recently arrived from their supplier in France, it was sublime. But of course to start with they would have a bottle of champagne surely? The diners agreed and the waiter flitted away to fetch the bottle whilst the group studied the contents of the menu.

Whilst decisions were made Benjamin made use of the time to inquire about David's circumstances.

"Now David; your turn, tell us of the Dei Gratias." David had settled upon his choice of food by this time so he was more than happy to tell his friends all about how he came to Captain this particular vessel.

"It is a very similar story to yours Benjamin. I own a fifteen percent stake in the Dei Gratias, the rest is owned by a wealthy businessman from Boston. The cargo of petroleum is from his company that has struck oil in one of his many land holding. It will be sold in Genoa. As I said this morning, we leave on the sixteenth of this month."

"That is an incredible coincidence" responded Benjamin. "Our course across the Atlantic takes us to the Azores and then Genoa before our final port of Venice."

"Where in the Azores? We will make port at Sao Miguel before continuing to Genoa" asked David.

"We shall dock at Villa do Porto on Santa Maria before proceeding to Genoa and then Venice. If we are in port together at Genoa we must meet up again" offered Benjamin. It was not out of the question, an eight day head-start did not necessarily mean that the Mary Celeste would arrive at Genoa eight days ahead of the Dei Gratias. Weather, wind and currents may well conspire to make it a real possibility of docking more closely together.

"Then that it what we shall do" affirmed Sandra "if we are in port at the same time in Genoa we will find the Italian equivalent to Claude's and dine together again." Realising that Penelope would be absent Sandra quickly added.

"You shall be with us in Spirit Penelope. I shall write and tell you everything that we speak of over dinner" she smiled hoping that her condolence would be accepted; it was. Penelope was about to put into words her approval of the Genoa dinner plans when the waiter returned to the table carrying a bottle of Louise Pommery Champagne. He went through the usual ceremony of popping the cork and carefully pouring the sparkling wine into the cut crystal glasses. Then he insisted upon telling them all about the chef's most popular dishes. He was very animated and made each of the starters and main courses sound as if it simply had to be chosen. Decisions were made and their orders taken.

"Very good" he said before retreating to see to their wishes.

***

Dinner had proceeded splendidly. The food was as succulent and tasty as the waiter had described. The reputation of the restaurant was well-earned. Dinner conversation had covered detail about the Dei Gratias and the Mary Celeste and the crew manning each. Then it had turned to the wedding of David and Penelope around a year ago, and what had happened in the interim. It appeared that David and Penelope were very happy living in Boston and had no plans to leave. The fact that the Dei Gratias was based in New York was the only sore point. David was going to try and influence his majority owner to run the Dei Gratias out of Boston so that he did not have to make the journey from Boston to New York and back again between voyages.

At the point where the mains were almost finished Penelope asked where the couple had come from when they encountered each other earlier in the day.

"The insurance company that is underwriting the policy for the ship and the cargo" said Sandra. "It was such a high premium" she complained "because the alcohol is flammable, how ridiculous! Nevertheless it is better to be insured than not. We have too much to lose if this maiden voyage does not go as planned" then contemplating her words, added.

"It is a strange thing, that should we lose the entire cargo and ship but somehow escape with our lives, the insurance payment would be worth more to us than three years of freighting cargo back and forth across the Atlantic. Isn't it funny how insurance works?" her rhetorical question raised a small laugh from the diners.

"Let us pray for a safe journey for both of our vessels then" offered David. He raised a glass of wine and proposed a toast.

"Here is to none of us collecting on our overpriced insurance policies" it was a comical toast that they all delighted in by clanking their glasses together to acknowledge it.

Benjamin called an end to the evening.

"We sail at noon tomorrow, so it is best that Sandra and I get a good night's sleep". The usual platitudes were exchanged wishing each other a safe voyage; or in Penelope's case a safe journey back to Boston. The bill was ordered and paid and after the diners had had their coats and hats returned and left the premises they farewelled each other one more time, outside at the base of the stairs leading into Claude's restaurant.

"Let us hope that fortune favours us both and that we see you again in Genoa David" said Sandra underlining their plans to meet up should they be there at the same time.

"Indeed dear lady" he said in a very gentlemanly way. He kissed her gloved hand and they completed their goodbyes. David and Penelope headed off in a different direction to Benjamin and Sandra, but for some reason Sandra stopped and turned around to watch them depart. Thinking this unusual behaviour Benjamin queried his wife's action.

"What is it Sandra; have you forgotten to say something important?" at first it was if Sandra hadn't even heard him but then she shook her head as if to clear her mind of a fog. She looked at him and said

"It is the strangest thing Benjamin; but I feel as if we are never going to see them again." As if hearing her own words had somehow brought to light how ridiculous her suggestion was she admonished herself.

"Silly really; I am sorry Benjamin, I don't know what came over me!" she gave him an apologetic smile which he accepted.

"Not to worry my dear, I am sure that it's nothing. David is a fine Captain and the Dei Gratias is a brigantine, just like ours. They are proven ships for these jaunts across the Atlantic. There is nothing that he or his vessel cannot handle." He looked at her hoping that he had assuaged his wife's unusual fear. She nodded gratefully.

"Of course you're right, let's go home I still have some packing to do before tomorrow" He offered his arm which she took and they made in the direction of their city abode.

Chapter 3: The Anchor & Chain Tavern

In another part of the city, one where the restaurants did not have a maître d'hôtel, the four German crewmen of the Mary Celeste were celebrating their last night on dry-land together. Vaughn and his younger brother Bill, Hans and Adrian had chosen the Anchor and Chain Tavern because it was boisterous and the ale was cheap. It appeared to be favoured by men of the same ilk. That could easily be seen in the way that the customers of the tavern dressed. Ships crews all managed to dress in a similar fashion whether they were on dry-land or working aboard a ship at sea. The tavern was full of sea-farers. The walls were panelled with dark wood and littered with superstitious paraphernalia. Horse shoes, rabbits feet of all shapes and sizes, some of which could be considered dubious as to whether or not they ever belonged to a rabbit. Wishbones too were scattered on the walls, large and small and every size in between. Finishing off the set of four types of lucky-charms were various four-leaf clovers cast in bronze, copper, silver, lead and some which were made of metals that could not be easily identified as they had been painted green.

The main bar ran the length of the front-wall closest to the entrance. It too suffered an oversupply of symbols meant to represent luck as well as the usual taps for dispensing the golden brews. There were bottles of every shape size and colour behind the counter. They may as well have been only for decoration though as the patrons rarely ventured beyond their beloved mildly effervescent habit. The Germans were sitting together in one of the booths that ran down each of the remaining three walls, about two thirds of the way down. The centre was filled with circular tables and chairs. Only a couple were empty. Even though it was a Tuesday night, the tavern was positively roaring with business.

Hans was saying something, but it was difficult to hear him over the ambient noise. Vaughn and Bill indicated that he should say it again but louder this time.

"I said, what do you make of our Steward, Edward? I hope he is a good cook. I always have a healthier appetite when at sea." It was a valid concern. The Steward was the main cook the crew of a sailing ship. The crew worked hard and expected to be fed well. Not just a generous amount of food, more than that. The crew should have sustenance that was flavoursome, rather than just palatable. Adrian attempted to address Hans's concern.

"The Captain would not have hired him if he had not tried his food first, yah?"

"I hope you are right Adrian, it is a long way to Venice to endure poor cooking" Hans sounded less than convinced. Bill could not resist the chance to mock his fellow shipmate.

"Only ever thinking of your stomach; that is why it is so big!" he said and laughed loudly at his joke accompanied by Adrian and Vaughn. Hans was less than impressed and gave Bill an admonishing look. Adrian however slapped Hans's back to remind him that the gibe should be taken in good humour. He relented and gave a small laugh. A man was standing at the edge of their table. This eventually caught the attention of the small group. They looked up. He was a cruel looking man with narrow lips and a sour expression. Without a word he pointed to Vaughn and indicated that he should leave the table and speak with him slightly away from his friends.

Vaughn did not introduce the man that was clearly known to him, instead he said

"This will not take long. Please excuse me" He shuffled out of his seat and accompanied the man over to what was now the only vacant table in the room. The general noise covered their conversation essentially making it private up to a point.

"Who is that?' asked Adrian. Hans shook his head. They both turned to Bill hoping that he may be able to shed some light on the situation. At first he looked a little ashamed, but thinking that if he couldn't trust his own countrymen and shipmates then who could he trust, Bill revealed the identity of the rude man.

"He is a debt collector for one of the underground gambling houses" he indicated with a point of his head to the west of the city. Adrian and Hans assumed that that was where the illegal gambling house must be located.

"Debt-collector; Vaughn must be in trouble for not paying his debts?" said Adrian. It was a summation of the facts but also a question that required verification. Bill nodded whilst looking down at the table a look of disappointment and gloom on his young features. It was then that the voices of Vaughn and the unwelcome interloper could be heard over the crowd. They were exchanging heated words. Some of the people at the tables nearest to them turned to see what the fuss was about. Vaughn could be seen trying to calm the man down with gestures of his hands. The debt-collector stood up and pointed his slender finger directly at Vaughn's face in a threatening way. Then with a thump on the table from his other hand he walked away and left the tavern. A few of the faces watched him go; then the atmosphere was back to its normal boisterous self again.

Vaughn got up from his chair and walked over to his compatriot's booth. He could see from the look on their faces that Bill had told them who the man was, or at least what he did for a living. They waited for him to speak.

"It is a bad thing to have a debt hanging over one's head. But the wages from this voyage will more than pay him off and I will see no more of him or his kind." He hoped that his explanation would smooth over the incident and they could get on with the evening and forget about it. Bill offered some words of support.

"You know that you can rely on me to help you out Vaughn. Blood is thicker than water yah?" Bill looked up at his elder brother as he spoke. Vaughn could see the sincerity on his face and hear it in his words. But he had no intention of availing himself of his younger brother's finances or any other help that he may be offering.

"Believe me" he said looking at them all in turn "This voyage will save me from any repeat of this nonsense. And I will not be returning to the gambling house where I suffered such losses. I do not believe that it is an honest institution." The thought of course was absurd, that an underground gambling house could or would ever be run honestly. Nevertheless the sentiment was willingly accepted by his shipmates. Clearly Vaughn had learnt his lesson and would not be getting himself into a situation like this again.

"Vaughn has seen the light" exclaimed Hans, inferring that Vaughn had suddenly found religion. They all laughed at the ludicrousness of the assertion.

Wanting to change the subject whilst the mood was good, Adrian picked up the folded paper that was on the table. He had been meaning to read it and this seemed like a perfect opportunity.

"What is in today's paper? Let us see if anything exciting is being reported?" He read out a headline about the stock market but it was met with a resounding *Nein* from the men, who were not interested in such things. Then he saw a sub article about a robbery from a local museum.

"Rare set of diamond rings stolen from museum" he was fascinated already. As there was no objection he continued to read.

"*Police are baffled about a robbery in the private museum in Winthrop Street. On display was the entire jewellery collection of the late Dame Victoria Madison totalling one hundred and twelve separate pieces; however only three rings have been reported missing by the museum curator. The rings are perhaps the most valuable in the entire collection as they have the largest diamonds. Each of them is flawless and has a seven carat diamond as the centre stone. One surrounded by smaller diamonds. One surrounded by dark blue sapphires. And the last surrounded by small emeralds. The white-gold rings were the work of renowned French jewellery house Chaumet. Police have no witnesses to the robbery which took place on Monday night the sixth of November.*" He was about to go on reading when he was reminded of something quite coincidental.

"Hans, you went to see that exhibition on Monday!" he said. The others all looked at him.

"So?" he asked, shrugging his shoulders with nonchalance.

"Did you see the rings that were taken that night? Did you see anybody acting suspiciously? You may be able to help the police with their investigation?" said Bill.

"Why would he help the police?" gibed Adrian "He saw the rings liked them and crept back that night to take them!" Adrian laughed at his own accusation of Hans as did the others. Hans however was unimpressed at the allegation and it showed. He scowled at them all. Seeing that this was annoying Hans Vaughn pressed the point.

"Where were you last night Hans?" This gave rise to another chorus of *ahhhh* from the men. He looked even more annoyed and brushed aside their indictment.

"I was where all sea-faring men go before a long stint at sea" he said with quite some conviction. They waited expectantly for the answer.

"At the local bordello!" he said and slapped Adrian on the back. They all burst out laughing.

"More ale!" exclaimed Vaughn.

"Well what are you waiting for?" goaded Bill, "Go and get us some" realising that he had effectively volunteered to shout the next round Vaughn got up and headed toward the bar.

"Anyway" said Adrian finishing off the topic of conversation. "If you did rob the museum Hans and I found out about it, I would want my cut" he mimicked the actions of the debt-collector and pointed his finger at Hans's face. Hans pushed Adrian's finger away from him and said.

"If I did have those rings I would not be sharing them with the likes of you."

"How much are the rings worth; does it say?" asked Bill. Adrian scoured the rest of the article for the appropriate answer.

"*Police will not disclose the exact value of the rings but it is thought to be a significant figure*?" he quickly read the remainder of the article and summarised it for his captive audience.

"They have no clues and the investigation continues." He said concluding the information that was printed before him. He began searching the paper for something else of interest.

"Imagine that" said Bill "Selling those rings and living without a care in the world for the rest of your life" he had a dreamy look upon his face as he imagined the possibility.

"Except the police chasing you to recover the stolen goods" reminded Hans.

"You are no fun Hans. I was just dreaming about what I would do with that sort of money; that is all" explained Bill.

Unnoticed by any of them the second mate of the Mary Celeste entered the bar with a pretty young girl on his arm. He looked around the bar and immediately saw the three Germans in a booth on the far corner. Then he spied Vaughn at the bar trying to grapple with four tankards of ale. He turned around and motioned for his lady-friend to exit with all due haste.

"What is it Andrew?" she asked.

"Not this place Wilomena; it is too crowded and noisy. I know of another place a few streets away that is better. Quickly" he said. Wilomena did as he said and they both exited the bar unseen by any of the other crew.

Chapter 4: Andrew Gill - Second Mate

Andrew and Wilomena hurried through the streets away from the Anchor and Chain tavern and toward something that Andrew had identified as the Lord Nelson Inn. Wilomena was not entirely sure why there were in such a hurry but any time spent close to Andrew was a thrill, so she did not mind the frenetic pace that he had set. Soon enough the Inn was in sight. It looked very quaint indeed thought Wilomena. Her opinion was reconfirmed upon entering the establishment. It was much quieter than the Anchor and Chain had been. Andrew was correct, this was a better place for them to spend some secret time together.

The Inn was smaller than the tavern that they had just left. But that made it more intimate. There were similarities in the design though; booths along the walls and tables and chairs in the centre of the room. This one had a roaring fire place which gave the room a beautiful glow even over the gas lantern lighting its interior. There was the typical dark wood panelling, but this one was covered with paraphernalia all surrounding the famous Lord Horatio Nelson hero of the Napoleonic wars. The bar was smaller and had a friendly looking old man behind it, with a beard and one lazy eye.

Looking around Andrew spied a free booth.

"Take that booth and I'll bring us something to drink" he smiled whilst nodding to the booth that he meant. Wilomena was only too happy to oblige.

"Alright" she replied and went to do as she was told. Andrew walked up to the bar and ordered two Sazerac's from the barman who promptly set about making the cocktail.

"How much?" he asked whilst the man was still busy mixing the concoctions. The barman answered and Andrew pulled the correct amount of money from his pocket bit by bit, and counted it twice before depositing it in a neat column upon the shiny wooden bar. By this time the barman had completed his handy work and giving the column of coins a quick look nodded his acceptance of the payment and said "Thankyou young man; enjoy. I make the best Sazerac in the city" It was quite a bold claim, and it amused Andrew but he did not let it show. Instead he replied

"Then my fiancé and I are in for a treat; Cheers"

Wilomena was waiting with a look of pure love on her face as Andrew approached with the drinks. He set them down gingerly not wanting to spill a drop and then settled in beside her taking her hand in his.

"There now, isn't this better than that noisy old tavern?" he asked. Wilomena agreed. Then Andrew laughed a little.

"What's so funny?" inquired Wilomena.

"I told the barman that you were my fiancé." He said "and I have to admit, it felt good to hear it." Now it was Wilomena's turn to laugh, although this was more a laugh of pithy than outright amusement.

"If only that were true Andrew" she said laconically. Andrew realised that he had touched a nerve and tried to sooth her feelings.

"You know that I will marry you one day don't you Wilomena? If it wasn't for your overbearing father I would have asked for your hand in marriage long ago and set a date for our wedding already. You could go with your sister and mother to pick out a dress and do all of the things that a woman needs to do to prepare for a perfect wedding." He gave her a mournful look like a tiny puppy hoping for a show of affection. She could not resist him when he gave her that look and conceded.

"If only you were the Captain of you boat" she began. Andrew corrected her immediately.

"Ship" he said

"Ship then" she said. "He so desperately wants me to marry into a family has as much wealth as our own or even more. But I think that he would make an exception for a *ship's* Captain. It is such a noble undertaking. Do you think that aboard the Mary Celeste you will be able to rise to first mate and then Captain someday?" Wilomena's question, although a little ignorant of the speed with which Captains are made, was still poignant. Andrew gave her a very broad smile, like he was keeping something important from her.

"I have a plan" he said somewhat mysteriously, then paused for effect.

"Well don't keep it to yourself, tell me what it is and if it will help us get married, or at least engaged". She was excited and could barely contain her feelings.

"I don't want you to worry, but I have found a way to make more money than any second mate normally would on board a merchant Brigantine like ours." He paused again trying to judge her features. How would she receive the news? Wilomena turned her head slightly sideways hoping that visual clue would spur on Andrew's explanation.

"I have smuggled aboard some additional cargo to the ship which I will sell in Italy. Furs that dress makers will make into fine fur coats for the women of Europe. I will effectively double the salary that I earn on this voyage. What would your successful businessman father think of that?" he said

"Andrew, that is very clever." Exclaimed Wilomena, impressed with the lengths that Andrew was going to in order to win over her father so that he could win her hand in marriage. Then a thought crossed her mind.

"You won't get into trouble will you?"

"Nobody will ever know! I have been overseeing the packing of the ship below decks whilst Albert, our first mate, has overseen it above deck. Nobody saw me secret the furs away and nobody will ever find them. And when we arrive in Venice I will take them to the best dress maker that I can find. American furs are in demand in Europe. I will get the highest price that I can and I will be able to do something similar on the way back. I haven't figured out what I will bring back from Europe to sell here, but I will find something of value. I am being enterprising, not dishonest, exactly" he said sounding like he had to convince himself as well as Wilomena.

Wilomena was impressed at Andrew's strength of conviction.

"I think that it is a brilliant idea Andrew, and when you are able to show my father that you can earn a good amount of money doing what you do then I am sure that he will soften his attitude toward you. He didn't make his fortune without stepping on a few toes of his own you know." She said and touched her finger against her nose.

"I'm glad you like my plan" he said genuinely relieved. He had wanted to tell her since he had thought it up, but was afraid that it would not be well received.

"Let's drink a toast to the voyage of the Mary Celeste, may it make me lots of money so that I can make you my happy fiancé!" Wilomena and Andrew touched their glasses together making a slight clinking sound and took a sip of the potent cocktail.

Chapter 5: Albert Richards - First Mate

Albert Richards had arranged to meet his brother for a very early lunch prior to departure. He was waiting outside the chosen eating house for his sibling. Even at a distance he could spot his kin from afar. Even though there was a year that separated them, they could easily have passed for twins. The resemblance between them left nobody in doubt that they were brothers; sharing a similar build and features. When they eventually came together Albert was delighted to see his elder brother.

"Finnius, you look well. How are our parents?" he smiled and extended his hand in a very gentlemanly manner. Finnius took the hand offered and in the typical sibling rivalry that they had both displayed for their entire lives together an overly firm handshake was given. Both men tightened their grip essentially playing a game of who could squeeze the tightest. Finnius thought that he would win as he had always done, but was surprised to find that he could barely take the pressure that Albert was exerting upon his hand. Eventually it became too much and he acceded.

"Alright; Albert, you win!" he said disappointed in his own performance. Albert gave him a smug smile and repeated his question.

"Are our parents are well Finnius?" he said in a smarmy manner.

"Yes, yes Albert, they send their love and wish you a safe and expeditious voyage to Venice and back". He gave Albert a look of minor brotherly contempt.

"What is the name of this ship? I know that you have told me but it slips my mind." He inquired.

"The Mary Celeste, merchant Brigantine sailing ship. Recently completely refurbished; it even has a small coal fired engine should we hit the doldrums. It has all of the comforts of home too. And as first mate I get my own cabin. What more could a man ask for?" He said completing his glowing critique of his new commission.

"I see that you are already packed" said Finnius pointing to the one large and one small clothing chest that Albert was standing next to. Finnius gave them both a cursory look and something odd stood out to him.

"Why are there holes in the top of both of them? Aren't these sea-chests supposed to be water-tight to keep your clothing dry?" it was a valid question. Albert shook his head.

"I am one step ahead of the old sea dogs that believe that Finnius. I want my clothing to be able to breathe so that they won't develop mould in the damp air."

"Uh-ah" snorted Finnius not really interested in the state or storage of his younger brother's apparel.

"Is this the place where we are eating? It looks closed" he said looking through the paned window to the interior. There was nobody to be seen.

"I know the owner, he has opened early especially for us to dine together in peace and quiet" explained Albert. Feeling somewhat privileged Finnius said.

"Then what are we waiting for let's go in. Here let me carry one of your chests." Albert was about to thank him for being so kind when

Finnius reached down and lifted the small one and gave Albert a cheeky wink before marching up to the door of the diner, gingerly opening the door, and marching through.

"Uh-ah!" said Albert sardonically and took hold of the large chest by two well positioned handles and swung it up over his back. It looked to be an awful weight but he seemed to throw it around like it was made of paper rather than seasoned timber. He followed his brother inside.

Finnius had already taken a seat at the table in the very centre of the room. Albert shut the door behind him and put the large chest to the side of the door. He joined his brother at the table.

"At least on this voyage you are going to a civilized country, not like that last one. Haiti; of all the places on earth to travel to for a holiday why that remote island, it is full of barbarians; what were you thinking Albert?" But Albert would hear no criticism of his choice for an adventurous holiday.

"It is exotic; mysterious, full of superstitions and history. I saw things on that island that few white-men have ever seen. It took a lot of effort on my part to persuade the natives that my interest in their culture and their voodoo magic ways was genuine and not just a passing interest of a bored tourist." Albert was speaking with such passion that it enraptured Finnius.

"What did they show you that they wouldn't usually show outsiders?" he asked in a hushed voice.

"I was allowed to attend one of their secret ceremonies where they raised from the dead a recently deceased man, a zombie they called it". Albert looked directly at his brother who was visibly shocked.

"You can't be serious? A man raised from the dead!? That is impossible for anyone except the Lord himself. Nonsense; you are spinning an old sea-farer's tall tale Albert and I won't fall for it." He said dismissively waving his hand as if to shoo away the ridiculous words from the air. "Now where is that *friend* of yours that owns this establishment, I want to order something."

"Perhaps I should go out the back, and find him? He is probably getting the kitchen prepared to begin cooking. Now let me guess, what will you have Finnius? A steak; well done, with fried eggs on the side and toast?" he offered looking at his brother for confirmation that he had appropriately predicted what he would order.

"You know me too well Albert" he laughed. "Am I really that predictable?'

"Yes" said Albert as he got up from his seat.

Chapter 6: Departure

Captain Brigges could see his wife and two-year-old daughter at the end of the gang-plank from his position in the wheel house. He hurried to the top of the plank and signalled for them to remain where they were until he joined them on the dock. Sandra and little Sara were accompanied by the cab driver that had taken them from their home to the dock. He had unloaded the three large chests from the back of the horse and carriage and was setting the final one down on the dock when Captain Brigges joined his wife and child. Benjamin paid the cabbie and the man thanked them. He nodded at the ship and wished them a pleasant voyage before he returned to his cab and with a *hiah!* ushered the horse and carriage into motion.

"A beautiful day to set sail" offered Sandra.

"It is indeed" responded Benjamin. He crouched down to better address his daughter.

"Are you excited to be travelling with Daddy on his ship?" he asked of the bright-eyed two-year-old. She nodded excitedly and managed a very definite

"Yes!"

"Why don't the two of you board and I will have the crew see to the luggage when they arrive? Come along" he said. He took Sandra's hand and Sandra took Sara's and they walked carefully in single-file up the gang-plank. The solidity of the wooden deck felt reassuring after the tenuousness of the long timber board. Something made

Benjamin look back to the dock. The four German crewmen were arriving; they each carried a large trunk of their own.

"You know the way to our cabin, why don't you show Sara around so that she knows where everything is?" he said. Sandra obligingly went to do just that. Benjamin called out to the men on the dock.

"The three large chests; to my cabin please!" he shouted at all of them. A couple of them waved their hands in acknowledgement of the order. They busied themselves setting down their own luggage and giving priority to the Captain's. Edward Heed, the ship's Steward and Cook arrived at that time and joined the small party on the dock. The five men quickly divvied up the duties to get all of the trunks on-board. It was decided that two men should carry each one for the sake of stability whilst on the shaky plank.

Vaughn and Bill, the two brothers, carried one of the Captain's trunks up the plank, each carrying one end. Hans and Adrian took one of the Captain's other large trunks. Not wanting to be look like he wasn't helping Edward looked around for a trunk that was small enough to handle on his own. He located one in the pile on the dock and carried that up after the four men.

Edward had a leather satchel slung over one shoulder. He left it on as he carried the luggage on to the deck of the boat. However he did not notice that the stitching in the strap had become frayed at the back. He had just set both feet firmly on the deck of the ship when it gave way and his satchel fell to the seasoned timber surface making quite a crash. Everyone turned to see that had happened. The leather satchel had fallen to the deck and splayed open revealing the contents.

Knives, of all shapes and sizes scattered around. It wasn't the fact that the cook had a bag full of knives that caught the men's attention; it was the number of them, and the number that looked to be far too large to be considered for normal use in the small galley that Mary Celeste was equipped with.

"Was ist das!" exclaimed Vaughn as he put into words what his three other compatriots were thinking. Vaughn quickly set down the trunk that he was carrying and set about gathering up the knives, placing each one back into the pouch that seemed to be custom made to carry them all in their individual places. Even Captain Brigges was a little alarmed at the sheer size of some of the knives that were on display.

"Good heavens man!" he said in his typically authoritarian Captain's voice "what on earth would you need cleavers the size of those for, on a voyage like ours!?' Such was the force of Captain Brigges inquiry that Edward stopped recovering the knives and cleavers and looked up. He seemed somewhat flustered that his collection was on display. He was shaking his head and at first looked a little lost for words.

"Tools of my trade Captain; I must be prepared for any contingency. What if I should need to butcher a beast for preserving? I would need the correct cleavers and knives to properly dissect the carcass." He did not wait for acknowledgement from the Captain that his explanation was sufficient and returned to gathering up his knives. The other crew members all looked to the Captain for his reaction. Captain Brigges raised his eyebrows and shook his head. There certainly wasn't anything wrong with Edward's explanation, at least nothing that he could put his finger on. So he simply made his way toward the wheel house to check once more the course that he had plotted for their voyage. There was nothing more to say on the matter as far as he was concerned.

Seeing that the Captain was not alarmed at the number and size of the knives in Edward's possession the other crew were a little more at ease. Nevertheless they all exchanged looks of being somewhat irked at the thought of having so many sharp utensils so easily available. They returned to the task at hand.

***

Sara was very excited at the thought of going to sea with her parents. She held tightly to Sandra's hand as they finished looking around their quite spacious cabin. The panelling was beautifully done. The main bunk big enough for two, had polished wooden sides to prevent the mattress and the occupants from rolling out in high seas. New highly-polished brass fittings glimmered with light from the portal on each side of the large cabin. It took up the entire aft section of this level, the one just below deck. Below that was the engine that could be used should the ship experience a lull in the trade winds whilst crossing the Atlantic. The Captain's cabin was accessed by a neat staircase from the wheel-room above. There was a small door of course to prevent just anybody from entering. Sara had her own bunk on the opposite side to her parent's capacious one, and appropriately the sides were much higher to prevent her from falling out. She was thrilled at the prospect of sleeping so high up the wall that she would need to climb a small ladder to reach it. Also there was the assuredness that comes from being able to see her parents sleeping just over from her bunk. This she felt was much better than their house where she had to sleep in her own room.

A companion in its own small section took up a part of the cabin. It was of course for the exclusive use of the Captain and his family. A small table and inbuilt bench-seat and a library of books behind brass rods made up the remainder of the space. All up it was a very pleasant cabin. A second door led out to the main corridor.

"Shall we explore the rest of this deck?" asked Sandra.

"Yes please Mummy" replied Sara. They opened the door and looked down the length of the hall. There were six doors visible; three to the port side and two to the starboard, and one at the far end of the passageway. The first door led to the coal room and the engine room that was beneath the stairs that led up from the Captain's cabin to the wheel house. Sandra and Sara looked over the amazing piece of engineering.

"What does it do Mummy" inquired Sara.

"This is the engine that Daddy will use if we need it" tried to explain Sandra.

"When will we need it?" asked Sara. Knowing that this was going to lead to a never-ending series of follow-up questions, Sandra decided upon telling the truth.

"I don't know. And do not ask me why I don't know young lady! Let's explore the other doors" she said hoping that the distraction would be enough to prevent a tirade of questions from the youngster.

The two next closest doors were the cabins of the crew. Sandra and Sara peaked into both the one on the port the other on the starboard. There were three bunk beds in each of them. This is where the crew will sleep. Moving up to the next two doors they had to duck around the stairway-come-ladder that led to the deck above. It was too steep to be considered a staircase, yet not quite a ladder either. This was the mid-ship hatch access. They reached the next two doors and opened the one on the port side. This had only one bunk in it. Although the same size as the other two, it would only have one resident.

"This is where the First-mate will sleep" said Sandra. Sara repeated the words.

"First-mate" and they closed the door. The door opposite Albert's cabin was the forward companion, the one that everyone else would use. There was only the door at the end of the corridor now. In order to get to it however one had to pass around the rather sturdy pole of the forward mast. It stretched through the ships decks to the keel unseen below. Sandra waked around it to the left and Sara to the right. Briefly releasing each other's hands Sara hurriedly took her mother's hand again as they met in front of the remaining door. They opened it.

"This is the Galley" explained Sandra to Sara, who did not know what a galley was and gave her mother a look of puzzlement. Seeing that she did not understand the reference Sandra explained as they entered.

"This is where Edward will prepare all of our meals and we will eat them together, just like a large family." Sandra pointed out the table fixed to the floor surrounded by fixed padded benches. There were cupboards on all of the walls. There was a ships-stove that would use coal from the small coal room below the Captain's cabin, beside the engine room. It had never been used as it was part of the significant refurbishment that the Mary Celeste had undergone prior to making this voyage. Sandra and Sara looked it over with interest. Beyond the galley a small storage room full of the food supplies for the journey completed the full length of the one-hundred foot ship. A ladder beside the stove led to the fore hatch and would be used by the crew to enter the galley from the deck above. This was a ladder though and not the odd hybrid that the mid-ships access was. A small round brass and glass portal was at each side of the galley. It allowed light in, but the majority of it was coming from the open hatch above the ladder. During high seas and at night the hatch would be closed, for both the forward and mid-ships access ways. Then the brass oil lamps affixed to the ceiling would provide all of the light necessary to enjoy their meals.

"Shall we look at the cargo that Daddy is carrying to Italy?" suggested Sandra. Sara was only too happy to agree. There were a number of ways that they could gain access to the cargo deck but Sandra chose the easiest way. Returning to the main corridor she stopped at the steeply arched staircase and reached down to pull on a flush fitting brass handle. The trapdoor lifted with ease and she locked it into place with a latch against the underside of the ladder. Looking around she located an oil lamp that was burning, but it was currently turned right down to offer a minimum amount of light. She adjusted the dial and brought the lamp to life. Unclipping the lamp from its ceiling fixture and kneeling down she lowered the lamp into the bottom most deck of the ship so that they could both see.

The cargo deck could not be stood upright in, it was too low. Hundreds of barrels took up every nook and cranny of the storage area. They were not likely to roll anywhere such was the tightness and precision of their storage, but they were all tied up in sections just to be sure.

"What's in them?" asked Sara innocently.

"Alcohol to fortify Italian wine" replied Sandra, immediately realising that Sara would not understand the explanation at all. Sara did not but said *oooohhh* as if she had. Lifting the lamp up, the cargo deck was returned to darkness. Sandra unlatched the trapdoor and put it back into place. Returning the lamp to where she had found it Sandra clipped it back into place.

"Let's us go and look at the deck. We can watch the sails unfold when we set sail" another offer from her mother that Sara was unlikely to refuse. Everything was so exciting aboard the Mary Celeste.

***

By the time that Sandra and little Sara came back on-deck the crew had successfully transported all of the chests and other luggage onto the ship. Andrew Gill had arrived and was setting his own luggage down with the rest. Various exchanges of good morning Ma'am and little Ma'am were exchanged between the crew and the Captain's wife and daughter. Andrew went so far as to say that he hoped that they would both enjoy the journey. There was an air of excitement building now that cast-off was so close. There was less than half an hour to go before their scheduled departure time at noon.

The luggage had to be stowed quickly and the preparations to make sail begun. Captain Brigges was shouting such and it caused a flurry of movement from the crew to quickly get their belongings stowed before beginning their seaman duties. Unnoticed in the general commotion, Albert had arrived and managed to get his large chest and smaller one up the gang-plank without the assistance of anyone else. He proceeded to stow it in his cabin similarly without aide. Sandra was perhaps the only one who noticed and assumed that he must be travelling lightly. The size of his large trunk was such that it must surely be empty for him to wield it so freely.

The tone of orders from the Captain increased in intensity as the hour of noon approached. Benjamin looked toward the dock to see if any of the other co-owners had come to see them off, but was disappointed. Nobody had showed up. They must have other business ventures that were taking their attention he thought.

"Come Sara let us stand to the side of the wheel house, we shall have a good view of everything and we shall not be in anybody's way". Sandra took Sara's hand and moved into position. From the elevated level of the wheel-house section of the deck they could see everything. The two tall masts and the spider-web of ropes and rigging that would soon be used to hoist a number of the fifteen sails that would be deployed at various times throughout the voyage. The lifeboat had its own position to the star-port side of the forward hatch on a slightly raised section called the deckhouse. Sandra leaned over to the right side so that she could see the new anchor in its position on the starboard side. As they were safely tied up in dock there was no need for it here in New York harbour. Sandra supposed that the first that that it would be used would be when they made port in Santa Maria in the Azores sometime around the sixteenth of the month.

"Look at the flag Mummy!" proclaimed Sara. Sandra turned to see what she was pointing at. The thirty-seven stars and stripes flew from the aft deck. Another much larger flag was now being raised by a couple of the crewmen on the lines leading up to the main gaff. All around there were people calling out to each other about various duties that now needed to be performed.

"Cast off!" Ordered the Captain. He had taken up position in front of the wheel house and Albert had taken the ship's steering wheel, inside the small room. Bill and Hans both scurried down the gangplank and one made his way toward the fore lines mooring the ship to the dock, the other went to release the aft. The ropes were set free and immediately the ship could be felt to move. The men raced back up the gang-plank before the boat drifted too far from the dock. Edward was there to retract the gang plank and safely stow it. This left Bill and Hans now free to join the others in untying the various square sails and the fore and aft sails that Benjamin had nominated to be hoisted.

Although it was November, it was a fine day. The sun was shining above there were small white clouds scattered here and there. You would never have believed that it was winter in New York. It now seemed a pity to leave. But Sandra was not fooled, she knew, as did the rest of the crew, that the winter would set in and the city would be cold and snow-covered by the following month. Leaving now was very timely.

"Daddy is so clever Sara. Look at all of the other ships that he has to navigate his way around so that we can safely leave the harbour." Sandra lifted up Sara to give her a better view of the other ships and boats in the harbour. Not fully understanding what her mother had said, Sara was happy to look at the multitude of masts and sails around her.

The Mary Celeste manoeuvred smoothly, gracefully as a lithe Brigantine should. More shouting of orders revealed that Benjamin was planning to make quite a display as they departed the harbour. He had ordered the preparation of almost all of the sails. The ship would look resplendent as it made its way elegantly through the crowd of other sea-faring vessels and toward the open sea.

With so much sail, the first mate had to judge the situation carefully. He did not want the maiden voyage of the refurbished ship to be tarred with any near-misses or other incidents. But he did well, with instruction from the Captain such as:

"Watch out for that sloop to the port" and "mind that Cutter just ahead" and soon enough the number of vessels diminished. It became easier to push the ship onwards. The wind was blowing just enough to fill the sails, but not push the ship at a frenetic speed. If the Captain had hoped for a stylish departure, that is exactly what he, with the help from his crew, achieved. The Mary Celeste left New York harbour and was on its way to cross the Atlantic Ocean. For now, to all of them, it seemed like nothing could stand in their way.

Chapter 7: The Captain's Journal

Thursday November 9th 1871

We could not have asked for a more perfect day to leave New York Harbour. I am certain that the Mary Celeste looked resplendent as we made sail in the favourable winds.

If the crew continue to perform as soundly as they did for our departure then I anticipate that this will be an easy journey. Everyone appears to get along well and I can foresee no clash of wills between any of the men, nor dark-horses that will cause problems in the future. Albert has stamped his authority as First-mate as he should and the men rightfully see him as the second-in-command. Although somewhat cautious about installing a crew aboard that I had no previous experience with, I feel now that the decision was a good one and that they will contribute to the speed and success of our maiden merchant trading voyage.

Thus far the ship has performed admirably. There are no teething problems that are apparent, as can be the case for a refurbished ship the age of the Mary Celeste. This is a testament to the workmanship of the men that carried out the refit in order to make it a larger and more contemporary vessel, capable of the tasks that she will be required to undertake.

Little Sara thinks that the whole journey is one big adventure. She has made friends with all of the crew and they are delighted at her talkative and inquisitive nature.

Having my Dear Wife and my youngest with me has eased the burden of my position as Captain. No longer do I pine for my family and for the comforts of their company. At this moment I feel that I could happily spend the rest of my years earning a respectable keep as Ship's Captain. All thoughts that I had harboured on land to start a hardware business with my brother have faded. Being at sea now feels more like home than our house in New York. It was a good decision to carry on serving at sea in this way. I am proud to have a wife made of such metal that can abide such a lifestyle.

Friday November 10th 1871

After such a perfect beginning to our voyage the inevitability of unpredictable weather at this time of year, has brought home the fact that we are at the mercy of the elements. Storm clouds threatened us all day but thankfully did not make good their promise of driving rain. The accompanying wind however saw the Fore Staysail rip. It became impossible to drop the sail as the rope had become entangled.

I mention this for the sake of commendation, as the bravery and skill of Vaughn Lorensen was put to the test as he climbed the Fore Mast to recover the sail. Although causing a great deal of anxiety from us all, he was successful and recovered the sail for repairs before the high-winds could do more damage to it. He insisted on repairing the sail and we all wait to see the result of his handiwork. We have a spare but I would prefer to have the original put back into place once repaired.

In spite of the rough seas we have yet to record one case of sea-sickness. I had feared that either my Wife or child would suffer from it at some stage, however there is no sign. I am grateful for this blessing. Therefore Edward's cooking is still in great demand from all present. Edward has turned out to be a fine Steward and an accomplished cook. Working from a recipe book that he tells us was his Grandfathers, who was also a cook aboard a ship, he has managed to surprise and delight us with his offerings. He has promised that when we get to Santa Maria, he will prepare a suckling pig whilst we are on dry land and preserve the various cuts of meats for the second part of our voyage.

Saturday November 11th 1871

Today was an easier day than yesterday. The winds have eased somewhat making it less of a burden to keep us on course. The crew does not have to work as hard hoisting and dropping sails as the winds become too much for the material to bear. They can concentrate upon more of the normal duties that a crew should undertake in such circumstances. I expect that every surface of the ship will be cleaned at least twice over by the time we make port at Santa Maria.

Vaughn finished repairing the Fore Staysail and all agreed that he had done an outstanding job. I too was very happy with the results. It is now back in place and ready to be used once more.

I have re-plotted our course and find that we are exactly where I had hoped we would be by the third day of our journey. All things being equal we should make port in the Azores on or about November the sixteenth.

Bill has a bruised leg and without doubt bruised pride. He slipped whilst descending the mid-ship stairs and landed awkwardly.

He was lucky to have not sprained an ankle or worse broken a bone. Little in the way of medical assistance was needed. He is a young man and will surely heal with the haste that is the purview of the youthful.

Sunday November 12th 1871

Another day of battling the weather, which to say the very least was dreadful. Rain has dampened our normally high spirits. Only Edward's fine cooking is keeping a sunny disposition amongst the crew.

The wind was of such ferocity today that had the Mary Celeste been a lesser ship, one or both of the Masts would have been forfeit. We were able to drop sails as quickly as can be expected under such circumstances. It is the other consequences of facing such adverse weather that caused me much more concern. Although only the fourth full day of our voyage, the crew are beginning to show signs of weariness. I fear that unless we can get past this storm that it will have dire consequences on the morale of all on board.

Sandra spent almost then entire day in our cabin reading to Sara, who was terrified of the thunder and the roaring wind. Only at dinner time did they venture out and joined Edward in the galley. We could not all meet together today as our duties under the adverse conditions prevented us from doing so. Edward ensured that there was a hot stew for those crewmen that I, in turn, sent below to take some well-earned rest.

I can only hope that the storm will pass, or that we shall sail beyond its influence. However my experience tells me that we are sailing with the storm and that it may endure for much longer than we would like to bear.

Chapter 8: Preparing for the Storm

Captain Brigges did not get much sleep. He woke on Monday the 13th of November knowing that the situation had not changed. He could feel it all around him. He could hear it and smell it in the air. Sandra was still very much asleep beside him. As she slept on the inside part of the bunk he was able to raise himself and prepare for the day without disturbing her.

"Daddy" it was Sara's small voice from her bunk. Benjamin finished buttoning his jacket and went to see her. She was visible from the small amount of light that the lantern was throwing throughout the cabin.

"What is it little one?" he asked in an equally small voice so as not to alarm her.

"When will the thunder go away? It frightens me" she said. Benjamin laughed a little in a way that he hoped would be comforting rather than mocking.

"The thunder cannot hurt you Sara. I won't let it" he proclaimed proudly touching the end of her nose with his finger to highlight the point. This seemed to have the exact effect that he had hoped for.

"That's good. Thank you Daddy" she said and settled herself back beneath her blankets. Amazed at his daughter's faith in him to deliver on such an intangible promise he stroked her head and gave her a parting kiss.

"Now go back to sleep" he advised.

***

When the Captain reached the wheel house he could see that all was far from well. Andrew was at the wheel and he looked tired. The wind and rain had not abated overnight. Checking the chronometer, Benjamin could see that it was past the time that the sun should have risen, yet it was still very dark.

"Any news to report from your watch Mr Gill?" the sound of the Captain's voice jerked Andrew back into the here and now.

"Aye Captain; forked lightening ahead and lots of it too!" Just as he was pointing a myriad of lightening glittered ahead. It was perhaps five nautical miles hence, but it would soon be upon them.

"And the sails?" inquired the captain.

"We are flying only the Mizen Staysail and the Jib Captain. Any more and we risk tearing them, and being taken by one of the sudden port cross-winds that we have been battling for the entire watch." Andrew finished his report to the Captain. It was now up to Brigges to decide upon a course of action. Benjamin did not take long to consider.

"We shall make power by propeller Mr Gill. Stoke the boiler engine with coal, and when we are able to make momentum via the engine alone, drop the remaining sails. This is a modern vessel and we need not be at the mercy of this storm as a sailing ship. It will be easier to steer her into the storm and through the other side without risking mast, boom, gaff and sail." The Captain's solution to battle what looked to be the very heart of the storm that they had been enduring sounded reassuring.

"I shall take over the wheel. See to the engine and then direct both Messer's Lorensen to take down the sails. Andrew acknowledged the Captain's order and looked at the way that the Captain had entered the wheel house. It would be the dry path for him to get below deck. After all the coal room was beside the Captain's cabin. However the Captain was not inclined to have Andrew disturb his wife and child's sleep simply to stay dry. He shook his head knowing what Andrew was asking for without using words.

Deflated that he now had to endure the wind and driving rain before he could make it to the mid-ship hatch he steeled himself and exited the wheel house closing the door quickly behind him. The wind and rain stung his face because it was hurled at him with such force. It was cold too, adding to the discomfort. Long before he made it the short distance to the mid-ship hatch he was already soaked through.

Clambering through the hatch he managed to close it before too much water followed him below deck. Then making his way to the coal room he grabbed a bright copper coal shovel and scooped up a generous quantity. He opened the boiler door and threw the coal in before reaching for some kindling and the large matches that were stored in a cupboard on the wall. He had been trained in the correct operation of the engine and was delighted although somewhat apprehensive about being able to put into practice his learnings.

He carefully lit the contents and took up the brass stoking rod and skilfully poked the contents to allow the correct amount of air in to properly ignite the boiler. Soon enough it had taken and he then began to fiddle with the valves to ensure that they were set correctly. Satisfied that all was in readiness, he left the engine to continue to build-up its pressure and went to rouse Bill and Vaughn from their sleep. He estimated in his head that by the time they had taken down the sails, the engine would have come to full pressure and would be ready to engage the propeller to give them forward motion.

***

By the time Andrew Gill made it back to the wheel house to report that the Captain's orders were being carried out, Brigges had had time to assess the forthcoming storm more carefully. Gill was soaked through and dripping wet when he burst back through the door shutting it loudly behind him to prevent too much rain from entering. He looked up from shaking off the excess water from his clothes as the Captain addressed him.

"This is a nasty one Mr Gill." He said "Perhaps the worst that I have ever seen in all my days at sea. I want you to alert all members of the crew to stand by for storm duty. I estimate that we will be in the thick of it within half of an hour." The grim expression and the tone of Brigges voice was enough to give Gill a heightened sense of urgency. Suddenly it did not matter that he was dripping wet and that he had to once more endure the lashing rain in order to return below deck. All that mattered now was the Captain's evaluation of the situation that they were all facing. If he of all people was concerned with what lay ahead then they all should be. Andrew almost gave a military salute such was his newfound eagerness to bring the news to the remainder of the crew.

"Aye aye Captain!" he said with gusto and rushed from the wheel house to do as he was told. This time Andrew hardly noticed the driving rain and wind assaulting his exposed flesh as he made his way to the main hatch. He almost lost his balance a couple of times in the rolling waves that were tossing the brigantine up and down. As he fumbled with the wet latch of the hatchway he looked up at the direction in which they were heading. The clouds ahead seemed blacker than black if that was possible. The lightening was frenetic and abundant; the sight filled him with foreboding.

The Captain's words echoed in Andrew's ears as he pulled the hatchway shut behind him and navigated the slippery staircase-ladder to the relative security of the deck below. Andrew made straight toward the First Mates cabin. He should be the first to be informed of the Captain's instructions. Knocking loudly upon the door there was a surprising and immediate response from within.

"One moment" Albert's instruction to wait was uncharacteristic. Andrew wondered what Albert could possibly be doing to warrant any delay. Surely he of all people knew that if somebody knocked upon his door then there would be good reason.

"Come!" Albert's follow up instruction put an end to Andrew's brief musings. Andrew opened the door and saw Albert holding a mug and saucer. The Saucer was full of milk which had been made from powder. Andrew gave Albert a quizzical look to which Albert responded.

"I spilt my milk in the rough seas, lucky I had the good sense to have a saucer beneath as I was drinking".

Uninterested in the trivial matter that Albert was outlining Andrew did not acknowledge it but instead gave a summation of the Captain's earlier orders.

"The Captain says that we are facing the worst storm that he has ever seen. All crew are to prepare for storm duty." He said, quickly and with urgency. Albert emptied the saucer into the mug and placed both on the shelf safely behind a brass rod that would hold them in place in the high seas.

"Very good Mr. Gill; please rouse the others from their sleep, and be sure to have Mr Heed make tight the galley".

"Aye Mr Richards" said Andrew enthusiastically and moved to the closest crew's quarters doors to do just that. This was the cabin that he shared with Edward and Adrian. He opened it and shouted to the two slumbering occupants.

"All crew report for storm duty, orders of the Captain. Mr Heed secure the galley, this is going to be a big one!" There was a general grumble from both men as they were unceremoniously awoken. Andrew did not wait for follow up questions he moved to the other crew's quarter's door. He knew that only Hans was sleeping there as he had previously woken the Lorensen brothers to take down the sails. They must surely have secured them by now. With a pang of guilt he opened the door. Hans had been on duty prior to Andrew taking over from him, so he had only had about four hours sleep. But orders were orders and the Captain wanted all crew to help get them through the storm. He flung open the door.

"Awake please Mr Gondeschall, Captain's orders; all hands prepare for storm duty". Hans sat up at the sudden intrusion into the cabin and his wonderful unconsciousness.

"What?' he said bleary-eyed and blinking at the sudden rush of words.

"Storm Hans, a big one and we're heading right into the heart of it. It even has the Captain worried. Worst that he has seen he says". These additional facts served to snap Hans back into the present.

"Alright: he said and looked around the cabin as if trying to locate where he had left his rain-coat and wet-weather boots. Andrew left him to his devices. At that moment the main hatch opened and produced the Lorensen brothers who scampered down as quickly as they could slamming the hatchway shut behind them. They stood at the bottom of the stairs wiping the water from their faces.

"The sails are down and safely tied-off?" asked Andrew as he joined them. Albert too had come out of his cabin, now fully dressed for wet weather. Edward pushed past the contingent and made his way to the Galley to make sure that everything would be braced for the storm. Adrian too joined the small party at the base of the steps. Vaughn answered.

"Safely tied down Mr Gill" he said. Bill reiterated the affirmation.

"All done" he said. Albert took over at this point.

"Mr Gill, what is the current situation?" he inquired.

"We have dropped all sails. Mr Heed is seeing to the galley and the Captain is at the wheel. I have stoked the engine boiler with coal, it should be ready to engage the propeller by now" he said summarising the recent events.

"Very good, see to the engine Mr Gill and get us some forward motion" instructed Albert. Andrew went to do as he was told. The general commotion must have alerted Sandra, as the cabin door was opened and she stood in her dressing gown looking at the gathered men.

"Mr Richards. What is the matter?" she asked as look of concern on her face. Albert left the small contingent and went to speak to her.

"The Captain has ordered all hands prepare for a storm. May I suggest that you and Sara stay in your cabin?" he advised. Sandra looked over to Sara who remained fast-asleep.

"Nonsense Mr Richards, I shall help in any way that I am able. What should I do?" she asked. Albert looked over to the sleeping two year old.

"But Sara?" he began, thinking that it would be best for Sandra to watch over the toddler.

"Sara will sleep through anything" she replied "Providing it is dark the little darling will sleep. If it is light however, she will be awake at the crack of dawn. I have pulled the curtains over the portholes to prevent the lightening from waking her up. She will be fine, and will call out if she needs anything. Now believe me Albert, I am willing and able to help." Albert was impressed with Sandra's pluckiness.

"Very well Ma'am. Edward could do with some help in the Galley. The rest of us" he said turning so that they could all hear him properly "Will stand by with buckets to bail-out any water that gets through the hatches and that the pumps cannot handle. I want all oil lamps checked to ensure that they are securely fastened. All cabin doors secured. We should expect lightning strikes and saint-Elmo's fire. Get ropes ready to tie around the waist of anybody that needs to go up on deck so that they don't get washed off in the high-seas. If any of the rigging breaks we have to be prepared to fix it before any damage is done. I want a man with the Captain in the wheel house to help him keep an eye on fore and aft."

"I'll go" volunteered Bill. He was about to make his way up the main hatch when Sandra stopped him.

"No Bill, this way please, it will be safer. Under the circumstances I don't think that Benjamin will mind" she pointed out the way through the main cabin and up through the stairs and hatch that led directly to the wheel house. Sara chose this moment to awaken and sat up calling to her mother. Sandra indicated to Albert that she would take care of this little crisis first and then go to assist Edward in the galley. Bill was heading up the stairs in the Captain's cabin when Sandra moved to comfort the youngster.

"What's happening?" she asked in a feeble voice, still partially asleep.

"Daddy is steering the ship through a storm and safely to the other side, but we both need you to stay down in your bed safe and warm whilst we make sure that the ship is safe. Will you do that for us both please Sara?" such was the sincerity in Sandra's voice that Sara answered immediately.

"Yes Mummy" she replied, although not fully understanding exactly what she was agreeing to.

"Good girl" said Sandra affectionately and pulled up the blankets as Sara snuggled down in her bunk once more. Sandra gave her a kiss on her forehead.

"I'll be back soon" she promised and left the cabin closing the door behind her. The men were a melee of activity. Ropes and buckets were being gathered together in preparedness for use. Lamps were being checked. Sandra navigated her way through the activity and into the Galley. Edward was busy tying a rope around the handles of the various cupboard doors. He looked up when Sandra entered.

"I am here to help" she said simply. Edward looked relieved.

"I could do with some help here please; could you tie this off whilst I see to the lower cupboards?' he asked. Sandra needed no further encouragement. It was obvious that he was securing the cupboards. Even though they all had latches, he wasn't taking any chances and was tying all of the cupboards that were on the same level, together so that they would be additionally secured. Sandra dutifully took over from him allowing Edward to begin on the remaining cupboards.

"When we are done I want to secure some of the stores in the provisions room" he said. Sandra nodded. They went about their work as quickly and efficiently as they could.

Chapter 9: The Storm

Captain Brigges inquired about Sandra and Sara from young Bill.

"Missus Brigges is assisting Edward securing the Galley Captain, and little Sara has been told by her mother to stay in bed."

"And Mister Richards?" he further inquired.

"Has instructed Andrew to start the propeller, and tell all of the crew to secure everything, prepare to bail water and repair damage to the rigging and masts if any occurs. There are ropes ready to ensure the safety of crew working on-deck" responded Bill.

"Excellent" said the Captain now assured that everything was ready for the situation that they were facing. He had detected forward motion and could hear the engine over the thunder that was rolling around them. The flashes of lightning became more frequent and brighter.

"Go below and tell Mr Gill to give me all of the speed that the engine will bear and then return to me, the storm is upon us." The Captain nodded to the hatchway leading to his cabin, it was now the safest and fastest way to communicate to Andrew in the tiny engine room.

"Aye Captain" said Bill and scurried through the hatch shutting it noisily behind him.

***

By the time he returned matters had worsened. Bill was about to report that all was well in the engine room and that they were making maximum speed out of the small engine when extended multiple flashes of sheet-lightning lit up the way ahead of them. Both the Captain and Bill saw it at the same time; a huge wave behind a deep trough. Both of their eyes widened, pupils dilating and then constricting with fear. The trough was at least as tall as the ship from keel to the top of the main mast. The wave beyond it was at least twice as big as that. There was no time to warn anybody, the Mary Celeste began the descent into the trough.

"Hang on!" shouted Brigges. He was white-knuckled his grip upon the wheel was so tight. Bill held on to the brass railing in front of him for dear life. The entire ship lurched downwards. It felt like it was tipping over forwards, almost as if it were doing a tumble turn. There was a sudden increase in speed, everybody on board felt it. The ship careered down into the trough of water and crashed into the wall of water that was beyond it.

Everywhere on the ship there was absolute mayhem. The sudden deceleration followed by the sharp change in pitch from down to up threw people from their feet. In the Galley all of the contents of the cupboards tested their brass and rope moorings as plates, cups, bowls, cutlery and saucers all tried to fly from their secured places. Sandra and Edward were thrown forward and then rolled backwards as the ship began to climb the mountain of water that it now had to contend with.

The men in the main corridor were similarly hurled to the front of the passageway and then backwards. Not one escaped injury either against wood, brass or one another. They attempted to scramble to their feet but found it almost impossible. The angle of the ship was now reversed and it felt like she was about to tip over backwards. So steep was the incline that nobody could properly compensate for it. They had to content themselves with clinging on to anything that was fixed to the structure.

In the engine room, Andrew had fared better than most, he was holding onto some brass valves when the ship lurched forwards, and the security of the fittings more than held his weight as the ship suddenly smashed into the wave and changed angle altering its direction.

Sara was thrown from her bunk but mercifully landed on the Persian rug that was fixed to the floor of the cabin. She instinctively reached for anything to hold on to and found the leg of the table that was bolted to the floor. She held on as tightly as she could and screamed for her mother as she did so.

Brigges and Bill could see a wall of water covering the front of the deck ahead of them it travelled down the length of the deck and smashed into the wheel house. How the windows did not break was nothing short of a miracle. At some point Bill realised that he had shouted a profanity at the top of his lungs as the water approached. Now that the water was washing away from the portals, he suddenly felt embarrassed.

Captain Brigges however was not paying attention to the young man he was trying to see ahead through the rain that had somehow managed to become even heavier. It was as if the all of the available air ahead of them was taken up with millions of huge drops of rain.

The ship reached the peak of the massive wave and began its downhill slide. Brigges could see for just an instant that there was another trough and wave behind this one, smaller than the one they had just faced, but not by much.

"Another one Bill; hang on!" he bellowed. The wheel felt like it was being wrenched from his hands. The rudder must have been facing incredible forces, all of them trying to take the ship from its heading.

"Give me a hand with the wheel, keep her true Bill!" Brigges moved over so that he could take the left side of the wheel and Bill could take the right. Together they had to fight to keep the rudder on track. The wheel pulled right and left threatening each time to overpower them both, but they held on to if for all that they were worth. Both sailors knew that if the ship was left open to the forces of the waves around them then it would certainly capsize. And in a storm the scale and ferocity of this one, there would be little to no hope of survival for any of them.

Down in the corridor some water had managed to get through the hatch.

"Check the other hatch" ordered Albert". Adrian somehow managed to crawl and stumble to the galley door and get it open enough to get in. he had no sooner done so when the ship, now at the bottom of the second trough, hit the next wave. The door slammed shut. Inside Sandra, Edward and Adrian were once more thrown backwards. Adrian crashed against the galley door, Sandra and Edward landed at his feet. As Adrian had suspected there was water coming through the forward hatch too. Not much, but any amount was always a concern. Unless they could find their feet and begin shoring up the hatches, or bailing water then a little water over a long period could do a lot of damage to the interior of the ship.

"How much more of this can we take?' shouted Sandra over the noise of water hitting every exterior surface of the boat. Edward answered something, but it was lost in a crack of thunder that drowned out everything else.

"I must get back to the cabin and check on Sara" said Sandra. Both men nodded in agreement. Adrian reached down and took the forearm of Sandra, who reciprocated. He pulled her up and they both fell once more back against the Galley door. Adrian shuffled over to one side and motioned for Sandra to do the same. This put her in a position to open the door so that she could exit to the corridor. She fumbled with the latch and managed to free it. It took a lot of effort to open the door but she managed. The boat was luring forward again. She gave both Edward and Adrian a knowing exchange. They had been through this enough to realise that it was a repeating pattern. Down into a trough, a wall of water and up over the next gargantuan wave. This was her opportunity and she seized it.

"Go now!" exclaimed Edward. Sandra heaved herself through the door; Adrian doing his best to hold it for her as she did so. She managed to get into the corridor. All of the men looked up, they were busy getting to their feet and trying to grab on to anything that would brace them for the next descent.

"Sara!' was all that she could manage to say before the ship was once more hurled against the bottom of the trough of water. Sandra flew through the air and landed on the deck of the corridor. She scurried forward on hands and knees and grappled with the mast pole that lay before her. Wrapping her arms around it she steadied herself.

Albert came to Sandra's rescue.

"Quickly, as we climb the next wave run for your cabin door, I'll help you" he said. Sandra let go of the mast pole and took Albert's hand. With all of her might she pushed herself forward as did he. Together they scampered to the end of the corridor and made it to the main cabin door. Albert had just managed to open it and began pushing Sandra through when the ship mounted the peak of the wave and began its break-neck tumble down the other side. Sandra almost lost her balance and fell backwards out of the cabin and into the corridor once more but a concerted effort from Albert to stop that happening diverted the adversity. With his help Sandra managed to heave her body into the cabin. There she saw little Sara on the floor clinging onto the table.

"Sara!" she shouted with both concern and relief at the same time.

"Mumm!" cried Sara. Sandra dived across the floor and grabbed on to another leg of the table that Sara was using to keep herself from being thrown about the cabin.

"Mummy's here darling, hold on, baby hold on!"

Captain Brigges and Bill were continuing their battle with the wheel. Another fortuitous smattering of sheet-lightning afforded them both a view ahead. The next trough was smaller this time, still bigger than either of them would have liked to face, but definitely not as large as the previous ones. Similarly the wave that lay behind the trough was not as large as the ones that they had scaled successfully.

There was even room for a tiny bit of contempt toward it, in relation to the others.

"Not so bad now eh Captain?" said Bill with a hint of indifference in his voice. Brigges was not as glib with his response.

"Steady does it Mr Lorensen. No time for flippancy until we are safely through this storm".

"Aye Captain" said Bill a little remorsefully. Just at that moment a forked lightning strike accompanied by a deafening clap of thunder jolted both of them. The main mast had been struck. It lit up as if it were a gas lantern. The light was blue-white with a halo of green.

"Saint Elmo's fire!" shouted Bill. He had never seen it before. Both men were treated to the rare atmospheric occurrence. It was amazing to see. The light somehow managed to both remain static and move at the same time. It was almost impossible to describe.

"Incredible" said Captain Brigges. He had only encountered it a few times before himself in all of his years at sea.

"It's just like the northern lights, but around our mast" he said to Bill. "Beautiful" Both men were mesmerised. The ship hitting the next wave shook them out of their enthralled state. The water spraying the window blurred their vision. A loud wood-upon-wood crack alerted them both to a new danger. The main boom appeared to be careering out of control.

"The boom has broken it stays" observed the Captain with grave concern. The lightning strike coupled with the sudden and violent lurching of the ship must have broken both pulleys and ropes that kept the main boom in place. One of the wooden pulleys was now loose and smashing against the outside of the wheel house. For now what mattered most was finding the opportunity to fix the boom back into place before it damaged the intricate rigging that was the part of the structure.

"Look ahead Sir" exclaimed Bill. "The waves are getting smaller". Captain Brigges looked forward. The waves indeed were getting smaller, but were still larger than he felt comfortable with. He tried to judge the forces that were pulling at the wheel.

"I can handle the wheel Bill. Get below and tell Albert what's happened. We need to get that boom tied down as soon as possible".

"Yes Captain" replied the enthusiastic young man. When Bill hurried down the stairs and into the main Cabin he found Sandra and Sara clinging onto the table, both of them on the floor.

"Are you right Ma'am?' he inquired with some concern.

"Are we through the worst of it Bill?" asked Sandra.

"It is easing, but still rough seas ahead. The main boom has broken loose. We need to repair it as quickly as possible."

"Don't let me stop you Bill, we're fine" said Sandra motioning with one hand for Bill to go about his assignment.

Bill stumbled through the door to the main corridor as the boat heaved this way and that.

"Repair duty gentlemen; the main boom has broken loose!" Bills exclamation garnered everyone's attention. Albert took over.

"Two ropes, Hans and Vaughn" Albert barked his abbreviated orders. "Adrian!" he shouted toward the shut galley door. Adrian appeared, Edward could be seen behind him. "You and Edward keep an eye on things down here we'll go and fix the moorings for the main boom, they have come loose. Let Andrew know what's happened!" he finished his directions and made toward Bill, motioning for him to precede him back the way that he had come. Accessing the two points where the main boom was tied down would be easier from the wheel house. One rope and pulley lay at the very aft of the boat, and the other directly in front of the wheel house.

Still struggling to keep their balance in the high waves the repair party hurried as best as they could under the circumstances up the stairs and into the wheel house. It was now very crowded with five grown men inhabiting the finite space. Captain Brigges offered some advice.

"If you can repair the aft fixture first then it will be easier to repair the front one". Albert nodded having come to the same conclusion. He tied one of the rope lengths around his waist making a typically perfect nautical knot to keep it in place.

"Vaughn" he said indicating that Vaughn was the other man chosen to venture outside to repair the fitting. Vaughn tied the other rope around himself and emulated the perfect knot. Albert then stated the obvious. "Bill and Hans, keep tight hold of those ropes, we could easily get washed off deck in these seas." Everybody was thinking the same thing. They indicated that they were ready. Bill and Hans braced themselves either side of the wheel house door.

"Ready?" he asked looking at both of them. They nodded. Bill opened the door, the rain and wind swept into the small room. The boat lurched again as the two men exited. The deck was slippery, coupled with the high-seas it made the deck a treacherous place to be. The main boom was swinging left and right like a clock's pendulum just above their heads. Through the driving rain they could see the aft pulleys, one hung from the boom, the other was still in place tied to its rope affixed to the deck.

Albert pointed to the pulley and rope on the deck; that was their first objective. Both men stumbled and fell as they walked only the few steps that it took to reach it. Recovering themselves they could now use the rear bannister to steady themselves. Albert picked up the pulley and rope.

"It's not broken, just undone" he said. This was good news; they would not have to replace the rope for this section of the system. Albert looked up trying to judge the motion of the boom.

"When it comes back we will both grab it" he shouted over the howling wind "providing it is not moving too quickly" he added the sensible caveat. The ship lurched again and the boom began to swing toward them. Vaughn kept an eye on Albert for his assessment of the speed of the boom. He made a snap decision and shouted "Now" indicating that they should both reach up and take hold of the boom. They grabbed on to it and did their best to brace their legs against the deck to stop its motion. They were only partially successful as it managed to push both of them to the side of the deck in the direction that the boom was travelling.

Albert grabbed the pulley and rope hanging from the boom.

"No hold on whilst I tie them back together" he said, and began to thread the rope through the pulley system to correctly anchor the device safely once more. It seemed to take much longer than either of them would have liked. The rain and wind and motion of ship made it difficult to do anything with alacrity. Eventually though it was done.

Vaught let go of the boom, it was anchored in-place once more. They both gave the fitting another look-over to ensure that it was going to hold and then Albert pointed to the forward fitting. Instinctively, Albert moved to the port of the wheel house as Hans was on the port side in the wheelhouse holding Albert's safety rope. Vaughn moved to the star-port because Bill was on the star-port side. That way their ropes would not tangle. They met at the front of the wheel house and located the pulley hanging from the boom. This was the one that had been knocking against the wheelhouse.

"Lucky" said Vaughn indicating that this too was a simple case of retying the ropes once they were correctly threaded through the pulley. Both men set about the task at hand without any need for further communication. It was obvious what had to be done. The task was just as difficult as the first one though. However with some perseverance they both managed to get it done.

"Good work" complimented Albert of Vaughn's handiwork. He had no sooner said the words when the ship lurched suddenly to the port side as a wave struck the star-port side covering them both with a wall of water. Vaughn was knocked down by the force. Albert lost his balance and fell backwards the water sweeping him overboard.

"Man overboard!" shouted Captain Brigges from within the wheelhouse. Vaughn scrambled to his hands and knees looking around him. Albert was nowhere to be seen. He scurried to the side of the ship and grabbed on to the bannister and peered overboard. The rope that was tied to Vaughn was tense and could be seen disappearing into the foam and dark blue waves. There was no sign of Albert though. He ran to it slipping over once on the way, and took hold. Looking back at the wheel house he shouted.

"Pull. Give it everything you've got!" He pushed his left leg against the side of the wooden hull and heaved on the rope with all of the might that he could. He could feel that Hans and no doubt the Captain were assisting him from within the wheelhouse. There was definitely a weight at the end of the rope. This let him know that Albert was still at the end of the rope, but not what condition he was in. Had he been knocked unconscious when he was swept overboard? Had he taken water into his lungs? If he had hit the hull of the boat was the blow that was delivered a fatal one? All of these thoughts managed to go through Vaughn's head simultaneously filling him with dread.

He heaved and heaved, Albert must surely be out of the water by now and hanging just over the side. Vaughn was about to chance a look when two hands grabbed onto the side of the hull. Albert was alive. He hauled himself up with apparent ease and scrambled over the side and onto the deck.

"Thank God!" shouted Vaughn. "I feared the worst" he added, relieved that none of his misgivings had come to pass.

"I am well" is all that Albert managed to say. He pointed to the wheelhouse indicating that they should return to its shelter. Glad to oblige, Vaughn ushered Albert ahead of him. Once safely inside Captain Brigges gave an uncharacteristic show of emotion and grabbed Albert by the shoulders heartily.

"Bill take the wheel" Brigges directed and then turning to Albert asked with concern "Are you well?"

"Yes Captain, quite well thank you" replied Albert apparently none the worse from the harrowing experience. None of them could believe the composure that Albert was showing under the circumstances. He had nearly lost his life but either did not seem to acknowledge it or more likely did not want a fuss made of something that may have happened, but did not. Guessing that his sanguine response was alluding to the latter, Captain Brigges gave him a slap on the back and ordered him back below.

"Very good; get dried-off" he ordered. Vaughn and Albert untied the ropes from around their mid-sections and coiled them up neatly.

"The storm may have eased a little, but it is far from over" warned the Captain. Hans, Vaughn and Albert returned below deck to continue to see to the safety of the ship and cargo.

Much later Captain Brigges recorded the incident in his log and how the ship and crew fared through the extended storm front.

Monday November 13th 1871

The ferocity of the storm that we encountered on the morning of this day was unlike anything I have seen before in all of my years at sea. Waves twice the size of the Mary Celeste battered us as did wind and rain. Thunder rolled all around us and lightning covered the sky. We were privileged to witness Saint Elmo's fire around the main mast, but as sea-faring legend would have it, such a thing is portents of looming disaster. Although I do not believe in such superstitions it was hard to ignore the fact that we almost lost Albert Richards when he was washed overboard whilst repairing the fixtures for the main boom.

Sensibly, ropes had been used to assure the safety of Vaughn Lorensen and Albert so we were able to avert disaster. That however was only the beginning of our troubles. The storm lasted most of the day and seemed at various times to be abating only to once more whip itself up into a frenzy over and over again. If it had not been for the forward motion provided by our propeller and small engine then we may not have fared so well.

At various times the bilge pumps were overwhelmed by the amount of water that managed to penetrate the cargo deck. The men were rotated constantly to keep them from tiring too much. But the relentlessness of it ensured that the entire crew had reached the point of exhaustion by the day's end.

The storm finally did pass by about four o'clock in the afternoon. I have arranged shorter than normal shifts for the night-watch to allow each man to recover their strength.

My good wife took over the duties of the Steward and has made us all a hearty stew for our dinner. As I write this we are gathering in the Galley to celebrate our safe passage through the storm and eat a well-earned meal before retiring for the night.

Chapter 10: The Celebration

Captain Brigges finished his journal entry and shut his log book. He looked up as Sandra placed a steaming hot bowl of thick stew before him.

"Thank you my Dear" he said graciously. He put his journal on his lap so as to make more room on the table for everybody's bowls. The serenity of the scene was relaxing. Vaughn was the only one absent. He was at the wheel. Everybody else was here with the exception of Sara who had been fed already and was fast asleep after her harrowing day.

"Now let us say Grace and thank our Lord for seeing us safely through the storm" said Sandra. Everyone bowed their head. Sandra said the blessing.

"For what we are about to receive may the Lord make us truly grateful. Thy saving power has seen us safely through the storm and we give thanks; Amen" which was chorused with an *Amen* from everyone.

"This smells wonderful Missus Brigges" said Bill clearly enthusiastic about the meal that had been prepared. His sentiments were echoed by the others. Forks and spoons went into the stew and initial tastings all confirmed that the dinner was as good as it promised. They were eating in relative silence when Captain Brigges made an observation.

"Albert, I seem to recall that you had a much healthier appetite when you served beneath me aboard the Stanstead". This got the attention of all present. Albert did not seem to be eating with the gusto that the other were. He hesitated before answering as if he were trying to find an adequate explanation for his apparent lack of hunger.

"It's still a little too hot for me; I'm waiting for it to cool a little." The response was completely plausible but somehow sounded contrived; although Captain Brigges could not quite put his finger on how or why this would be the case. Mrs Brigges playing the perfect dinner host rescued them all from what could have turned into an awkward situation.

"We are all clearly very grateful to have come through such a fearsome storm with our wits intact. I don't mind admitting to everybody here that I was afraid for all of our lives. But having come through such a fear and to now be safely on the other side of it, leaves me wondering if that was the most frightening thing that I have faced in my entire life. I don't believe that it was." Sandra stopped speaking, dangling the intriguing thought in front of them like a tempting piece of exotic ripe fruit. The men were all looking at one another as if to see which one of them was going to ask her to tell them what they wanted to know. It was Bill that eagerly pleaded for Sandra to continue.

"Please Missus Brigges, tell us what it was then? What have you faced in your life that was more frightening than the storm?" he looked at her in anticipation. The others too gave their encouragement in various verbal forms; *yes please*; c*ontinue by all means*; *hear-hear*; and so on. They all leaned forward their attentions held captive.

"Well, many years ago, before I met William; I was in the employ of the renouned Psychic, Madam Athalia. I was her personal secretary arranging appointments, billing clients and preparing correspondence on her behalf; all of the usual duties that you would expect of a young girl in that kind of position. Madam Athalia was born in Moldavia and reportedly came from a long line of sensitives. She had moved to England which is where I came into her employ. My father was stationed there, a part of the diplomatic corps from the United States. My mother had met Madam Athalia in her professional capacity wanting desperately to get in contact with my Grandmother, her mother who had died shortly after my birth. I never did find out the exact nature of the initial inquiry, but the results of the few visits to Madam Athalia that my mother made were astounding. She was absolutely convinced that Madam Athalia was the genuine article and had somehow contacted my Grandmother and come up with the answer to the question or the solution to the conundrum that had so perplexed my mother. I was never allowed into the sessions, the séances but I saw the effect that they had had on my mother; it was amazing. With her solution found, my mother offered Madam Athalia my services as her secretary. As a sixteen year old girl, I was duty-bound to do as my mother wanted, but was very apprehensive about working for such a....well I don't mind saying it.....such a spooky lady!" Sandra finished the introduction to her story with a flourish by leaning in and widening her eyes looking around at all of them in turn.

The scene was set, the men were enthralled; they were all imagining the young Sandra in the employ of a supernatural practiser.

"What happened?' asked Bill excitedly.

"One particular séance, I remember it clearly, for a member of the aristocracy, I won't say who out of respect for her privacy, I had to attend in order to make up the numbers seated around the table. There always had to be a minimum of five, never six, seven was acceptable, not eight and a maximum of nine people. Well in this instance one of the expected guests had taken ill quite suddenly and was unable to attend. I was the only available person. It was in the winter, the days were short; the nights seemed to come around faster and faster. Although a late afternoon séance, it was absolutely dark outside by the time we were all assembled and Madam Athalia went into her trance." Sandra shifted uncomfortably in her seat. Retelling the incident had brought with it all of the emotions that she had encountered as a young lady.

"We all joined hands and Madam Athalia called out to the spirit world. Don't ask me how or why, but just believe me, I felt a presence enter the room. There was a cold wind even though all of the windows were closed and the fire place well stoked. The gas lights in the room dimmed of their own accord. Madam Athalia was to my right, her grip on my hand suddenly tightened. I could not free myself of it even if I had wanted to, and I wanted to more than anything that that point in time." Everyone had stopped eating and was hanging on to every word of the beguiling story.

"Then I saw it! I saw it with my own eyes. A disembodied woman, glowing; floating across the room toward the table; eyes afire; I screamed at the top of my lungs. I have never been so frightened as at that moment." Then Sandra surprisingly paused. It was too much for Adrian who tried to get the rest of the story from her.

"But what happened then? Did it reach the table? Who was it? Was it the person that they were seeking to contact in the after-life?" Adrian fired a barrage of questions. All of which Sandra answered but not with the detail or the outcome that they were expecting.

"I feinted. I have no more memories until I came around, revived by Madam Athalia over half an hour later. The other guests had left by this time. I queried Madam Athalia on the vision and the outcome of the spirit visitation. What had transpired whilst I was unconscious? All that she would ever say about the incident was that the client had made contact with the woman that she had hoped to and that the spirit had given her the guidance that was sought. No more than that. I begged my mother to allow me to leave the employ of Madam Athalia. Thankfully my mother relented and shortly afterwards, my Father was transferred back to the States so we were all able to return home. I could not wait to leave England and the most frightening incident that I have ever had in my life." Sandra concluded her tale of horror and looked around to see if there were any follow-up questions from the men.

They were all silenced by the very thought of encountering the spirit of a long-dead person. Satisfied that her tale had had the effect that she wanted, Sandra turned the attention to her husband.

"What about you Benjamin. What is the one incident in your life that has scared you more than the storm that we have just weathered?' Sandra asked. Knowing only too well that there would be no way to dodge this as a topic of dinner conversation Benjamin relented.

"Well my Dear, it is funny that you speak of dead people, because it was not so much an incident that has scared me more than anything, but a book; The Modern Prometheus by Mary Wollstonecraft Godwin-Shelley. It is the tale of a man of science completely obsessed with the reanimation of the dead. Has anyone here read it?" He stopped to see if there were any. All around him people were shaking their heads, even Sandra; although Sandra did admit to having heard of it.

"It was very popular back in the early eighteen hundreds was it not?" she inquired.

"That it was, and I do believe that nobody has since written anything as terrifying as it. I read it as a much younger lad of course, but it frightened me so much that I could barely sleep for a month. A crazy man piecing together a creature from pieces of dead people in his laboratory and then successfully bringing the abomination to life; it's enough to scare anyone. So the storm that we have faced-down seems tame by comparison; to me at least". Captain Brigges story was nowhere near as dramatic as his wife's but it did serve to keep the atmosphere of the dinner table moody and contemplative. Benjamin decided to keep his wife's theme going and nominated the next in line to tell their story of fear.

"Albert, your turn, what tale of dread do you have for us" he said firmly handing the mantle to his first mate to take up. Albert did not have to think for long.

"All of this talk of communicating with the dead, and reanimating the dead makes me think of one thing. I have recently returned from Haiti, an island full of beliefs in the occult. The natives have a spiritual practice there whereby they are able to raise from the dead a recently deceased member of their brethren so that it may serve. There has to have been some crime that the person must pay for in their death that they never did in their life of course. It is not something attempted on all of the Islanders that die. Being a white-man from the United States of America, I thought that it would be nearly impossible for me to ingratiate myself to the natives in such a way that they would allow an outsider to see such a ceremony. But I was tenacious and befriended a local Voodoo Priest and convinced him that my interest was not superficial. He took me under his wing and I was allowed to attend a ceremony to raise the dead."

Just as Sandra had captivated everyone at the table, now Albert had similarly gripped everyone's attention.

"The ceremony began at midnight, drums, many of them beating an infectious rhythm for well over an hour. We had to eat certain preparations and drink certain native beverages, in a very specific order. There was chanting over and over and over. The recently deceased man had been accused of a horrible crime that I will not repeat in the presence of a lady. But you can probably guess what it was. The victim, a young girl had demanded from the village elders that the perpetrator be raised from the dead and become her servant for the crime that he had committed against her." There was no need for Albert to elaborate, all present easily guessed the man's crime.

"His body was dug up and placed where everybody could see it. The Priest shook bones and skulls around the lifeless corpse and as surely as I sit here telling you this, the dead man's eyes opened and he sat up of his own volition." Sandra gave a small stifled scream that startled the listeners. She apologied and begged Albert to continue.

"I returned to America shortly after, but I can assure you that this dead man was walking and following around his new master dumbly and doing rudimentary things that she asked of him. She had her slave, returned from the dead to serve her." Everyone was absolutely stunned. It was almost too impossible to contemplate. A well-educated man claiming to have seen Haitian natives reanimate a corpse, just as in the novel by Mary Shelly those many years before.

"You can't be serious!?" said Edward.

"I know what I saw, and this dead man came back to life, I swear it".

"The very thought is sending shivers through my entire body" admitted Hans.

"Take heart though, apparently the ceremony only works on the native Haitians. At least that is what the Priest told me" said Albert finishing off his tale of horror. Before any more questions or statements of doubt could be levelled at him, Albert thought to deflect them by nominating the next in line to tell their story.

"Andrew, your turn; tell us all about the most frightening thing you have lived through?" Andrew could be seen to be thinking and then as if his mind had settled upon one particular thought, he got a far-away look in his eyes. Then through the abject silence he muttered one word, beneath his breath but still loud and clear enough for all to hear.

"Alcatraz"

The looks of surprise on his compatriot's faces snapped Andrew back into the present. He suddenly needed to explain to them exactly how he came to be in the notorious Prison in San Francisco Bay. He stumbled at first such was his haste to put to rest any fears that they may have after his bizarre admission.

"You see it was like this; not what you are thinking; I was not an inmate, just stranded." He looked around and realised that his overly abbreviated explanation had done little to end the apprehension in their expressions. He took a breath and calmed himself and tried to think of the most logical way to tell his story.

"I was sailing a small skiff in San Francisco bay, part of a race for a local sailing club. But out of nowhere a storm came, not as fierce as the one that we have just passed through, but enough to swamp a small sail-boat like mine. The prevailing winds pushed me in the opposite direction to where I needed to be in order to make it back to shore safely. I was dragged further and further out into the harbour. Any hope that the organisers of the race could come to my aid was quickly dashed by the heavy rain and hail that began to pelt me."

"Oh dear!" exclaimed Sandra. Andrew nodded his agreement and continued.

"My canvas sail was tearing as a result of the wind and hail. Visibility was hardly ten feet in any direction. I was at the mercy of the elements when I saw rocks ahead. Too late to try and avoid them I initially thought them a blessing. Even if I was wrecked on them I could at least try clinging to the solidity of the rocks in the hope that the storm would pass and I would be spotted and rescued." Andrew paused to gather his thoughts and his breath. It was too long a pause for Bill who hurried him up.

"When then Andrew, what happened?"

"I realised that the rocks were part of Alcatraz Island and did my best to navigate around them in the hope that I would find a way to beach the skiff safely. As luck would have it, that is exactly what happened. I chanced upon a safe entry to the island and ran the skiff aground. I was comparatively safe. I managed somehow to take down the sail and tied it up. But that is not the end of this story of unease. I made my way toward the prison. It could be seen through the rain and hail. Knocking upon the door I was not greeted with the kind of welcome that you would expect of a stranded sailor. Instead the guards seized me and took me to a room for questioning."

"But Why?" asked Edward

"They assumed that I was part of some elaborate scheme to help one of the prisoners break out. Can you believe it? Can you even imagine me masterminding the break-out of prisoners from a fortress the likes of Alcatraz? Ridiculous!" he said slamming the table with the palm of his hand.

"I was outraged but unable to disprove any accusation that they made. I pleaded with them to see reason and allow me to show them my wrecked skiff. Eventually they relented and we ventured out into the rain once more. It had eased but the wind and rain were still too heavy for me to contemplate leaving them and attempting to make shore once more. Once the guards and one of the senior prison administrators had seen my boat they began to soften their attitude towards me. However that too is not the most frightened that I have been." He said building up his story and enticing his audience with the promise of more.

"Stop teasing us Andrew" warned Adrian "tell us what happened that was so terrifying". Andrew looked around the table. And spoke in a lower slower voice for better effect.

"Darkness came before the storm relented and I was forced to spend the night in Alcatraz military prison, a guest of the Commandant and his men. Never have I been so scared in all my life. They told me that often the hardened murderers escape from their cells at night just to satisfy their lust for killing. They never make it out of the walls, but that is not their intention. Slit your throat whilst you sleep with a knife stolen from the mess-hall, and sharpened against the stones of the cell. That's what they told me. Although sure that it was just a joke that they were playing on me I barely got a minute's sleep all that night. It was just horrible. I never wish to be anywhere near Alcatraz again. That is my story of dread. What do you think?" he said throwing open his story to critique from everyone.

There were nods of appreciation that it would indeed be a distressing situation to be in. But that it was the eventual outcome had everyone more interested? Bill put into words the question that they all wanted answered.

"What happened the next day, did you get rescued?"

"Oh yes. The race organisers had guessed that I would have found shelter, such as it was, on the Island and came to retrieve me and what was left of my poor little skiff." Andrew felt that it was now his duty to nominate the next person in turn to tell their tale of woe. He chose Edward.

"Edward. What tale will you tell us all?" he asked. Edward did not have to be encouraged to tell his story. He settled himself and clapped his hands together.

"Your story of a creepy institution reminds me of when I was a boy. I was completing a course in butchery at an abattoirs in Mississippi. How old would I have been?" he said questioning himself whilst looking at the ceiling trying to pull the information from his memory.

"Fourteen and terrified of my own shadow; that is how old I was. I was part of a small class that year, there were only five of us that made it through the butchering part of the training. But it is a necessary part of any cooks role to know how to properly butcher a beast and get from it the choice cuts of meat, how to separate the offal how to drain the blood......" Edward was oblivious of the effect that this line of conversation was having upon Sandra Brigges.

"Oh Edward please, spare us the excruciating detail" begged Sandra. Realising that the present company did not have the same interest in exactly how to butcher a beast as he did, he changed the direction of his story.

"Well as if it wasn't scary enough being in the abattoirs in the first place. The teacher and the staff liked to play pranks on the students that were sent to their institution to learn. We were in residence for a month, sleeping in dormitories that were in a separate wing of the building. Large dormitories meant for much larger class numbers than we had. The five of us huddled together and slept closely to each other. Such circumstances can either make men out of boys or leave scars for life. I am still not certain which applies in this case." The quite frank admission raised a couple of eyebrows around the table, but nobody pushed Edward to elaborate upon his odd remark. He continued with his story oblivious to the vexed expressions around him.

"The five of us took up three beds on one side of the dormitory and two on the other. I was in the group of two. The bed next to mine was empty. But one night the staff and teacher had worked us particularly hard and then insisted that we drink warm powdered reconstituted milk before retiring for the evening. The combination ensured that we were fast asleep so that they could get up to mischief. A noise awoke me at some point during the night. I remember it as though it were yesterday. The moon was full its light streaming into the room. I could see everything clearly in its bluish hue. And then I noticed that there was a figure in the bed next to mine. But it should have been empty. I looked around the room and counted. There were now six beds occupied. How could this be; I thought to myself." Everyone was now entranced. Who was the newcomer? When did they arrive?

"I got out of bed and walked over to the bed to get a closer look to see who it was that had joined us while we were asleep. But the blankets were pulled up over the head of the person. A large head, it was abnormally large. I didn't have the courage to pull back the blankets so I scurried over to the closest bed of my fellow students and woke him pointing out the newly occupied bed. We alerted the others as quickly and quietly as we could. Soon we were all discussing what we should do? And as you can imagine with such inquisitive youths, and with the courage of numbers we decide to pull back the blankets to reveal the stranger." Edward paused deliberately to build the suspense.

"We crept over and surrounded the bed. I was somehow nominated to pull back the blankets, something about it being me that noticed the stranger and woke everyone so it was my responsibility. I reached down and slowly pulled back the blankets. There was the head of a huge boar there. We all muttered in disgust at the practical joke that was played on us. And then without warning the beast came alive. A man with the head of a boar leapt out of the bed and grabbed me with both arms growling as he did so. I screamed louder and longer than I had at any point in my life before or since. It frightened me completely and utterly out of my wits. I swear that it gave me grey hairs even at such an early age. As it turns out it was our teacher. The head was a properly taxidermy boars head that they had hollowed out, removing the straw and sawdust. The ritual was one that they played upon all new students visiting the abattoirs. But I did not then, and still do not see the funny side to it." He said. His tone was sincere but the listeners were mixed in their reaction to his tale.

Sandra chorused her support that it was a cruel joke to play upon such young boys. Hans and Bill thought that it was just plain hilarious and could easily imagine the young Edward being scared silly by the incident. Captain Brigges backed up his wife's opinion and Albert and Adrian agreed that it was unconscionable but amusing nevertheless. Once the follow-on discussion had subsided Edward carried on with the unspoken but agreed process for nominating the next in line to tell an anecdote of terror. He could choose from Adrian, Bill or Hans. Now that it was up to him he realised that it was more difficult to choose a successor to the storytelling than it had seemed up to now. Hesitantly he chose Adrian.

"Adrian, you seem to have been amused by my story. Tell us the time in your life that you were so scared that you could not think straight?" he said in a mildly mocking tone. Adrian scratched his chin.

"I will continue along the same theme. In this case institutions that have scared me half to death. It all happened about ten years ago. So I would have been twenty-five at the time. There should have been nothing that could possibly scare me, or so I thought." With the scene set and the attention of everyone held, Adrian began his story.

"My aunty on my mother's side went completely mad, we don't know why, and murdered her husband, my uncle." There was a collective gasp from the diners.

"What happened?" inquired Bill

"Tell us the details please Adrian" begged Sandra. Adrian seemed to have been deflected from telling the climax of his story and was now resolved to give his eager listeners the background information that they so desperately desired.

"It was a funny thing. She had seemed a little eccentric for the entire time that I had remembered her, even when I was a child. My mother called her the *unusual* sister within her family, which by the way had no brothers, only sisters, no brothers at all. Anyway, her funny ways, talking to herself and looking around the room as if she was hearing conversations other than those actually taking place were all quite harmless, or so we thought. My uncle seemed to love her eccentricities as a part of her character." He paused briefly to gather his memories and put them in some sort of order that would best explain his deranged Aunty and her predicament.

"We lived in the same town when I was growing up. Aunty Beatrice and Uncle Adam were only a short walk through the centre of the village. They had a humble house and were dealers in crockery. They imported some, made their own and otherwise sold locally produced items as well. One set that my Aunty had designed was the subject of some consternation however. She had designed a dinner set with scenes of dismembered body parts on it and my Uncle and indeed everyone that she had shown her designs too were horrified. It could never be made and put on sale; nobody in their right mind would buy such a horrific thing. That is what everybody told her. But she would not listen. She went ahead and hand-painted a complete set of this awful crockery. Uncle Adam was incensed. It was a complete waste of their kiln, dyes and paints and time and money. But Beatrice would not listen. It would fetch a fortune from the right buyer was how she justified it."

"Dreadful" agreed Sandra; the others nodding in agreement of her assessment.

"Well eventually it was done and against Uncle Adam's wishes it was displayed in their shop. As you can imagine it drew the chagrin of all that saw it and word soon spread. You know how small townships can be? Uncle Adam felt that he was the laughing stock of the entire townspeople. But try as he might, Beatrice would not remove it from display. Eventually it became too much for him and he had quite angry words with her and removed it from their showroom against her wishes. There was an argument, in front of customers, and a number of pieces were broken whilst Beatrice tried to wrestle them from Uncle Adam's grip." He looked around waiting for a reaction. The expressions of *what next* encouraged him to continue.

"That night after the store had closed for the day, without a single item sold and news spreading fast about the scene that had taken place. Aunty Beatrice became inflamed with Uncle Adam and blamed him for deliberately breaking some of the plates. He thought to calm her, but, and we are not entirely sure what happened next because we only have Beatrice's version of the events. But the *voices* in her head told her that the set could now never be sold because Adam had desecrated it. She waited for him to turn his attention away from her, apparently he was reading the newspaper and she struck him in the head repeatedly with the brass fire stocker. He died from the wounds. His skull shattered in multiple places. That was from the report that looked into the cause of death"

"Horrible" said Bill.

"Hideous" confirmed Andrew. The others mumbled in agreement.

"Aunty Beatrice was taken away and tried for the murder but found to be insane and not responsible for her actions. Her sentence was to be committed for life in an asylum for the criminally insane. My father often commented that insanity ran in *that* side of the family" There was another collective inhaling of breath at the revelation.

"My tale of horror begins when by some strange sense of family commitment to her sister my mother took me to visit Aunty Beatrice in the asylum. Never in my life have I been so scared. Think of exactly the type and place of such a building and it would be absolutely true. The institution was in a remote place near the shore high on a cliff-face with a shear fall from one side of the building. There were waves constantly pounding the craggy rocks below. The walls of the asylum were high and fortress-like. The *staff* were enough to scare you from being able to sleep for a week, but of course the inmates that were littered everywhere were an absolute fright too. The less dangerous ones were allowed to roam around. The very dangerous ones like Beatrice were locked up in small cells as far from the common areas of the other inmates as they could be."

"Why?" asked Captain Brigges, although he could probably accurately guess exactly why that would be the case.

"The screaming Captain, the relentless crying out from the most hardened and insane of them all; it was more than I could bear even at the age of twenty-five. I will never forget going to that horrible place and enduring the multitude of crazy people as long as I live!" he ended his story by pointing directly at the table to make his point.

"Needless to say, even my mother was traumatised and we only ever made the one visitation to Beatrice. As far as I know she is still in the asylum and still screaming along with the others. It gives me the shudders just thinking of it even here and now, hundreds of nautical miles away from her and that horrible place". Adrian looked around to see the effect that his story had had on the others. He was pleased to see that his story had held up well in the company of so many other yarns of similar ilk. But now it felt as if it was up to him to nominate the second last in the story-telling line. He chose.

"Bill, your turn, what do you have that will scare us this evening?" He looked expectantly at Bill. And far from the doe-eyed null response that he was expecting, young Bill had already prepared his story and was itching to tell everybody about it.

"When I was a teenager, I served aboard a riverboat that travelled the Danube ferrying cargo between the principalities of Moldavia, where Madame Athalia was from" he said nodding to Sandra in reference to her earlier tale.

"Moldavia to Wallachia" he said completing the summation of the regular course of the riverboat.

"Most of the crew were from either Moldavia or Wallachia. These men were from countries that have been steeped in folklore and superstition for centuries and didn't mind telling an impressionable youngster all of the most horrifying stories at every opportunity. The most scared that I have ever been was at the retelling of the most famous or rather infamous of these legends. We had finished our shifts and were gathered together, much like we are now, finishing off our final meal of the day. The men were talking in their bizarre dialects, which I could almost interpret but found it difficult to do so. They seemed to be discussing amongst themselves whether or not they would tell me of *the* legend." Bill had his listener's attentiveness; he could see it all around him.

"Whatever *the* legend was I was curious and had interpreted enough to force their hands and I demanded to know more about it. They relented and the oldest of them seemed somehow consigned to tell me all about it." Bill shifted in his seat to get more comfortable before continuing.

"During the war in the fourteen-hundreds there was a Prince called Vlad the third of Wallachia. He was charged with keeping the Ottomans out of Wallachia which they had claimed as part of their empire. I think that it was the Sultan Mehmed or something like that. The Sultan had sent envoys to Vlad demanding a tribute be paid to help fund the Ottoman army. Prince Vlad sought guidance from Pope Pius the second who responded by decreeing a crusade against the Ottomans."

"That doesn't sound so bad" said Hans, less than impressed with the horror story.

"Ah! But it was what Prince Vlad did with the envoys that make this a truly unnerving story. He impaled them on stakes outside of the town's walls. In that way every successive envoy with demands from the Sultan had a chance to see what would happen to them should they enter and make their demands on behalf of their ruler."

"And of course the Sultan's men would not turn away and report back to the Sultan that they had not completed their mission" said Albert correctly guessing the next part of the story.

"Exactly! So the number of impaled men grew and grew. Here is where the legend turns into a tale of absolute terror. Word apparently reached Pope Pius who though that Vlad's methods were too un-Christian and had him excommunicated. A political decision for sure. If Wallachia was no longer part of Christendom, and the Sultan invaded then there would be no need for reprisals or retaliation. Furious that he had been abandoned by the Pope, Vlad had the messengers from the Pope impaled outside the city walls as well. He effectively declared war upon both sides. Anyone who trespassed within Wallachia from either side was impaled. The numbers grew to be in the thousands before he was eventually toppled from power and killed."

"Horrible, yes, but absolutely frightening, no" commented Edward.

"Vlad did not stay dead!" Bill's twist to his tale caught them all by surprise.

"What?" echoed a chorus of all present.

"He haunted the land then and apparently still does today!" Bill observed the impact that the climax of his story had on everyone and was satisfied.

"He roams the streets near the township that harboured his castle, and still wanders the streets and haunts the surrounding forest. It is said that if you are not a native of the land he will know, find you and impale you if he can catch you alone and travelling through the night. They all believe it and warn all outsiders of the legend. It is absolutely frightening. I could not sleep at all that night, knowing that we were heading directly into Wallachia the following night aboard the riverboat. Terrifying!" he said. "When we made port at Wallachia, I resigned and spent the whole day searching for a vessel that would take me as far from there was possible. Luckily for me I found another riverboat that was in need of help and was not due to return to Wallachia in the near future. I signed on as quickly as I could. To this day I have not spent a night in the principality of Wallachia, and I never will!" the resolve in Bills tone was quite apparent.

The diners, now all completely finished with their dinners were adequately satisfied with Bill's story. Now there was only Hans left.

Everyone turned to him and he realised that it was his turn to present to them all.

"I have a similar story to Bill. It involves a riverboat." There didn't seem to be anything too startling about that, but Hans was able to surprise them anyway.

"This riverboat travelled the Amazon!" he had succeeded in capturing all of their imaginations.

"This all happened about five years ago. I had tired of the usual sea-farers life and wanted to do something that was different. I had served aboard a vessel on which one of the crew had previously worked on an Amazonian riverboat. He gave me the address of a Captain for one of the boats that worked the mighty river. I wrote to him with my particulars and in time he wrote back and said that he would be happy to employ me if I ever made it to the region. Well, as you can imagine with such a tempting proposition before me, I packed my bags resigned my then commission and booked passage to Santaremo. I had an adventure before me like no other. The mighty Amazon was awaiting me, full of tribes of natives that have never seen the outside world; beasts that I had only ever read about. The journey there was arduous. But when I eventually arrived at Santaremo, it was exactly as I had imagined it; a frontier town, with only the façade of civilisation to cling on to. I found out that the Ayapua, the riverboat that I had been offered work on, was due to arrive back in dock in the next couple of days. I spent the time looking around the small town. When the boat arrived, I met with Captain Manaus and my working arrangement was set. I was however quite unprepared for what lay ahead."

"Whatever do you mean Hans?" inquired Sandra echoing the thoughts of all of the listeners.

"The heat, the humidity, the leaches that seemed to jump from the water and onto my skin; the mosquitos that seemed to be much larger than any others that I had encountered in my life, it all made an honest day's work an absolute chore. But I soldiered on because this was my greatest adventure. Our course took us from Santaremo to a number of smaller townships that sat along the length of the Amazon. We were carrying supplies from one to the other, each feeding the link in the chain. At night, the crew spoke of the wonders that they had encountered in their travels."

Hans paused and drew breath before continuing.

"I did not have to wait long before I had encountered all of them for myself. There was a boa-constrictor, a snake that was twenty foot long that somehow managed to slither on-board one night. It had crushed to death and eaten one of the pigs in the hold before it was discovered. Eaten in whole! Disgusting, but still somehow fascinating, you could see the shape of the pig inside the body of the snake."

There was a collective groan from the listeners as they all imagined what it must have been like.

"There were flesh-eating fish called Piranhas that would strip the flesh from a bone of meat thrown into the water. Some of the crew knew the areas that the fish lived and showed me by throwing into the water a bone from the galley; frightening. But none of it compared to the tribe that we had to make contact with at the end of our journey. Captain Manus had some kind of deal with this particular tribe. He gathered traditional carvings, weavings and masks and gave them in return knives and other hunting instruments. They lived inland rather than on the river so when we made port, such as it was, at the smallest and most remote township on the river, we had to trek inland for a day to reach the tribe."

"ohhhh" said Sandra imagining the scene in her mind's eye.

"When we got there all that I can say is thank God that the Captain was on good terms with them. Because they were the most feared of all legendary tribes of the Amazon; they were head-hunters and cannibals!"

Sandra actually screamed and Captain Brigges had to take her hand to comfort her.

"Not just that, but they had a strange practice of taking the heads of the victims that they had eaten and somehow shrinking them to the size of a dolls-head, it was without doubt the most bizarre and unsettling thing that I have ever seen in my entire life."

"You saw them, these shrunken heads?" asked Bill completely wide-eyed.

"Yah, horrible it was. We had to spend the night with them and return to our boat the next day. I did not close my eyes the entire night. That was the most scared that I have been in my life".

The entire evening's story-telling had taken its toll on everybody. Captain Brigges called an end to it.

"Thank you Hans for that unsettling story and with that my dear wife and I will say good night. We have all had a harrowing day, and now it would seem that we have had just as harrowing dinner conversation." Everybody laughed at the comparison. There was general agreement that the dinner conversation was lively and disturbing at the same time. Captain Brigges and Sandra stood up and he offered his arm to her in the very gentlemanly way to which he was prone. She took it and they nodded their good-nights to everyone and made a graceful exit.

The remaining men did some hearty back-slapping in appreciation for the good story-telling that they had had bestowed upon each other. But the call of the sleeping bunks was overpowering and eventually they all decided to call it a night. Santa Maria of the Azores would be practically in sight by the morning's light following tomorrow.

Chapter 11: Santa Maria

As predicted and as ably navigated by Captain Brigges, the Azores southernmost island was spotted about sunrise two days later. Captain Brigges made his entry into his journal.

Thursday November 16, 1871

Santa Maria and Villa do Porto are in sight. We have come through some of the most ferocious weather that is possible to endure from the Atlantic. The sight of the port was very welcome indeed. We are all looking forward to spending some time on dry-ground.

My wife and I are planning a day trip up to the hill-top fort of Sao Bras. The crew all have their various plans. Edward for example has promised to butcher a pig and somehow preserve the meats for us in a very short amount of time so that we have pork available for the next leg of our journey to Genoa.

With good fortune and God's grace we will have an easier time for that part of our journey. But for now it is enough that we enjoy the simple comforts that solid land can provide.

***

Benjamin and Sandra and Sara were walking up a disused road, now little more than a track heading toward the fort high upon the hill overlooking the small port of Vila do Porto. From where they were they turned and looked down. It was very pretty. The sun was shining. The breeze blowing, it was not too hot or too cold, in fact it was just perfect. Sandra commented on the scene that they were taking in.

"How pretty are the white buildings against the lush green trees, can you see Sara?" she asked of the wide-eyed two year old.

"Yes Mummy, pretty!" she exclaimed. The smattering of old Spanish-type buildings that made up the centre of Vila do Porto could be seen from this height. The numbers of buildings dissipated further away from the actual port. People could be seen wandering about their business, in no particular hurry. Such was the lifestyle here in the Azores. Time did not seem to matter. Somehow, the journey that Benjamin and Sandra chose to make with little Sara up to the disused fort was out of kilter with the general disposition of the inhabitants. They were almost in a hurry on an island where nobody hurried or seemed short of time.

They pushed on and eventually reached their destination by about noon. The vista from the fort was amazing. All around them lay Santa Maria one of the many islands of the Azores that made up the archipelago. It was absolutely breath-taking. The sounds of birdsong surrounded them. The scent of the many wildflowers filled the air. Having taken in the view of the port below they all turned their attention to the abandoned fort.

"It would have been absolutely magnificent in its time" observed Benjamin as he looked up at the high walls of the old building. Sandra agreed and then sought to reaffirm her understanding of why the building was constructed in the first place.

"It was to ward off attacks from the marauding pirates of the time, back in the sixteen hundreds?" asked Sandra.

"Yes, and very effective for its day too no doubt" replied Benjamin confirming his wife's appraisal of the reason that the fort was constructed.

"Shall we go in?" he asked. It was a rhetorical question. They both took one of Sara's hands and walked through the now permanently open gates to the fort. As they did so Sandra looked back at the twisting road that they had come up. For just a moment she thought that she saw something moving. But when she tried to focus her vision upon it, there was nothing. Dismissing it as a trick of the eyes she turned to face the direction in which they were going.

They moved through the gateway and into the main courtyard of the fort. The high white walls were all around them. There were abandoned carts that would have been powered by horse or donkey, wheels which were hanging on by a thread or completely off and lying next to the broken down vehicle. There was a well that looked completely overgrown. But through it all it was still possible to see the feat of building engineering that it took to construct such a building a couple of hundred years ago.

"Magnificent" was all that Benjamin could say as they looked around taking in the magnitude of the building.

"Shall we climb the battlements and take in the view?" asked Sandra. Sara nodded excitedly, understanding only the part about climbing. They looked around for a possible entryway that would lead them up to the battlements. Benjamin pointed out an archway.

"There appears to be a stairway through there" he observed.

"Let's see" confirmed Sandra, and they walked over to it. Peering through they realised that it was indeed a staircase leading up to the battlements of the fort.

"Come along Sara" prompted her mother. The three of them could barely fit on the narrow cast-clay staircase, but they managed. They climbed to the very top and landed on the battlements and Benjamin lifted Sara on to his shoulders so that she could see over the top of the wall.

"Look Mummy we are in the sky" shouted Sara excited at being so high above the amazing vista that lay before them all. The town, the port and the ocean lay beneath them. It was somehow more beautiful when looking down upon the water than it was when sailing upon it. Sandra couldn't quite understand how that was and discussed the difference with Benjamin.

"It is all in the view my Dear. From here the ocean seems calm, beautiful. But of course we know better. It is ferocious and demanding some days and serene on others. This is an illusion, nothing more." He concluded. Sandra agreed.

"Lets us walk around the full length of the battlements, if we are able and see everything that we can" she suggested. They both looked around them. It appeared that some parts of the battlements may be impassable such was the deterioration, but it was worth a try at any rate.

The trio took their time and ambled around the battlements stopping frequently and admiring the scenery over and over. Sandra commented that she could never tire of such a beautiful panorama. It took quite some time to go around the full circumference. There were parts that had to be navigated with some care, but eventually they managed to see the island and the sea and sky from all of the compass points that the high-wall offered. They had returned to the staircase when Sandra got the oddest feeling that they were being watched. By chance she glanced over the side of the wall into the internal courtyard below. Just for a moment she saw movement.

"Benjamin!" she called out. He joined her in looking down into the courtyard.

"What is it?" he asked.

"I thought that I saw somebody down there." Sandra motioned with her hand in the general direction of the scene. Benjamin looked down; he could see everything that was to be seen.

"I thought that I saw somebody ducking back into that doorway to the left of the water well" she further explained.

"Could you make out if it was a person? Perhaps it was a stray goat?" he suggested. The thought did not detract from Sandra's feeling that somebody was there and scurried for cover when they realised that she may have seen them. She looked at him with concern on her face. There was nothing firm that she could offer him by way of proof though, so she hesitated to labour the point. However the coincidence of now twice seeing something, firstly on the pathway leading up to the fort and now within its walls had unsettled her. She thought for a moment to tell Benjamin of her first *sighting*, but thought the better of it. There was little to no proof that she had seen anything this time, how could she say with any degree of certainty that she had seen anything the first time.

"Perhaps" she said although she did not sound very convinced. Realising that his wife was clearly concerned but also knowing that she did not want to show it, Benjamin offered another solution to the problem.

"We have seen all that there is to see here, let's return to the port and see if Edward has managed to come up with a pig to roast for our dinner tonight?' his offer was thoughtful and Sandra knew it. It was immediately calming and she accepted it gladly.

"Yes, let's go and see how Edward is doing" she said, the relief clear in her voice. She looked again at the doorway. The old door that would have been there was in pieces and lay around the entrance. The sun was in a position that hid the doorway in deep shadow, it was impossible to see if there was anyone or anything lurking just inside.

They carefully descended the stairway and entered into the courtyard once more. Sandra knew it in her heart that somebody was watching them. She looked intently at the doorway on the opposite side of the courtyard.

"Do you want me to go and see if there is anybody there?" offered Benjamin. Although knowing that he was more than capable of looking after himself, the thought of sending Benjamin into the unknown filled Sandra with dread.

"No" she said quickly. "There is no need my dear. Let us return to the Mary Celeste." She gathered up Sara and they made their way out of the old fort. Their day's sightseeing done.

A set of malevolent eyes watched them leave; safely hidden in the darkness of the shadows.

Chapter 12: Death at Sea

When the Brigges family arrived back at the Mary Celeste, the crew had all returned from their brief morning shore-leave. All were engaged in the various duties that were needed to restock the galley supplies. It was agreed by the Second Mate that if the ship was adequately taken care of then the men could have the rest of the afternoon and the night-off. They could indulge themselves in the local culture provided all were back on-board ready to set sail the next morning.

As they approached the ship they could see that there was a fire burning in a stone pit about a hundred foot from where the ship was tied up. The majority of the port was stone and built on a natural outcrop. The pit must have been specifically used for the very purpose that Edward was now doing. He could be seen roasting a full pig over the fire on the spit.

"Edward found his pig to cook?" said Benjamin as they came to the end of the gang-plank. Andrew nodded.

"He is very happy about it too. He said that butchering it was all of the recreation that he needed from his shore-leave. Apparently it will take the rest of the afternoon to cook properly and then cure and dry the choice cuts. If you wish to eat aboard tonight Captain, he is more than happy to serve up a roast. But the other's I have promised can take more of their fill from the local Taberna."

"That sounds like a wonderful idea Benjamin. Let's not bother Edward. We should dine out this evening" suggested Sandra, warming to the idea.

"Very well my dear, we shall" agreed Benjamin. The Captain looked around and inquired of Andrew.

"Where is Albert?"

"Right behind you Captain" was the reply. They turned to see Albert walking up the gang-plank.

"Sorry that I wasn't back earlier, I was trying to negotiate with a local merchant for a keep-sake, but in the end we couldn't reach an agreement." Albert explained his slight tardiness from his duties. Benjamin thought nothing of it.

"I think that we might put Sara down for an hour or so. She has had quite a big day today. I will get to work re-plotting our course for tomorrow, and then we can go out to dinner later this evening." He said defining his plan for the next few hours.

"I have some sewing that I need to finish, this will be a good opportunity" said Sandra agreeing with her husband's afternoon plans.

***

By the time that the Mary Celeste left port the next morning, the men had had their fill of the local wines and foods. The Brigges had enjoyed a night out at a more salubrious establishment than the one that the crew had chosen to visit. And Edward had managed to cure and dry is pig so that it could be enjoyed for the next leg of their journey.

The tide and winds eased the Brigantine out of port and soon the island of Santa Maria was left behind them. It was a bright day but by the afternoon the weather had become increasingly cloudy. Strangely though, the wind had eased. The temperature was dropping and the barometer moved slowly from *fair* to *change.* Bit by bit the sails began to slowly droop, watched with some concern by any that were on deck or in the wheel-house.

"Ahead!" there was a shout from the forward part of the deck. Captain Brigges was in the wheel house looking at his charts at the time and looked up to see what the commotion was about. Albert could be seen at the extreme forward point of the deck pointing and looking back to check that Benjamin was seeing his motioning. Ahead of the ship was grey. Grey sky, grey sea. It took a moment for Brigges to realise what Albert was pointing out.

"Fog?!' He said aloud, the incredulousness audible in his tone. Adrian who was at the wheel at the time agreed.

"Unusual" he said. "I would have thought that it was a bit too early in the season to encounter fog?" he looked over at the barometer on the wall as did Brigges. They both read that it indicated a change was in the air, but neither of them would have attributed that to such a condition.

"Well it is good that the wind is down then, we will be forced to proceed with caution; although, there is nothing in the area that would warrant it." Brigges looked down at his charts just to make doubly sure. There was no sign of a reef or rocky outcrop. They had clear seas ahead of them, albeit seas that they soon would not be able to see very much of. The absolute greyness of the inbound fog was somehow unsettling. Shaking off his uneasiness Captain Brigges gave his instructions.

"Nothing for it but to wait it out and hope that the wind picks up and blows it away" Brigges orders were succinct and self-evident. He could see no reason to stay in the wheel-house as soon enough there would not be a view of anything, anyway. Brigges waved at Albert at the front of the ship, indicating that he had understood the situation that the ship was approaching.

"I'm going below. Call me in need"

"Aye Captain" responded Adrian. Captain Brigges opened the doorway that led to the staircase down to his cabin. Closing it behind him he walked down the five stairs. Sandra was reading a story to Sara. They both looked up and greeted him with smiles.

"The strangest thing my dear, we are going into a thick fog" he said.

"None of the men have weak chests do they? We should prepare a mixture in case" offered Sandra. Benjamin nodded and offered to take over the reading of the story to Sara whilst Sandra went to the galley to concoct the preparation.

"Better to be safe than sorry" she said as she left the cabin.

***

Edward was busy getting the dinner ready when Sandra entered the small galley.

"Fog ahead Edward, I want to make a preparation should any of the men suffer from a weak chest. Fog is the very thing to bring on such attacks you know." Sandra's news and rapid explanation of her visit took Edward aback.

"Certainly Misses Brigges. What do you need?" he asked.

"Castor oil, ether, some of the alcohol that we are carrying and if you have any dried lavender" the list was short. Edward thought for a moment.

"Yes all three, clearly labelled in the store-room" he said indicating the doorway to the supplies. I will have Bill retrieve some of the alcohol from the storage deck for you." He said and put down the spoon he had been using to stir the soup he was making. He left the galley and could be heard knocking on the door to the cabin that Bill shared and issuing the instruction to fetch a barrel of the cargo. When he returned Sandra had found the castor oil but was struggling to find the dried lavender.

"Dried lavender?" she inquired.

"Top shelf, to the left" he replied. He knew the exact whereabouts of everything when it came to his galley supplies. Sandra located the small parcel and retrieved it. Edward had his doubts about whether any of the crew did in-fact suffer from a weak-chest. It would be very unusual for any sailor to take on a life at sea if they did. He had even more doubts about the list of ingredients that Sandra was planning to combat the as yet-undiagnosed condition in any of them. Thinking that the concoction was a formula of some aversion he offered an alternative.

"Perhaps we should call for an early dinner. I have prepared a ham and pea soup that will surely stave off any attacks of weak-chest" he offered. Sandra could smell the soup that Edward was making. It did indeed have a wonderful aroma. She asked

"Only if it is no trouble and you are ready?"

"No trouble Misses Brigges; and the soup is good and ready."

"Very well, I will muster the diners" she offered and went to do exactly that. Edward breathed a sigh of relief.

***

Soon enough they were gathered in the galley and Edward was serving the soup. Albert however had insisted on staying topside and at the front of the boat looking hopelessly into the grey void. And of course Adrian too was absent as he was still at the wheel.

"This smells absolutely wonderful Edward" complimented Bill as his bowl was filled. He reached for a piece of bread to have with it. The loaf was brought on board earlier that day and was still fresh. Bill examined the two foodstuffs. How could something so simple be so satisfying he thought to himself. The now customary grace was said before they began eating and then it was a merry feast of pea and ham soup and fresh bread. They all chatted about their various experiences in Villa do Porto on Santa Maria.

Meanwhile on deck in the wheelhouse Adrian was getting very bored very quickly. He could barely see to the mid ship hatch, no not even that far. The fog was quite unlike any that he would have thought to encounter in this area of the Atlantic and at this time of year. But if seafaring had taught him anything, it was to expect the unexpected from the sea.

He looked down at the chart that the Captain had so ably plotted their course upon. Along with the sextant and spyglass on the chart table they were of very little use in the current circumstances. He allowed his mind to wander. His mind went back to the tavern in which he and his three German companions were celebrating their last night in New York before leaving the harbour. He remembered how oddly Hans had reacted about being accused of the theft of the rings from the museum across town. The miniature scene played itself in Adrian's mind over and over again. Yes, there was definitely something about Hans and those stolen rings, but he couldn't quite put his finger on it.

Adrian had devoted so much time thinking about the odd scenario that he had lost track of time. When he eventually pulled himself back to the grey reality of his duty he had decided that perhaps Albert could take the wheel and he could go below and get some soup. He would appreciate the company. He tied off the wheel and left the wheelhouse to find Albert. Adrian had only walked as far as the mid-ship hatch when he spotted Albert at the front of the ship through the fog. There was something strange about the way that he was standing. It was a stance almost like a marionette. The rocking of the boat exacerbated the odd movement that Albert was making.

"Albert" Adrian called out expecting the murky figure to turn around. There was no response. Adrian immediately felt that something was wrong. He walked a little closer to Albert. By the time that he had passed the row-boat he could tell that something was terribly wrong. Albert seemed to have his neck resting upon one of the ropes and wooden pulleys that fastened the nearest main-spreader to the deck. A particularly thick cloud of fog momentarily obscured Albert from Adrian but Adrian walked toward Albert nevertheless. The fog cleared just as Adrian rounded Albert to face him.

***

Below in the galley everyone was having a lovely meal when it was interrupted with a blood-chilling scream from the deck above. Everyone momentarily froze.

"What was that?" asked Sara nervously.

"Up" was all that Captain Brigges said, and the men went scrambling for the ladder that led directly to the forward hatch and the deck. Vaughn and Hans were the first to emerge and take in the scene that met them. They recoiled in shock and disbelief. Captain Brigges was next on to the deck followed closely by Bill and Edward and Andrew. Sandra and Sara had wisely decided to stay below. Captain Brigges tried his best to not react to what he saw.

Albert had somehow become strangled by the rope and pulley from above. His face was purple his tongue swollen and protruding. His eyes were bloodshot to the point of hiding any colour that was originally there. There was a look of absolute torture fixed upon his bloated face. The men were all shouting in disbelief *how could this have happened* and *oh my God* and similar utterances. There noise gave Captain Brigges something to focus upon in the here and now.

"Quite! Quite please everyone!" he motioned for them to calm themselves. He turned to Adrian.

"Adrian, what happened?" he asked forcefully. Adrian was shaking his head.

"I came out to get Albert to take the wheel so that I could join you all below and I found him like this! How could it have happened Captain, a man of his years of experience; how could he have bound himself in the rope?" Adrian was at a loss to understand the scene before them all. Captain Brigges made a closer inspection. Somehow the rope had managed to loosen itself enough so that it could be wrapped around Albert's neck once. The rope and pulley system did not look to be out of kilter or otherwise out of order.

"Could he have run into it in the fog and somehow managed to choke himself?" asked Vaughn trying to make sense of it all. His explanation of the tragic accident though did ring a chord with the other crew members. Bill and Hans agreed with the theory and asked for the Captain's opinion on it.

"Yes Captain, surely that must be the way that it happened!" exclaimed Bill.

"What other explanation could there possibly be?" asked Hans. But Captain Brigges was not so easily convinced. He looked steadily at Adrian searching for any evidence of a guilty conscience. But he could find none. He looked around at the expectant faces. They were all awaiting a determination from him over the bizarre event.

"See that Sandra and Sara stay below" he instructed Andrew, who hurried to comply. Captain Brigges moved around the corpse studying it from various angles. Edward offered another potential solution.

"Perhaps he was resting against the rope and fell asleep, the motion of the boat managed to quietly strangle him; he would have never known what was happening to him?" Edward looked around for support for his thought on how the accident may have occurred. There was general agreement with this theory too. Captain Brigges was deep in thought, his brow furrowed, and his hand upon his chin. It was easier to believe even such an implausible explanation than it was to believe that Adrian had strangled Albert. There was no ill feeling toward one another, not that he had noticed.

But then Benjamin remembered the story that Adrian had told about his murderous aunty found guilty of her husband's murder and locked away in an asylum for the criminally insane. What was it Adrian's father had said about his mother's side of the family? 'Insanity ran in *that* side of the family.' For just a moment Brigges entertained the thought that Adrian had inherited the murderous tendencies of his aunty. He pondered it for a while and it began to ring true, but just as quickly he dismissed it.

Snapping himself out of his ridiculous musings, he brought himself back to the situation at hand. If he accused Adrian of such a thing, the remainder of the voyage would be tainted with the thought that a murderer was amongst them. How would he cope with detaining Adrian and keeping him apart from the rest of the crew aboard such a small ship? The logistics and impact of such an accusation would be impossible to navigate. And he had absolutely no evidence. Could he even damn this man on the crimes of one of his Aunties?

"No" said Brigges aloud, not realising that he had made verbal his ultimate decision.

"Captain?' asked Vaughn curious as to what he was saying no to. Brigges looked around. The men were waiting on him as though he were a judge handing down a verdict. And for all intents and purposes, that is exactly what he had to do in these circumstances. It was expected of him by is rank.

"No, I don't believe that it could have been anything else other than a tragic accident" stated Brigges with as a resolute tone as he could muster. The men all appeared more at ease. His findings, such as they were, were having the desired effect on the crew.

"Vaughn and Hans; get Adrian's body down from there and prepare a proper covering for him. We have a duty to his mortal remains and we are honour-bound to do the right thing. Our First-Mate has died under tragic, *accidental* circumstances. Place his body in his cabin for the time-being. We must make immediate preparations for a decent Christian burial." The decisive action that Brigges commanded help focus the crewmen. There was a definite plan to follow, orders to carry out; and upon deeper reflection sensible ones at that. Even though the overall temperature was quite cool now, Albert's body would not last long in the cabin before rigor mortis set in and then soon enough he would begin to decompose. A burial at sea was not only the decent thing to do; it was the pragmatic thing to do as well.

Vaughn and Hans moved to disentangle Albert's lifeless body from the ropes; Bill and Edward moved to lend a hand.

"I will explain what has happened to my wife" said Brigges and moved to descend the ladder into the galley. When he reached the bottom Sandra was holding Sara a look of great concern on her face.

"Andrew told us to stay here Benjamin, what on earth has happened? Who was it that screamed?" her questions were anticipated. Benjamin moved to stand closely to her and stroked Sara on the head who blinked at him unknowingly.

"Prepare yourself for a shock my dear. It is Albert. A tragic accident has occurred he has become entangled in one of the ropes in the fog-bound deck and choked to death." He finished his summation. Sandra gasped loudly but then looked at the reaction that it was having on little Sara and then tried to compose herself as best as she could.

"Terrible" was all that she could manage to say. She closed her eyes.

"Mummy what's wrong?" asked Sara her innocent face close to her mothers.

"It is time that you were in bed darling, I will tell you tomorrow?" she said.

"But it's not bed-time yet Mummy" protested the toddler unable to comprehend why she had to go to bed so early in the evening.

"Don't argue with your mother precious. Come along we will both tuck you into your bunk" offered Benjamin as a way of smoothing over the objection.

"Alright" answered the little girl delighted at the prospect of both her Mummy and Daddy putting her to bed for the night. Benjamin opened the galley door to the corridor and allowed his wife and child to go through following them afterwards.

"What will happen now?" asked Sandra as they walked the short distance to their cabin.

"We will have a proper burial at sea first thing tomorrow morning. The body will be prepared in Albert's cabin." He answered. Sandra nodded her understanding of the events that were in the near future. She looked over at the doorway to Albert's cabin. It was closed. The thought that his body would soon be interned there, and for the rest of the entire night filled her with unease. Benjamin must have guessed what was going through her mind he spoke softly to her.

"Try not to worry Sandra. We must face this adversity with all of the dignity and fortitude that we can muster." Benjamin's words were somehow strangely comforting. They reached the doorway to their cabin and Benjamin opened it. As she walked through Sandra glanced backwards at the galley door, it was a little ajar and she could see the men lowering the lifeless corpse of Albert down into the room. She quickly turned her attention to Sara.

"Let's prepare you for bed" she said and did her best to give a warm smile to the toddler.

Chapter 13: Saturday November 18th 1871, Morning

Captain Brigges was reading his journal in the wheel-house. He had his quill in hand and wanted to write about the recent events. He thought that it would help him make sense of a situation that made no sense at all. But he came up with nothing; he could think of no way to start the next entry in the log. Again he read the last entry which was about the Mary Celeste making Villa do Porto on Santa Maria. Still nothing came to him. He put down the quill in frustration. He looked out at the pleasant day that had dawned only an hour before. It was hard to believe that he now had to say farewell to his friend and First-Mate Albert Richards.

A knock at the door interrupted his thoughts. It was Andrew.

"We are all assembled Captain" he said. Brigges looked to the deck where Albert's sheathed body now lay on the gang-plank ready to be buried at sea. The men were all standing around heads lowered. Sandra chose that moment to enter the wheelhouse from the main Cabin shutting the door gently behind her.

"Sara is still asleep bless her. I thought it best not to involve her in this morning's proceedings. She would not understand" Sandra said. Benjamin nodded in understanding and support of his wife's decision. He reached for the small bible that he would use to read from and then offered his arm to Sandra.

"Shall we?" he asked. She took his arm and they left the wheel-house together.

***

"For man thou art dust and unto dust thou shall return. We commend the body of our shipmate Albert George Richards now to the sea. May he find peace in the arms of the Lord our God, and we bless him in the name of the Father and of the Son and of the Holy Spirit" Benjamin finished the rather lengthy version of the service and indicated that the plank should be lifted to allow Albert's body to slide overboard. Andrew and Vaughn lifted the plank and all watched as the bound and covered remains of Albert slid off and splashed into the Atlantic Ocean. There was silence. Nobody could think of anything to say that would sound adequate. Realising that he would have to break the impasse Captain Brigges pointed out the next step in the tradition of burying a shipmate at sea, the wake.

"I believe that we have some wine aboard Edward?" he asked

"Yes Captain" Edward replied.

"Then I think it only fitting that we fortify a small amount of it with the alcohol that we are carrying and all raise a glass to the memory of Albert as is customary." The thought of being able to have a glass, or rather tin mug of fortified wine appealed to all of the men. They needed something to help dull the sharpness of grief that they were all feeling. Even Sandra expressed her appreciation of the idea.

"I shall go and see if Sara is awake, and bring her along to the galley" she said and made toward the wheelhouse. She looked up at the minimal sails that were propelling the ship. They fluttered in the wind just as they always did. To Sandra it was a stark reminder that no matter what had happened aboard the Ship, the Mary Celeste would continue to operate as it had done the day before and would do so tomorrow as well.

The men were entering the lower deck through both the front and mid hatchways.

"The wheel is tied-off and we have minimum sails and a clear run ahead of us according to the charts. We shall leave the ship to find its own way for the next twenty minutes, then Mister Gill, if you could take the wheel please, that would be very good indeed. I think that we should all attend the wake, no matter how brief." Captain Brigges gave his orders. Andrew responded in the affirmative and allowed the Captain to precede him down the mid-ship hatch. Just as he got to the bottom of the curving staircase-ladder there was a horrifying scream from his cabin, it was Sandra.

All of the men were galvanised into immediate action. Even without thinking they ran to the door of the cabin flinging it open. Sandra was screaming again. She had opened the curtains and the ensuing light had revealed a horrible scene. A huge boa-constrictor was coiled around Sara. From the angle of the toddler's head her neck was clearly broken. Sandra screamed again, unable to move from the fright that the snake had instilled into her. She wanted to intervene and rip the hideous thing from the body of her daughter but was rooted to the spot. She was shaking uncontrollably and sinking to her knees in abject horror.

Brigges had to do something. He didn't even think it through first. He ran to the bunk and grabbed the sizeable head of the snake and wrenched it backwards in the hope of breaking its grip on Sara. The snake responded by baring its huge mouth. Benjamin forced the snake's jaws shut with an almost inhuman strength that he developed from the shock of what was happening. By now Andrew and Vaughn had thrown aside their fear and were trying to wrench the snake from Sara's body. It was having little effect. They could not believe the strength that the thing was using to crush Sara's body.

"Help us!" was all that Andrew could say to the others frozen with fright just a few steps away. It was all that they needed, Bill, Edward, Adrian and Hans all raced forward and the group somehow managed to grab a different section of the snake and as one they attempted to uncurl and disentangle it from Sara. It wasn't working. Benjamin looked around the cabin for something to help. The small table held a letter writing kit that was open. Within it he could see a brass letter-opener with a mother of pearl handle. It was blunt but resembled a knife enough for Benjamin to run across the cabin and grab it. He ran back and hesitated for a second trying to think where best to stab the creature.

Again he grabbed the head of the snake and thrust the letter-opener through its jaw. There seemed to be no effect. Angered and terrified at the same time he repeatedly stabbed the boa constrictor through the head each time entering from the soft underjaw. Blood oozed out and covered the blade, such as it was and Benjamin's hand.

"It's working" shouted one of the men. He did not know which, but gave the snake another three successive punctures.

"Pull" said one of the other voices behind him. The snake began to go limp and give up the incredible strength that it had used to crush the little girl to death. It was like untwining a rope from a sack of grain. With some coordination which was agreed as they went, the boa constrictor was finally freed from Sara and thrown to the cabin floor. Sandra raced forward and reached out to hold Sara's tiny head in her hands. It was completely flaccid. Sara's eyes were open looking lifelessly at her mother. Sandra sounded like she was choking; she did not seem to be able to catch her breath. But this turned into a sobbing and then a wailing as the reality of the situation enveloped her. Even Benjamin, not disposed to showing emotion couldn't help himself he wept openly as he held Sara's shoulders in his hands. A couple of the men were similarly disposed and made no attempt to hide their grief. The others were in a complete state of shock.

For a long time nobody could bring themselves to speak. Sandra and Benjamin's loud crying had died to a regular stammering sound of grief when there was one word spoken in the cabin. It was said by Edward.

"Where?" He said looking at the dead snake. "Where did it come from?" He looked up and at the others. Some were able to meet his gaze others could not. Nobody could think properly.

"Let's throw it overboard!" shouted Bill out of revulsion for the despicable thing that lay on the cabin floor.

"Yes" seconded Andrew. He looked to Captain Brigges who managed a stiff nod in agreement.

"Help me" Andrew said. Vaughn and Bill both reached down and lifted the snake. It was heavy.

"Up this way" he said indicating the door that led to the wheel-house. Without being prompted Edward made toward the door first to open it and allow the others easy access. He preceded them up to the wheel house presumably to open the door and allow the trio access to the back of the deck where the snake would be jettisoned.

Sandra watched the men take the creature out of the cabin and once more looked down at her child. Another overwhelming wave of grief flooded through every part of her body and mind. She could think of nothing else than her desire to have Sara somehow miraculously spring back to life. All that she wanted was for Sara to live once more. She did not even feel the comforting arm of her husband around her shoulders for a long time. When eventually she did notice it she looked into his face. There written as plainly as anything was the torture of a father that had lost his youngest child.

Sandra broke down and began to cry again. It was more than she could bear. At that moment in time she wanted to be dead so that she did not have to endure the suffering that had been inflicted upon her, upon them both. No parent should outlive their child. How can I go on without her? Why is there absolutely nothing that I can do to bring her back? Thoughts like these went around and around in her head until she thought that she would go mad.

At some point she realised that she was crumpled on the floor and Benjamin was holding her. She had lost all sense of time and could not remember how long she had been there in his arms. She looked up at him, now able to put into words a small part of how she was feeling.

"Our beautiful baby, Benjamin, what are we to do? How can I live without her?" He could offer no words of comfort as much as he wanted to. Benjamin did not want to agree with Sandra even though that was exactly how he was feeling. He shook his head in the hope that it would go some way toward answering her unanswerable questions.

He helped Sandra to her feet and they both looked at Sara's lifeless body. Benjamin tenderly and gently repositioned her head so that it was no longer at an awkward angle, and then straightening her hair and nightgown and putting her small body in a position of repose, he closed her eyelids and slowly lifted the sheets and blankets over her body covering it completely.

Somehow that felt as if it were a new dagger in Sandra's heart. It was an acknowledgement of the finality of Sara's fate. She began to cry anew.

"Come; Sandra" said Benjamin quietly. "Let us leave Sara in peace and grieve in the galley". There was no sense that Sandra could make of what Benjamin was suggesting, but she could find no words to object to the idea, no strength to offer any resistance.

They spent a long time in the galley, all of the crew Sandra and the Captain. Instead of a wake for the untimely death of Albert, it was a collective grieving for the loss of such a young soul.

Chapter 14: Saturday November 18th, 1871, Evening

Something was nagging at Sandra's memory. Somebody had spoken of a boa constrictor earlier in their journey. But for the like of her, she could not remember the details. The more that she tried the more that it eluded her. Frustrated she asked everyone in the galley.

"Who was it that said that they had encountered Boa Constrictors?" Sandra's question caught the attention of everyone. All had continued to mope in the galley unable to comprehend the events of yesterday and today. There was general confusion about the context of Sandra's question to everyone. People indicated their confusion by shaking their heads and looking perplexed. Sandra put further context around her inquiry.

"When we were telling our stories of horror, after the storm, somebody told us of boa constrictors, but I cannot for the like of me remember who it was or what it was in relationship too." Sandra had given them all enough information now to make a proper determination and supply an answer to her query.

"Hans" said Bill "His story of the Amazon riverboat included a boa constrictor killing a pig aboard his boat". Everyone looked at Hans. He suddenly felt that he was on trial for the mysterious appearance of the boa constrictor aboard the Mary Celeste that had so tragically killed Sara Brigges. He looked around him. All eyes were focussed upon him. He felt guilty but could not ascertain why.

"What?" he stumbled "What do you mean, why are you asking me this now? It was coincidence that I happened to mention a story from mine past but it has no bearing on what has happened now yah?!" Hans' German accent was suddenly very pronounced. He was normally so adept at covering it up. But he was stressed and felt like he was on-trial for Sara's death. Captain Brigges moved to diffuse the potentially hazardous situation. He knew that it would not do to begin accusing people of anything at a time when emotions were running so high.

"Nobody is accusing you of anything Hans" he said quite definitely. He looked around at everyone as if to drive home the point. None could meet his gaze. They all looked to the flooring as if ashamed of their sudden suspicion.

"But tell us Hans, as somebody that has encountered the snake before; are they are they to be found on Santa Maria? Could it have somehow secreted itself aboard and found its way to our cabin?" Benjamin's question seemed less accusatory but somehow it felt no less of a burden to Hans. He wracked his brain for the answer. He was sure that he had had a conversation with the other crew men aboard his Amazon riverboat about boa constrictors. He had to try with all of his might to resurrect the memories from his mind so that he could accurately disseminate the information to everyone. They all so desperately wanted to know.

"Um" he stammered and then as if someone had suddenly lit an oil lamp the information that he so desperately wanted was revealed to him.

"Central and South America and the islands of the Caribbean" he said with a note of pride in his accomplishment.

"So not Santa Maria, in the Azores?" asked Brigges confirming the geographic domain of the species.

"No mine Captain, definitely not from the Azores" he said with resolve. There was nobody that heard the answer that disbelieved him. After all he was the only person that had any first-hand experience with the snake. There was more silence as they all pondered the implications of their new-found knowledge. If the snake had not come aboard from the Azores, where had it come from?

"Perhaps it had come from another boat that was also docked and found is way aboard the Mary Celeste? One that had come from the Caribbean or from South America" offered Edward. People listened and contemplated the possibility. It did not seem outside of the realm of probability. Then out of the silent contemplativeness came a voice that seemed to pierce their ears; not just because of what he said, but because of the implications behind the theory.

"Perhaps Albert had taken it aboard in one of his chests as a pet and when he died and could no longer feed it, it came looking for a meal on its own". Everybody looked at Bill as though he were completely mad. But the longer that nobody objected to the absolute foolhardiness of the accusation, the longer it took form as a distinct possibility. Andrew seized upon the idea and expanded upon it.

"Could the snake have been kept alive by feeding it milk, milk from a saucer?" he asked Hans looking intently at him and waiting expectantly for the answer.

"Yah. I suppose. But…." Hans' reply was cut short by the excited interjection of Andrew.

"I caught" and then reconsidered his choice of words. "I interrupted Albert in his cabin. When I entered he had milk in a saucer that he said he had spilt, but maybe he was feeding his hidden pet boa constrictor?" he finished his piece of deductive evidence and looked to the others for support.

"When was this Andrew?" asked Captain Gill.

"Just before we hit the storm" he said, defining the timeframe in which he recalled the incident. The others contemplated this new piece of what now seemed like crucial information. Benjamin continued with the proposed chain of events.

"If he had not had time to feed his....pet, since the storm, perhaps it was hungry and broke out of its confinement. But where did he have this thing hidden?" he said pointing out the deficiency of the group-led hypothesis. It was Sandra that offered a piece of information.

"His trunks, the large one and the small one, they both had air holes in them. I had asked him at some time during the voyage about this oddity and he claimed that it would stop his clothes from becoming mouldy in the sea air. But now it just seems odd. And it supports the idea that he had brought the snake aboard with him for whatever bizarre reason." Her eyes were distant as she remembered the various memories that made up the thought. Bill interjected with an expansion upon the current trail.

"Maybe the snake strangled Albert up on deck and then made its way below?" the insinuation sounded completely hollow and ridiculous. It threatened to untwine the web of guilt that they were collectively weaving around the dead man; the only one of them that could not defend himself from the allegations. Sensing that this was indeed what was happening, and like the others still desperate to make some sense of the death of Sara, Vaughn interjected.

"Albert was in Haiti before he came on this voyage, he must have come across the snake when he was there!" the piece of the puzzle was absolutely damning. Everyone including Captain Brigges mumbled in agreement.

"Yes, and as we thought, it escaped when he died and then horribly killed Sara" Edward finished off the jury's finding of guilt upon Albert. There simply did not seem to be any other explanation that made any sense. They had all been gathered for the entire day trying to come up with something, anything that would help ease their pain. And this was it. The circumstances surrounding the appearance of the boa constrictor on board the Mary Celeste and how it came to kill Sara Brigges had been surmised by the men and woman aboard. There was a collective feeling of ease that permeated the air. It did not make accepting the death of such a bright-eyed beautiful toddler any easier, but it did help them all make sense of how it came to be.

More silence filled the cabin as thick as the densest smoke. But this time there was a tinge of enlightenment. If Albert's death was to be considered a tragic accident in the fog, then Sara's could be considered a horrific outcome of Albert's death. There was nothing more on board that could hurt them now. All of the bad luck that any voyage could ever have was spent by now. Everyone was tired. The energy that had gone into the burial of Albert, the wrestling of the snake away from Sara's body, the grieving for the toddler's untimely death and more recently the desperate search for answers had taken its toll on everyone. They were all exhausted.

It took a long time but eventually the silence was broken by Captain Brigges.

"Sandra and I will prepare Sara's burial shroud. And we will lay her out to rest in Albert's cabin until morning, when we will have another burial at sea. I suggest that we all resume out duties and continue onwards. Vaughn, please take the first watch". The definite plan helped people focus them all on something other than their grief.

"Sandra" Brigges offered his arm to his wife. She took it and did her best to make a dignified exit from the galley.

***

Sandra and Benjamin had made a death-shroud from some material that Sandra had been keeping to make a new fine dress for herself. It seemed only fitting, said Sandra. Benjamin carried Sara wrapped inside her finery down the corridor and Sandra opened the door to Albert's cabin. Benjamin placed her gently on the bunk and looked down at his covered daughter. Sandra however was distracted. She was looking at both trunks with holes drilled in them in order to circulate air. She moved toward the first one and reached out to open it.

"What are you doing?" Benjamin's voice startled her and she spun around in fright. She became annoyed and rebuked him.

"I want to see" she said. Then turning again to the trunk her hand hovered over the latch and she undid it. Taking both hands she separated the two halves to reveal the capacious emptiness inside. There were very few clothes hanging in the space. It was exactly as she had thought when she saw Albert carry the large trunk aboard, he was indeed travelling very lightly. She turned her attention to the smaller trunk, also with holes drilled in the top of it. This *must* have been where his deadly pet snake had resided until this morning when it had freed itself at the expense of Sara's life.

Benjamin seemed mesmerised as she reached down to open it. She flung it open. It was empty except for some toiletries, a shaving kit and some other unmentionables. Nothing was out of the ordinary. Nothing indicated that a boa constrictor had been resident there for the length of their journey. But neither of them was in a mood to disbelieve a truth that they had come to accept. Sandra slammed it shut.

"I shall not be able to sleep Benjamin" she said setting the topic of conversation to anything other than what they both did not want to talk about.

"Nor I. But we must try Sandra. We have to bury our youngest tomorrow." He forcefully took her hand into his and met her gaze. She could see the anguish still in his eyes. Somehow, that helped her manage her own grief. She suddenly felt as if she was a hard and cruel woman, incapable of returning love and tenderness when it was extended to her. Guilt surrounded her, even tighter than the snake that had killer her daughter. She was remorseful and wanted to let Benjamin know it.

"You are right, my dear, of course you are. I am sorry. I will do my best to get some rest before sunrise, I promise" her words were gratefully received by Benjamin. He squeezed her hand.

"Come along" he even managed the smallest of smiles and she responded in kind. They both left Albert's cabin, with one last look at their lost daughter lying on the bunk, then they closed the door.

Chapter 15: Sunday November 19th 1871

It was a much more sombre burial than Albert's the previous morning. The crew fought to hold back their tears as Captain Brigges read the passages from the bible. He had chosen different ones this time, but it all seemed so much more tragic because of the potential that had been so horribly snuffed-out. Sara Brigges innocence of youth had been taken far too soon in her journey through life. Her death was more of a tragedy somehow than Alberts. There was even guilt festering within the men for feeling this way. It was as though they had not felt enough grief for Albert's death and feeling more for Sara's was doing him an injustice. It all compounded and made the funeral service so much more difficult to endure.

Eventually though Captain Brigges signalled Andrew and Adrian to lift the board that held the tiny body of Sara and just as Albert's remains had done yesterday, she slid into the ocean but this time with the smallest of splashes. It was too much for Sandra who wailed loudly. Hearing the absolute agony in her crying was like having a rod pierce through the hearts of all who heard it. Captain Brigges did his best to comfort his wife under the circumstances, but it was clear that he too was barely able to contain his own grief.

He motioned for Andrew to come forward. Andrew did so and leant in to listen to the Captain's orders.

"There will be no wake. I think that it would be best for the men to return to normal duty immediately to keep their minds off the funerals." Benjamin's directions were sensible. Adrian nodded his understanding.

"I'll see to it Captain" he said.

"Missus Brigges and I will be in our cabin" Benjamin added, with that he guided Sandra, still sobbing toward the wheel-house.

***

The rest of the day had passed by the time Captain Brigges emerged from his Cabin. He entered the wheel house. Hans was at the wheel and greeted him.

"Good evening Captain. We are on course, there is a good wind and the weather has been fine. It looks like we will have a clear night with a half-moon to help light our way." The summary of the current status of the journey was welcomed by Brigges.

"Thank you Mr Gondeschall; carry on" Captain Brigges left the boat house to wander around the deck for a while. His hands were behind him and he looked out to sea. The sun was setting in quite a spectacular display of colours and cloud formations, but he was oblivious to the magnificence. He was staring out over the Atlantic, watching the moving seascape, but not taking in any of it. Bill was fussing over a rope and pulley and tying a knot over and over so that it was just right. He finally decided that no matter how many times he did it he would not be completely satisfied so he settled for the job he had just done.

"I'm heading for the galley Captain, is that anything that I can get you?" he asked, concerned that he and his wife had been in their Cabin all day without eating. At first it seemed that Brigges had not heard Bill, but just as the young man was preparing to repeat his question the Captain responded.

"I should go to the galley and take something to Missus Brigges" he said. His voice was flat, there was little emotion in it.

"Yah Captain" said Bill, affirming that it would be a good course of action. Brigges looked at the young man.

"I shall be along in a few minutes" he said indicating that Bill should not wait for him. Bill nodded and made toward the mid-ship hatch so that he could go below. Captain Brigges looked out to sea once more, but this time he took-in more of what he was seeing. His mind turned to the theory that they had all managed to piece together from the facts that they knew. What if it were all not true, he thought. What if the elaborate sequence of events that had led to a boa-constrictor coming aboard and killing his daughter were false? Then, he would be none the wiser about Sara's death. He felt no closer to a believable answer for Albert's death either. The very thought of not being able to explain two sudden deaths on a ship beneath his command was frightening to him, but he could never let it show. The crew would lose faith in their Captain and it would make the rest of the voyage unbearable.

There was nothing to it, he concluded, everyone would have to continue to believe the story that they had collectively conjured to explain Albert and Sara's deaths. But he would give it much more thought. There had to be more to it than they were giving it credit for.

He made his way toward the front hatch so that he could climb down the ladder directly into the galley. Shutting the hatch above him he descended the ladder and turned around. Bill was there being served a bowl of something by Edward. The remainder of the crew must have been in their cabins.

"Can I get something for you Captain, a bowl of stew perhaps?" asked Edward. Brigges looked at him and nodded.

"Two please Edward. I will take one to Missus Brigges" Edward hurriedly served off two bowls of what was a very nice smelling stew and put them onto a small tray with appropriate utensils and two small buns. Edward must have made them during the day at some point because they looked very fresh each with a golden crusty top.

"Thank you Edward" he said and went to the door. Bill jumped up from where he had sat down to open the door for Benjamin. Brigges thanked him quietly and left the galley, Bill shutting the door gently behind him.

There was nobody in the corridor. Benjamin navigated his way around the main mast and balanced the tray in one hand so that he could open the handle to the door of his Cabin. Sandra was sitting at the small table looking out the open star-port porthole. There was a breeze coming through it, and the remnants of the sunset could be seen in the dusk sky.

"I have something for us to eat Sandra" he said placing the tray down before her. She looked down at it and shook her head.

"I'm not hungry Benjamin" she said so quietly that he could barely hear her.

"Please try" he said hoping that she would change her mind, but knowing that she would not. He sat in the space opposite her. He looked at the stew and as appetising as it may have been, all of a sudden he had no appetite whatsoever. He could hardly insist that Sandra eat something to keep up her strength if he could not. Looking around for something to inspire him he saw his log book. He had to find a way to write down the events about Albert and Sara. He picked it up and opened it at the last entry. And for what seemed like an eternity he just looked at it. He was completely unable to write a single word.

By the time he came out of his dumbfounded trance, it was night. Neither of them had eaten anything. A wave of tiredness enveloped Benjamin. He accurately guessed that Sandra too must be exhausted. Grieving can take a lot of energy even if it appears to be a solitary and static emotion; it saps the strength from the body and the mind.

"Let us retire for the evening" he suggested. Sandra had absolutely no will or energy to resist. And right now it gave her something to focus her attention upon other than the loss of her daughter. They both silently prepared themselves for the night. Climbing into their bunk, Benjamin dimmed the lamp. They lay quietly together wandering if either of them would be able to sleep. But mercifully it came and soon they were both fast asleep.

Chapter 16: Monday November 20th 1871

Very little conversation happened between anybody the following day. The crew went about their chores. Captain Brigges wandered around the deck not directing anybody to do anything in particular. He had convinced Sandra to leave their cabin and she had managed to sit quietly at the back of the ship for a few hours before retiring again to the privacy of the main cabin. It was as if it was too difficult to talk to each other just at the moment. Some in the crew likened it to not enough time having had passed after the double-deaths aboard the Mary Celeste.

But in their silence to each other held the glimmer of disbelief; thoughts turned to the way that both deaths had occurred. Bit by bit people began to question the veracity of the story that they had all come up with to explain the situation. Nobody said anything to anybody about it, but at some point most of the people aboard had doubts about the validity of the explanation that had solved their dilemma. One mind however did not have any doubt about how the deaths had occurred. That person was certain that the alone were responsible for both. And now it was a waiting game to see which of them would be the next easiest to mark for murder.

***

Lunch was being served by Edward in the galley. Bill was at the wheel and the remainder of the crew were assembled. Edward had been making pork sandwiches for each of them. Large chunks of bread with large chunks of pork. There was a relish of some description that tasted of apples and onions. They were eating in contented silence when Captain Brigges entered the galley. Andrew asked him a question that had been nagging at him for a while. Now that he had had the chance to objectively assess their situation he felt it necessary to ask for the Captain's opinion.

"Captain Brigges" he began. Brigges closed the door and gave Andrew a look as if to say *please go on*. "I was wandering if we should not return to the Azores and report the deaths of Albert and Sara to the authorities there. Perhaps they will want to do an investigation?" his question was fair enough, but it stunned everyone nevertheless. All eyes moved from Andrew to Brigges to see what his reaction would be to the assertion. Brigges in his usual way gave the question a good amount of contemplation before he answered.

"No Mister Gill. I have thought of this and you are correct, two deaths so closely together at sea certainly warrant an investigation of some description. But I would prefer that this be reported to the Italian authorities when we reach Genoa rather than the Spanish ones in the Azores. I have had dealings with the Spanish authorities in some......" and he waved his hand dismissively "past circumstances and have found them to be overly officious and intrusive. I believe that we have ascertained how both of these tragic deaths occurred. The Italians will treat the investigation with more care. We need not unnecessarily delay our voyage by retracing our steps to the Azores. Our destination lies ahead."

"Yes Captain, of course" said Andrew, feeling somehow chastised for stating the course of action that he had. Then something occurred to him and he asked a follow-up question.

"Will the Italian authorities search the ship?"

"I imagine so, but no more than the usual port customs and taxation agency would so do." He saw a look of concern on Andrew's face.

"You appear worried Mister Gill?" he said. Everybody looked at Andrew. He realised that he was making too much of a fuss about the situation that they would face in Genoa when they arrived. His immediate concern was the furs that he was smuggling in amongst the barrels of alcohol below in the cargo hold. If the Italians found them and suitably taxed him on their importation he would not make nearly the profit on them that he had hoped. Andrew felt that it was best to leave the subject alone completely. He gave the Captain a nod of understanding and a wry smile. He hoped that it would be enough to end the discussion that he had inadvertently brought upon himself. Brigges made his way to the counter where Edward was putting together the luncheon sandwiches

"Two please Edward. I think that I shall be able to convince Misses Brigges to eat something today."

"Very good Captain" said Edward and skilfully put together two sandwiches for the Captain and his wife. Andrew meanwhile looked around him at the faces of the others. They had all returned to enjoying lunch. He cursed himself for asking Captain Brigges his question in the first place. As tragic as the deaths of Albert and Sara were he could not let the situation get in the way of his plan to make at least double his pay from this voyage. If he could do it this one time, then he could do it again and again and eventually earn enough money to earn the respect of Wilomena's father. Then the old man would surely give them his blessing and allow them to marry. Now more than ever he had to remain focussed upon his goal. He took a bite out of his sandwich.

The others eventually finished their sandwiches and drifted out of the galley. Even Edward had tidied up and left. There was only Bill who remained. Andrew looked up at him.

"You almost gave the game away Andrew" he said with a cheeky smile and a wink. Andrew was confronted and defensive.

"What do you mean?" he asked trying so hard to sound innocent that he managed to sound exactly the opposite.

"Your *extra* barrels below, the ones that contain furs." Bill clearly knew of Andrew's secret smuggling operation, there seemed little point in denying it now.

"But how?" he stammered.

"I noticed that there were more barrels on board when we first began loading and that you insisted in packing the very front of the ship yourself before turning over that drudgery of a task to me. And the barrels that you used are not quite the same as the ones that contain alcohol. I have managed to spend enough time down in the cargo hold to re-arrange enough of the barrels to bring to the surface one of the unusual ones, and I have opened it to see what was inside. I knew that it certainly was not liquid." Bill had indeed uncovered Andrew's scheme. He was a little frantic.

"What are you going to do?" he asked suspicious of Bill's motives for being so investigative in the matter.

"Nothing" he answered with complete sincerity.

"Nothing?" Andrew inquired incredulously.

"None of my business Mister Gill; if you want to make more money on this trip than your wage; that is entirely your own affair. Nothing to do with me at all." He sounded as though he was speaking the truth. Andrew was amazed. He wasn't sure what to say next.

"Uh, you don't want to know why?" he asked cautiously.

"Of course I do. Would you like to tell me?" he said his eyes lighting up in anticipation. Andrew looked at the ceiling briefly and then back at Bill.

"No." he said simply, hoping that the answer would be enough to end this awkward conversation as quickly as possible.

"Ah, well, that is that then" he said with disappointment evident in his tone. He got up from his seat and gave Andrew a small bow.

"Then I shall take my leave of you. Good day Mister Gill" he said and left the galley via the door leading to the corridor. Adrian assumed that he was going to his bunk. Left alone in the galley Andrew thought through everything that had just happened. Would Bill tell anybody else? That single question dominated his thoughts. Why didn't he simply ask Bill when he had the chance? He would have to find a suitable time in which to do so. He wandered when that would be. His mind went over the crew schedule and a possibility became clear. Bill would be steering the ship tomorrow afternoon. If he could finish lunch quickly enough, he could make his way to the wheelhouse and ask Bill. Or even sooner if the opportunity presented itself.

Then his mind turned to other motivations that the young man may have. Perhaps Bill intended to ask for a cut of the proceeds in order to maintain his silence? That possibility did not sit well with Andrew at all. He had to know what Bill's intentions were. Surely he would not have gone to such trouble to uncover the smuggling scheme and not want some recompense for it. He couldn't bring himself to believe that Bill was simply a curious young man and would mind his own business under these circumstances. That would be just too much to hope for.

Chapter 17: Tuesday November 21st 1871

The sunrise on the following day seemed to bring with it the promise that things were going to get better. Sandra had begun eating again, although not very much, it was at least a start. The winds had been favourable and progress along their plotted course was good. The ship was in excellent shape. The crew had busied themselves cleaning the deck. It did not need it, but nevertheless the result was welcomed by the Captain.

A pod of dolphins that began to swim alongside the ship gave the crew something to amuse them helping to break the spell of mourning that had fatigued them for the last few days.

***

Captain Brigges was in the wheel house staring once more at his log. He had still not managed to write a single word about Albert or Sara's untimely deaths. He knew that the authorities in Genoa would want to read his log about the incidents. He dipped his quill in the ink and brought it close to the page. Not a single word entered his head. He could not even bring himself to write a date and at least mark out the beginning of the next entry; nothing came.

"Perhaps tomorrow" he said aloud. Bill was at the wheel at the time and asked for clarification as to what the Captain meant by his softly spoken sentence.

"I am sorry Captain, what is it?" he asked.

"Nothing Mister Lorensen" answered Brigges. Tomorrow is another day he thought to himself. Perhaps this unwillingness to write about the deaths would leave him by then. He pondered briefly why he was incapable of making the next entry in his log. Perhaps because it would force him to relive the death of Albert and then the death of Sara over again; that was it. He promised himself that he would steel himself and begin his Captain's journal once more the following day.

Brigges had noticed that nobody spoke of Albert or Sara. He had wondered if that was a way of coping with the dual loss. Perhaps it was a way of being polite. Whatever the reasons, it somehow made the crew more able to go about daily duties, and that was a good thing. If the crew were busy then he was satisfied.

Andrew broke into Captain Brigges thoughts by opening the door to the wheel house.

"Captain, Edward is serving lunch. Bill would you like me to bring you something?" Both men turned to respond to Andrew's notification and question.

"Thank you Mister Gill, I shall come along presently" said the Captain.

"Yes thank you Mister Gill. Whatever Edward is serving would be very welcome indeed." He smiled his acceptance of Andrew's kind offer.

"Alright then, I shan't be long." He said closing the door when he left.

***

By the time Andrew arrived in the Galley lunch was in full swing. He then quickly busied himself compiling a small tray consisting of another one of Edward's chunky sandwiches and a mug of tea. This is what he would take to Bill in the wheel house. He was leaving the galley as Edward inquired.

"Will the Captain and Missus Brigges be joining us today Andrew?" he said

"I believe that the Captain is at this moment trying to convince Sandra to join us for lunch". It was almost a promise that Sandra was getting better and recovering from the incredible grief that she had suffered.

"That would be very nice" he said politely. His offer was chorused with a myriad of *yeses* from the others.

Andrew continued on his mission to bring some lunch to young Bill who was for sure by now alone in the wheel house, steering the ship. He left the galley quietly. The remaining men in the galley were eating quietly and not engaging with each other, Hans decided that it was too quiet and thought to start some conversation. He directed a question at Vaughn.

"Do you have any plans when we reach Venice, Vaughn; sight-seeing or anything like that?" it was an innocent enough question.

"Yes I do. In fact I am keen to see as much of Venice as I can" he continued.

"I want to see Saint Mark's square and have a gondolier take me on a tour of the canals"

"I want to see some of the famous Venetian glass being made." Edward joined in the conversation. "But even more than that, I want to avail myself of the local markets to see what I can source for our voyage home. I'm sure to come up with some tempting Italian foods for us all. That is something to look forward to." He said. Edward had a slightly far-away look in his eyes as he pondered how exciting it would be to shop for Italian produce from the locals.

"What about you Hans?" asked Vaughn. "What wonders in Venice do you want to experience?" he had just finished asking his question when Andrew re-entered the galley.

"Was young mister Lorensen grateful for his lunch?" asked Hans. Andrew nodded.

"Oh yes" he said and then sought to change the subject immediately. "What are you all talking about?" he queried of the group. It was Vaughn that answered.

"We were just about to find out what in Venice Hans most wants to do?" he had just finished asking his question when Adrian interrupted.

"Nature calls, I'll be back in a minute. Don't say anything interesting without me". He left the galley clearly heading for the forward companion. His desire to not miss out on any conversation was not honoured by anyone. They started to exchange short stories about what each of them wanted to do whilst they were in the romantic city of Venice. After a while Adrian re-entered the galley and wanted to know what he had missed out on. He was still speaking when a loud noise cut through the air. The noise was a constant clanging of metal against wood, long and loud and very out of place. It was instantly recognised by Vaughn.

"The anchor!" he shouted above the din.

"It's been released?!" exclaimed Hans as he stood up.

"What?" Adrian began his obvious question but the men were all up by now and crowding around the ladder to get up through the forward hatch. Vaughn was first followed by Adrian. Hans and Edward ran through the galley door to rush up the mid-ship hatch. As they did so Sandra opened the door of her cabin and called to them.

"What was that noise?" the look of concern on her face was obvious.

"Anchor Missus Brigges, it has been weighed for some reason" he said and then continued his ascent up to the deck.

"What? Here, in the middle of the Atlantic?" Captain Briggs suddenly appeared from behind Sandra with a follow-up question that went unanswered. Edward had now made it up the steep staircase-ladder by now. Sandra and Benjamin followed them both via the corridor and then up the mid-ship hatchway. They climbed up to the deck.

Everyone was there looking over the front of the boat at the chain that now disappeared into the waves below it.

"Where is Bill?" asked Captain Brigges. They all turned to see through the wheel house window, Bill was nowhere to be seen.

"He didn't go below did he?" Brigges looked around him for confirmation. People all shook their heads indicating that they simply did not know.

"Was he at the wheel when you left him Adrian?" Vaughn wanted answers.

"Yes, he was at the wheel when I left him and came back down to the galley." Adrian looked as dumbfounded as the rest of them.

"Where could he be?" asked Vaughn, he was agitated. Where was his little brother? Vaughn ran up to the wheel house in the vain hope of seeing Bill crouching down hiding from them for some inexplicable reason. He flung the door open, the small room was empty. The wheel was unattended, and not tied-off.

"He is not here!" shouted Vaughn with increasing anxiousness.

"Get this anchor up, Hans, Adrian. The rest of us will search the ship. Perhaps he went below to the forward companion or the cargo hold, the coal room or the engine room?" all were possibilities. But the obvious question was how. It was infeasible that he could have made it down the mid-ship hatch without any of them seeing him. Adrian and Hans got to work with the anchor system and began to winch it back up. Vaughn did not need any further instruction he ran to the mid ships hatch and disappeared below.

"Help him search" Brigges ordered Andrew who disappeared down the forward hatch to comply with his new orders. Brigges was looking out to sea, and all around the edge of the boat. Sandra followed him in a very quick circumference of the ship's deck.

"Do you think that he fell overboard?" she asked with a shocked look on her face. He did not want to alarm his wife after all that she had been through but there was no way to cover up what he was doing.

"I have to be sure, I don't want to overlook any possibility" he said. She nodded and joined her husband in scouring the water near the ship, concentrating on the back of the ship looking for a man waving in distress. But there was nothing. Just the waves and the wake of the ship as it sailed through the deep blue water.

"No sign" said Sandra confirming what Benjamin already knew. This filled him with both hope and dread at the same time. If Bill had not somehow fallen overboard then he must still be aboard somewhere. But then the sense of dread took over; an overpowering feeling that all was not well. There was simply no need for Bill to hide aboard the ship. Something was amiss and Benjamin knew it.

They moved to join Hans and Adrian who were still slowly winching up the anchor. The entire length of the anchor's chain had descended into the waters of the Atlantic and it had reached its end, so bringing it all back would take some time.

After a while Vaughn and Andrew appeared on deck once more via the mid ship hatch.

"Nothing!" shouted Vaughn with more than a hint of hysteria in his voice.

"Calm yourself Vaughn, there must be some explanation" said Brigges, sounding anything but convincing. Just then there was a cry from Edward. He was looking over the side of the ship at the anchor being raised. It had finally broken the surface of the water. Entangled by one arm in the chain was Bill's now lifeless body. Everybody rushed over to see what Edward had indicated. Sandra screamed. Even Captain Brigges had to stifle back a cry of shock. Vaughn upon seeing his little brother screamed at the top of his voice.

"Nooooooooooooo!" the despair and anguish cut through all of them.

"Bring him up, bring him up!" instructed Brigges. Adrian and Hans began to winch the anchor up to its mounting point. Vaughn and Andrew and Edward reached over the side to grab onto Bill's slumped form and try to bring him on-board. Vaughn had to untangle Bills arm from the chain before that could be done successfully. They lowered his body to the deck. Vaughn wept openly at the sight of Bill laying before him; dead. He crouched over his brother and wailed with tears and despair. The rest stood around almost unable to comprehend the reality of yet another death. Sandra could not stand to look at Bill's opened eyes and shocked expression and buried her head in Benjamin's shoulder and began to cry.

For a long time nobody was capable of any action other than grieving the loss of the young man. No one could think of anything else to do. The situation was so unbearable that it enveloped them in a cloud of misery and desolation. A sharp turning of the ship broke the spell of despondency for Captain Brigges. The wheel was unattended and the ship was at the mercy of the wind and waves.

"Andrew, take the wheel, get us back on course" he said in a feeble voice. But the affirmative plan was welcomed by Andrew. It gave him something other to think about than the scene that was before them all. Andrew stumbled numbly toward the wheel-house to do as he was told.

Vaughn had reached down and was hugging Bill's lifeless body. It was then that Edward noticed something at the back of Bill's neck.

"What is that?" he asked pointing and drawing the attention of everyone except Vaughn.

"There" he indicated pointing "at the back of Bill's neck". Sure enough there was a black ball with spikes coming out of it in all directions lodged in the back of Bill's neck. Hans who was kneeling beside Vaughn leant over to take a closer look.

"I think that it is a sea urchin of some description" he said. "It must have lodged there when Bill was dragged below the water by the anchor".

"What are you saying Hans?" demanded Captain Brigges. Hans suddenly felt that he had said the wrong thing. He stuttered and shook his head.

"Nothing Captain, just a sea urchin, nothing more" he managed to get out after a while.

"No what I meant was what do you mean about Bill getting dragged-down by the anchor, how do you think that it happened?" Captain Brigges question gave them all pause for thought. Even Vaughn had managed to contain his sorrow for long enough so that he could try and make sense of what had happened. However, being presented with this as a starting point though vexed everyone.

"Why was Bill at the anchor in the first place?" asked Edward. Nobody replied.

"How did he become entangled in the chain?" asked Hans.

"How did the anchor get released?" asked Captain Brigges. Again there were no easy answers. The lack of answers to such obvious questions gave them all a feeling of uneasiness. Adding that emotion to the situation made it even more tense than it already was.

"Who was the last to see him alive?" asked Brigges. He then realised that it may very well have been him and added "He was alive and steering the boat when I went down to my cabin to convince Sandra to join us for lunch. Andrew said that he was going to come back with some lunch for him". Brigges looked backwards toward the wheel-house. Andrew could be clearly seen steering the boat. Hans offered his summation of the events in lieu of Andrew being able to answer for himself.

"Andrew came into the galley and took a tray up to Bill. But he had returned to the galley by the time that the anchor was released." It seemed to be the exoneration of an alibi by a witness in a crime-scene. Again the silence was unbearable for Brigges. Either the crew were coming to their own conclusions and not willing to voice them or they were as stumped as he was. Neither prospect was very appealing right now.

Vaughn was trying to grab a hold of the sea urchin that had embedded its sharp quills into the back of Bill's neck. He managed to take hold of enough of the quills to pull it out and although briefly studying it with a sour face he threw it overboard.

"There was no reason for Bill to leave the wheel-house" he said now able to talk again.

"Perhaps he saw that the anchor was coming loose and went to refasten it, just as he was doing so, it broke from its mooring and dragged him down with it?" Sandra's sudden inclusion into the conversation was jarring at first. But the more that her words were left to be pondered, the more it seemed likely that that was exactly what had happened.

"What else could it have been?" said Edward adding his voice to the theory that Sandra had offered.

"Yes my Dear" said Benjamin adding his support "Bill somehow became entangled in the chain and it broke free tragically killing him." The neat and tidy explanation was left to linger for a while longer. Vaughn looked from Sandra to Captain Brigges and then to Edward and Hans and Adrian. Hans indicated with a shrug of his shoulders that it may very well have been the truth. Vaughn did not want to believe them. It couldn't have been as simple as that. But for the like of him he could not think what else it could have been that drew Bill from his steering duties to the anchor.

"How did it become lose?" he said weakly. They all looked to each other for anything that would support their newly found explanation. Nobody could think of anything.

"Vaughn, take Bill below, to Albert's cabin and lay him in repose" instructed the Captain. At first it looked from the expression upon his face that Vaughn was going to argue but he just shook his head, still unable to comprehend that Bill was no more.

"Please Vaughn" said Brigges sympathetically. "Edward and Hans can help you"

The offer of help somehow galvanised Vaughn into action. He did not want anybody else to touch Bill's body.

"No, I will do it" he said forcefully, his strength returning. He scooped up Bill and carried him toward the mid-ship hatch. Hans ran to descend the ladder first in order to assist Vaughn down the steep curving decline. Vaughn turned around before he attempted to navigate the steps.

"This ship is cursed!" he said spitting the words at Captain Brigges. Brigges closed his eyes as if the words had physically injured him. Vaughn continued down the hatch. Hans appeared back on-deck momentarily thereafter. Clearly Vaughn had not wanted any help whatsoever.

"He is correct Captain" said Edward. Brigges looked at him and could see the absolute belief in Edward's face. He truly believed that the Mary Celeste was a cursed ship. A moment of panic erupted within Brigges. He could not have the crew believe that the ship and their voyage was damned. Not on his watch. He mustered every bit of conviction that he could and levelled his retort at Edward and Hans.

"This ship is *not* cursed Mister Heed. We may have suffered more tragedy than any ship has the right to expect on a voyage, but I will not have you endorse stupid superstition aboard my ship. Do you understand!" he was clearly angry. Edward could not meet his gaze and Hans too looked down at the deck rather than antagonise the Captain in his current mood. Adrian too did not want to inflame the situation so added only his silence.

"Yes Captain" Edward said, capitulating.

"Sandra!" he said sharply and offered his arm. Sandra did not dare to refuse. She took it regarding Benjamin with apprehension. She could see that he was angry.

"We shall continue on-course to Genoa" his orders were clear. He led Sandra to the wheel house, they were both clearly making their way back to their cabin. Left alone on deck, Hans and Edward and Adrian looked at each other. There was silence but the three of them knew that it had to be broken. Eventually Hans ventured into the uncertain territory that he had been assessing in his mind.

"Where were Captain Brigges and Missus Brigges when this happened?" he said. Edward shook his head.

"They appeared at their cabin door shortly after the anchor was released. There is no way that they could have been on-deck and then raced through the wheel-house and back down below. Hans stop what you are thinking. Captain Brigges and Sandra couldn't have had anything to do with Bill's death". Hans was unsatisfied with Edward's rationalisation.

"Andrew then; he said that he delivered lunch to Bill. Did he? He told us that he spent time at Alcatraz. Maybe he was in inmate for a similar crime. How do we know that he wasn't?" Hans was searching for answers. Edward pointed at the wheel house.

"Only one way to find out isn't there?" he said and strode toward the rear of the ship with Hans and Adrian in tow. They flung open the door of the wheel house and Andrew looked around at them. The three men were looking around the wheel house for the tray that Andrew had previously delivered. It was quickly located on the chart table. A single bite had been taken out of the sandwich. It somehow made Andrew's assertion that he delivered Bill's lunch and then returned to the galley seem more credible.

"What is it?" asked Andrew wandering what Hans and Edward and Adrian were looking for.

"Nothing" said Hans tersely and left.

"Nothing" confirmed Edward and followed Hans. Adrian said nothing and closed the door to the wheel house as he left. The three of them went below via the mid-ship hatch and went straight into Albert's cabin. Vaughn was there looking down at Bill's body. He did not look up as they entered the small room.

"How could this have happened?" he asked them not expecting an answer. Hans and Edward and Adrian had no answers for him.

"Come away Vaughn" Edward said hoping to get him out of the cabin to leave Bill's body in peace.

"No....later....I want to stay for a while" he said in a broken sentence.

"Not too long" Edward tried to sound as comforting as he could but felt that it did not come out that way at all. Edward put his hand on Vaughn's shoulder in a further effort to in some small way ease the man's suffering. Hans indicated that they should all leave Vaughn to his mourning. There was something else in the way that he motioned to Edward, like he had something more to say to him. Adrian did not see the body language. He went into the galley instead, perhaps to find something to drink. Hans and Edward went into the nearest crew's cabin and closed the door.

"Three deaths in such a short time" Hans said stating the very obvious. This annoyed Edward. He frowned at Hans indicating his irritation.

"All in unexplained circumstances; how did Albert choke on a rope? Where did that snake come from? And how did Bill become entangled in the anchor? And how did it become released? You cannot tell me that all of these things just happened by themselves!" Hans was raising his voice and realised it, bringing it back down in volume.

"Something is wrong, I tell you."

"What are you saying Hans, that somebody has caused these *accidents*, who? How? It doesn't make any sense. Who would benefit from this voyage becoming a sailing disaster?"

"That, Edward, is what we have to find out!"

Chapter 18: Wednesday November 22nd 1871, Before Dawn

It was very early morning; the sun was not even beginning to peak over the horizon. Edward was not in his cabin. Instead he was in the other crew's quarters with Vaughn and Hans. Hans was putting forward his theory of how all of the deaths were actually linked.

"Think about it, both of you. Where was Captain Brigges when Albert was strangled?" Hans looked to them both. It was difficult to think after all that they had been through over the last few days. Vaughn did not even try to recall. Edward had a furrowed brow and was trying to think of where the Captain was at the time.

"He was with us in the galley, wasn't he; or in his cabin?"

"He had more than enough time to sneak up to the deck and strangle Albert in the fog and then come back down to hide what he had done". Hans' damning accusation stung Edward and to a lesser extent Vaughn who was still numb from grief.

"You must be joking; yah!?" Edward said, knowing that Hans was not making light of the situation at all. Hans realised that he needed more circumstantial evidence to convict his suspected killer in front of his jury of two.

"And before he came on deck for Albert's burial service, he had time to put a snake on his sleeping daughter to kill her too. How convenient that he and Sandra were the last ones to see her alive." Hans' second theory actually managed to snap Vaughn out of his stupor.

"Murder his own daughter? Why?" he asked incredulously. Edward too gave Hans a look as if to reinforce the point.

"He is a killer, who knows how he thinks or why he has done what he is doing. We have to fear for our own lives now." Hans managed to side-step the question completely. Feeling a little short-changed by the *answer* that Hans had come up with Edward changed tact with his questioning of Hans' suspicion.

"What about Bill then, how did he manage to tangle him in the chain and then release it?" Edward's query brought Vaughn further back into the here and now.

"Ahh" said Hans now clearly excited. "That one is easy. He was in his cabin supposedly when it happened. What if he knocked-out Bill and carried him over to the anchor, tangled Bill's arm in the chain and then released it. Did you notice that Sandra was the one that opened their cabin door? He did not show his face until a little while later. He had more than enough time to run back to the cabin by the wheel-house and then come up on deck with the rest of us and pretend to be looking for Bill. All the time knowing exactly what had happened to him". Edward completed his summation of how Captain Brigges was behind each of the deaths. Vaughn saw a small supporting piece of evidence to assist with Hans' conclusions.

"It was Missus Brigges that came up with the explanation of how Bill died." He said.

"A story that they both concocted beforehand and then offered to all of us wanting desperately to know how this tragedy could have happened. And we willingly and stupidly accepted it!" Hans used the new point of view to bolster his argument. Edward however was still not convinced.

"But your suspicions rely on the fact that they are both in it together?" he said as if it were a hole in Hans' logic. Hans thought however that it was more support for his argument.

"They must be in it together, how else could they have made three murders seem like fatal accidents." He was clearly now convinced that he was right, Vaughn and Edward could see it in his eyes.

"But that would mean that Missus Brigges was responsible for murdering her own daughter Hans. Do you have any idea how incomprehensible that sounds?" Edward tried to talk some sense into the man. But Hans would have none of it.

"Both cold-hearted murderers for sure!" he said a little too loudly. Vaughn and Edward looked at each other. Even in the face of everything that he had said it was clear that they did not believe that Benjamin and Sandra Brigges were responsible for the deaths. Hans was frustrated at seeing the disbelieving expressions on both of their faces. He challenged them.

"Well who do you think killed Albert, Sara and Bill!?" he said tersely.

"Adrian" replied Edward with a tone of conviction that caught both Vaughn and Hans by surprise. They were momentarily stunned.

"Adrian?" asked Vaughn "I thought that he was your friend?! How do you come to that conclusion?" Edward looked down as if trying to gather his thoughts and then paused briefly before he spoke.

"Adrian was steering the boat when Albert was killed. At least that is what he said he was doing. He tied off the wheel and crept up on Albert in the fog and strangled him and then placed the body in the ropes to make it look like an accident. He somehow smuggled the snake aboard and left it outside the Brigges cabin before he came on deck for Albert's funeral service. And said he was using the forward companion shortly after Andrew had taken lunch up to Bill, but he instead slipped up the mid-ship hatch and strangled him too and then entangled him in the chain and threw him overboard. The extra weight on the anchor eventually made the lever give-way. He had arrived back at the galley just in time for it to unfurl." Edward neat and tidy damnation of Adrian was complete. He looked proudly at his audience. Vaughn and Edward were contemplating what Edward had said. Adrian was absent for a short time to use the forward companion just after Andrew had arrived back from delivering Bill his lunch. It somehow did not seem like enough time to kill Bill and then throw his body over the side.

However the shorter summation managed to hold a little more weight than Hans' rambling diatribe. It was true, Adrian was steering the boat when Albert was killed. There was no way to disprove that he had somehow smuggled the boa constrictor aboard and secreted into the Brigges cabin just before the funeral service. And it was within the realm of possibility that he had murdered Bill after Andrew took the young man his lunch. Vaughn gave Edward's theory a little more evidence.

"Wasn't it Adrian's aunty that was committed to the asylum for the criminally insane for murdering her husband? Maybe murderers run in the family?" This was just the icing on the cake for Edward that firmly believed that he was right and Hans was wrong. Hans however was not so easily dissuaded from his current conviction.

"Two theories; two possible murderers; sorry three" Vaughn corrected himself as he said aloud what he was thinking.

"We need to know which one of them is guilty; so we can protect ourselves from them. Do you think that the murderer or murderers whoever they are will stop at three deaths? We are all in danger. We have to defend ourselves. We do not know which of us will be next?" Hans was getting quite animated again.

"Captain Brigges was very definite about not turning back and reporting this to the Spanish authorities on Santa Maria. I think that he is planning to kill us all before we get to Genoa!" Hans hoped that Vaughn and Edward would see that his reasoning was conclusive and that they needed to act.

"What do you propose that we do?" asked Vaughn.

"After the funeral service today, we have to mutiny and put the Captain and Missus Brigges in chains." He stated exactly what he wanted to see happen. Edward would not be so easily recruited for mutiny.

"What if I am right and it is Adrian, not the Captain. You will face charges both from the either the Spanish or the Italian authorities. And even if by some miracle you escape their retribution, you will most certainly face imprisonment when you return to the United States." Edward's reasoning deflated Hans somewhat. It was true he would face a harsh penalty which would surely include imprisonment if he was wrong about the Captain being the murderer, and led a mutiny at high-sea against him. If only Edward had not come up with an alternative for the killer, then he would have been certain that he was acting in the best interests of everybody aboard by mutinying. But now, the element of doubt had crept into his mind. And the thought of being wrong now seemed like at least a possibility. Edward could see that his caution had had the desired effect on Hans.

"No more talk of mutiny Mister Gondeschall. But I believe that you are correct and we must take steps to protect ourselves. We must watch Adrian and the Brigges closely. We should not be alone with them, and if we are, then we should not turn our backs on them." The logistics of Edward's proposal were barely worth thinking about.

"One of us will be on night watch, steering the boat like Andrew is now." It was obvious that the plan of action was ill-conceived and impractical. But the mention of Andrew brought a new thought to them. Edward put it into words.

"Do we warn Andrew? It would be wrong to not warn him about what we are thinking. What if he is the next one to be murdered by....whoever it is?" he said acknowledging that there was more than one plausible theory on the subject.

"I will do it" volunteered Vaughn. "After the service today when he is resting in his cabin alone, I will tell him what we have been talking about here." Vaughn sighed. Edward and Hans were glad to have set in motion a message to Andrew that may very well save his life.

"Go back to your cabin, it will be morning soon. You should be there when Adrian wakes up. We don't want him to suspect that we are conspiring about him." suggested Hans. Edward was not even contemplating returning to his cabin.

"I will not be alone with Adrian" he said clearly unnerved by the thought.

"I thought you were convinced that it was the Brigges that are the murderers, what does it matter if you are alone with Adrian?" Hans' tone had a distinct mocking note to it.

"Just in case you are right, I will rest here, if it is alright with you Vaughn". Edward had started his sentence before realising that to rest in the cabin with Vaughn and Hans meant he would have to sleep in Bill's bunk. It suddenly seemed like the wrong thing to say. But Vaughn was sympathetic.

"It is alright Edward, you can try to get some sleep in Bill's bunk." With Vaughn's words, Edward breathed an audible sigh of relief.

"Let us get some rest then" he said. The discussions had been somehow draining. Each of the though suspecting that they would not be able to sleep attempted to do so anyway.

***

Bill's funeral service was as sombre as the previous two. The readings were a different set yet again. Hans could not help but feel revile as Captain Brigges read from the small black bible. He is a murderer and he is administering the religious rites. It was the ultimate hypocrisy he thought.

A proper sea-man's burial shroud had been used to bind-up Bill's body, and in a scene that had been repeated now too many times, the body was slid into the Atlantic Ocean. Nobody spoke for a long time. Some stared at the deck, others out to sea. Andrew was the first to break the silence.

"Captain Brigges. In light of what has happened I think that we should turn back to the Azores and report everything that has happened to the local authorities." The assertion drew the sharp attention of everybody. They all looked at Captain Brigges for a response. Brigges in turn, looked at the faces that were watching him so intently. There was clear determination in their expressions. They were asking him to agree to the second-mate's proposal. The silence dragged on as Captain Brigges pondered the situation.

"The Italian authorities are better equipped to investigate these deaths Mister Gill. I do not believe that the Spanish authorities will have the aptitude or interest in our tragic events to warrant us involving them." He concluded and looked once more around at the faces. It was clear that his answer had not pleased any of them. He decided to take more of an affirmative stance.

"That is the last that I will hear of turning the Mary Celeste around, from anyone, is that clear!" he was angry now and made no attempt to hide it.

"Have the deck scrubbed Mister Gill. I want it cleaned from front to back before lunchtime today!" Brigges adopted the air of strict Captain with ease. He stared right into Andrew Gill's eyes as if daring him to disobey his order. Gill backed down.

"Yes Captain" he said capitulating to his superior "I shall see to it".

"Good. I will be re-charting our course to *Genoa*" he said reemphasising the direction in which he intended to take them all.

***

There was much mumbling beneath people's breath. The orders from Captain Brigges were being carried out begrudgingly by the crew. Andrew who had been steering the ship through the early hours of the morning had retired to the galley to eat something before getting some shut-eye in his cabin. Adrian was now steering the ship and the rest of the crew including Edward were engaged in washing the deck. Mops and buckets were sloshing water everywhere and extra effort was being put into the task, perhaps because it was a way to vent the discontent the crew were feeling. Captain Brigges and Sandra were in their cabin. It was assumed that the Captain was making good on his promise to re-plot their course toward Genoa, the final stop before reaching port in Venice.

Andrew had finished eating in the galley and decided that he needed to use the forward companion before retiring to his bunk. He approached and curiously the door instead of being shut was slightly ajar. The seas were calm today which was lucky Andrew thought as he approached it, as rougher seas would have caused the door to bang against the wall. It was lazy to have not shut it, whoever used it last thought Andrew. At the same time he did concede that everyone had been through much over the last few days and could be forgiven for a minor lapse in sea-faring etiquette.

Andrew opened the door and a metal cup which he had not seen, that was perched at the top of the door came crashing down on his head. He jumped back in fright. The metal cup clanged to the deck. It had been full of a clear liquid that covered his head and back. It had a distinctive odour.

"What the hell!" he shouted as he cursed whoever had set the practical joke. "Of all the times to pull an idiotic stunt like this; who could be so stupid!?" Andrew was very annoyed. He took a breath and tried to calm down and think about it. Maybe he could figure out which of the crew would think that something like this would be funny. He bent down and snatched up the fallen metal mug. He went into the galley and threw it in the sink. Running his hand through his wet hair he smelt the liquid on his hand. It was their cargo. Alcohol to be used to fortify Italian wine; it stank.

There was no other way to find out who was responsible other than asking everyone directly. He hoped that whoever it was would have the gumption to stand up and take his rebuke for the childish behaviour. Andrew started up the ladder of the forward hatchway and climbed out onto the deck. It was soaked. The crew were now all at the mid-ship hatch mopping and cleaning the deck together. Andrew was just about to yell out to them when he heard a sound behind him. It was a very familiar sound, somebody striking a match.

He spun around just in time to see the match get flicked toward him. He only barely registered that somebody was there. Instinctively he tried to duck the oncoming lit match and let out a yelp as he did so.

The noise caught the attention of the crew mopping the deck only about twenty feet away from him. They looked up to see what was going on. The alcohol that had permeated Andrew's hair and clothes on his torso was a very high grade. He could not get out of the way of the match in time. The alcohol ignited engulfing his torso and head in a roaring flame in the matter of a second. He bellowed in unbelievable agony.

Edward, Vaughn and Hans all screamed in terror as Andrew ran at first seemingly toward them flames billowing up from his body. He was unable to think or even see as his eyeballs shrivelled in the onslaught of the fire. With arms flailing and trying desperately to slap out the flames he hit the side of the boat and fell mercifully overboard and into the water.

"Man overboard!" screamed Vaughn. The three of them ran to the side of the boat and looked over. Andrew could be seen thrashing about in the water below. The flames were out but a new problem presented itself. The fin of a shark was closing on the hapless man.

"Shark!" shouted Hans at Andrew not knowing if he could hear or understand him in his current condition. On top of that the boat was pulling away from the distressed Second Mate.

"Throw him a rope!" Edward shouted. They all looked around for the nearest rope. There was one nicely coiled and stored near to where they were, and Vaughn rushed to use it. By the time he had thrown it over the side, aiming it expertly at Andrew, Captain and Sandra Brigges and Adrian had joined the trio. The rope unfurled in mid-flight and hit Andrew in the head. It must have been a reaction to reach up rather than carefully considered thinking on his part, but Andrew grabbed the rope in his hands.

"Pull him up" commanded Captain Brigges. "Hang onto the rope for dear life Andrew!" he hollered. Whatever thought processes were left to Andrew in his current state there must have been enough to tell him to grip onto that rope for all he was worth. He was being pulled along with the Mary Celeste now, so there was no danger of him being left behind.

"Look!" screeched Sandra pointing to the shark fin that was identified earlier. It was closing on Andrew.

"Faster; faster!" Brigges called out, directing the men to pull for all that they were worth. Edward, Hans and Vaughn were doing their best to get Andrew back aboard.

"Tie the rope around you so that we can lift you up!" Brigges tried to direct Andrew now to help in his own rescue. It was a harrowing few seconds. Andrew had the presence of mind to do as he was instructed he could be seen wrapping the rope around himself. His determination to survive even after what had happened to him was incredible.

"Another one!" Sandra's warning was shouted along with a direction to follow. Her pointed finger indicated another fin closing upon Andrew.

"We have him!" yelled Vaughn. Andrew was now directly beside the hull of the ship and could be pulled up from the water. Suddenly before all of them a shark surfaced twisting its body sideways so that it could get its razor sharp teeth fixed around Andrew's torso and bit into him. Andrew's scream was unlike anything that any of them had heard before. The weight at the end of the rope was now more than Vaugh, Edward and Hans could handle.

"Help us!" Vaughn directed Adrian who ran to assist. Even the four of them were struggling with the weight at the other end of the rope. And then the unthinkable happened. The shark thrashed about not wanting to release its prize and separated Andrew's head from his body, taking a large chunk of his neck and shoulder as well. The shark fell back into the sea and disappeared beneath the surface. Sandra screamed and clutched the side of the boat before feinting and falling backward onto the deck.

"Horrible" was all that Captain Brigges could say. He looked at the stunned faces around him. The men were all frozen they did not know what to do. Pull the remains of Andrew aboard or not. The choice was taken from them as the second shark now latched onto the remnants of Andrew's body. It must have been excited by the blood in the water and was now in a frenzied state. Vaughn hurriedly let go of the rope. This prompted Adrian, Hans and Edward to do the same. The shark pulled its meal beneath the water just as the first one had done.

Nobody could believe what they had just witnessed. Brigges bent down to cradle Sandra's head in his hands. She was limp. He looked up at the men.

"What Happened" demanded Captain Brigges? The men all looked at him at a loss to put into words what they had just experienced. Vaughn was the first to compose himself enough to relay what they had seen.

"Andrew came on deck and burst into flames. He fell from the boat and ...." He trailed-off. There did not seem to be any point in completing the explanation, everyone had seen what had happened from that point.

"Flames?" Brigges was incredulous. "How?!" he was angry. There were no explanations forthcoming.

"Answer me, all of you. How can a man catch fire? Who was near him?" he looked around. They were all looking at each other.

"Nobody!" replied Edward. "We were all mid-ships mopping the deck when Andrew appeared at the forward hatch. He called, or made a noise of some description and we looked up and he was on fire and running across the deck." The explanation did not explain anything at all. Brigges took off his jacked and bundled it beneath Sandra's head to act as a pillow. He stood up and looked toward the forward hatch.

"There are no scorch marks on the deck?" he said accusingly. Sure enough now that the rest had time to examine the surrounds they too could see nothing that indicated the fire that they saw.

"The deck was wet, it would not have been marked by the fire." Vaughn felt like he had to justify what he had said.

"Where did he fall overboard?" asked Brigges in an equally accusatory tone. The three men that were on-deck at the time indicated the exact point. Brigges strode over to examine it.

"There is no sign of fire here either!" he said looking at Hans, Vaugh, and Edward with some distain. The three of them were confused, they knew what they say. Han's was the one to come up with an explanation.

"The fire was only on his head and upper body. He hit the side of the ship with his waist and tumbled overboard. " Brigges looked at Hans as if he were mad.

"We are not on trial Captain Brigges! We know what we saw!" Hans was quite angry and made no attempt to hide it. It felt like the three of them were being held to account for the bizarre occurrence that led to Andrew's death. Edward too had an outburst and with a definite tone of revile spat his question at Adrian.

"Where were you when all of this was happening Adrian!?" Adrian was stunned at the tone that Edward was taking with him. He shook his head at first and then managed to stammer an answer.

"I was….in here, I mean the wheel house, of course, steering the ship. Where else would I have been? What are you saying!?" he indicated the wheel house as his face showed how unhappy he was at being questioned so brusquely.

"You could have easily crept to the forward hatch through the Captain's cabin and set Andrew alight before covering your tracks by running back below deck and returning to the wheel-house via the Captain's cabin!"

"Are you mad!" both Brigges and Adrian spoke the same words simultaneously.

"Don't you think that I would have noticed if Adrian had entered our cabin?" Brigges put it to Edward. Adrian was far more alarmed at what he had heard from Edward though and concentrated his questioning on the accusation he had just suffered from the Steward.

"You think that I killed Andrew?" he was absolutely incredulous. He was aghast and once more stammered trying to find the words that he so desperately needed to defend himself from the verbal onslaught.

"Absurd.....How could I have? Why would I? How can you think that I could do such a thing!" he was turning red with frustration. The situation was getting out of hand and Captain Brigges could see that it could easily deteriorate further unless he acted now. What he needed was to distract the two men from following this conversation at all. Thankfully Sandra chose that moment to open her eyes and moan her way to a state of near consciousness.

"Edward help me get Sandra to her feet!" his bellowed order was exactly what was required to deflect Edward from making any more accusations. Everyone turned their attention Sandra. Edward and Captain Brigges helped her up. She was still very distressed at what she had witnessed. She was pale, whiter than the sails above them.

"I am!" she suddenly shook herself free of the two men and ran to the side leaning over and vomited loudly. Benjamin moved to comfort her. She straightened up only to repeat the experience. The sight sound and smell of Sandra being sick had a detrimental effect on the men. Without the argument between Edward and Adrian about the suspicion of murder to focus upon they all had time to reflect on the hideous way that Andrew had died in front of them. Benjamin looked around at them. All were showing signs of being distinctly unwell.

Hans ventured the thought foremost on his mind.

"We must turn back to the Azores....." he never got to complete his sentence. Captain Brigges in a roaring voice dripping with malice shouted him down.

"We are NOT returning to the Azores, we are sailing onwards to GENOA! And that is the LAST that I want to hear of it from ANY of you! Is that perfectly CLEAR!" His sudden outburst caught everyone by surprise.

"I will take Missus Brigges below to recover from this harrowing event and then I will see ALL of you in the galley to get to the bottom of this hysterical fantasy that we have a murderer aboard my ship! Mister Gondeschall, take the wheel. Two hours from now tie it off and assemble in the galley!"

Chapter 19: Wednesday November 22nd 1871, Noon

Captain Brigges and Sandra entered the galley. Edward, Vaughn, Adrian and Hans were already seated, waiting. They stood up politely as Sandra came in through the door. Both the Brigges' could feel the tension in the air. They guessed correctly that no small-talk had been bantered around prior to them arriving.

"Please take a seat my Dear" he said softly and Sandra moved to sit with the crew. Captain Brigges regarded each of the men making it clear that he could hold all of their gazes with ease. He wanted to present the air of a man that would not take any paltriness from any of them. He succeeded in conveying his demeanour.

"Now let me understand this correctly Mister Heed. You think that Adrian is responsible for the sudden and tragic death of Andrew Gill, because you think that he threw a lit match upon him, even though Adrian was in the wheel house at the time, and that match somehow mysteriously managed to set him completely alight, which resulted in Andrew falling overboard and......" he looked at Sandra guessing that she did not need to hear repeated what they had all just lived through. She still looked decidedly unwell. "....and the rest we all witnessed with our own eyes. Is that what you claim Mister Heed?" The way that Captain Brigges summarised it made it seem ludicrous. But Edward would not have his prize theory about the murderer in their midst's brought into disrepute.

He stood up so that he could look Captain Brigges in the eyes. His actions made it seem like a court of law in which he was giving evidence.

"You make it sound ridiculous, but hear me out. Adrian was with Bill shortly before he *somehow* became entangled in the anchor which dragged him to his death. Adrian was steering the ship, or so he says, when Albert *somehow* managed to choke himself to death with ropes that he as an experienced seaman would know so well as to make it unthinkable that he could have accidentally killed himself. And we do not know where Adrian was shortly before Albert's funeral service. Perhaps putting a boa constrictor inside of the Captain's cabin to kill poor little Sara!" he pointed his finger accusingly at Adrian, who too jumped to his fee.

"Rubish!" he shouted red-faced and flustered once more.

"Quite both of you, and SIT down!" Captain Brigges stopped the argument before it gained any further ground.

"Is that *all* of the *evidence* that you can come up with to convict Mister Martins?" Brigges deliberately emphasised the words to illustrate how unconvinced he was by the deliberations. Edward pulled out his final musing.

"Insanity runs in his family, so does murder!" he slammed his fist on the table. Adrian once more jumped to his feet and was ready to shout a tirade back at Edward but was once more intercepted by the Captain.

"SIT Down Mister Martins!" Adrian took in and let out a couple of loud breaths as he attempted to calm himself. He sat and gave Edward a glare.

"No reasonable man or woman could possibly believe this concocted story Mister Heed, it is complete rubbish." But even as he spoke Brigges knew that he would have to do more than just decry the theory, he would have to actively discredit it piece by piece.

"Adrian was in the wheel house, he never entered our cabin, he could not have possibly been responsible for Andrew's mysterious catching alight...." Brigges was still talking when Edward held up a burnt match. All eyes focussed upon it.

"I found this near the entrance to the front hatch" he said slowly and menacingly. "This is the match that set Andrew alight" he showed it around the table. The men for reasons unknown to even them retreated from it as if it were diseased in some way. Captain Brigges moved forward to take the match from Edward. He did so and inspected it.

"It could have been dropped there anytime, one of the men that smoke..." he began to theorise about how the match may have come to be there by completely innocent circumstances. He was interrupted rudely by Edward.

"The deck at the forward hatch had just been mopped Captain, how could it be a left-over from any of us smoking a pipe. And besides only yourself and Albert are smokers aboard. The rest of us don't use matches." He was going too far to explain the presence of the match on the deck.

"We all use matches to light the lanterns, and you especially Mister Heed use matches in the galley all of the time!" Brigges turned Edward's argument professing non-use of the device around and pushed it back on him. "It may have been dropped by one of the men mopping the deck, it could have fallen out of a pocket. Vaugh, Hans, Adrian, Edward empty your pockets on the table now!" Captain Brigges order was surprising. They initially did nothing and then looking at each other began to turn out their pocket contents on the table. Sure enough both Edward and Vaughn had both expended and still unused matches in their pockets. Brigges reached down and picked up one of the used matches that Edward had put back in his pocket after using rather than back in the box from whence it came.

"See" he said with an air of superiority to Edward, holding it in front of Edward's face to press home the point. Suddenly this one flaw in Edward's evidence managed to cast doubt over all of it. Even Edward was now feeling like he may have gone too far in accusing Adrian in front of everyone. Captain Brigges could see the doubt in his face and seized upon it offering an unpleasant alternative.

"If there is a killer aboard Edward, I do not believe that it is one of us" Benjamin's revelation stunned one and all. Even Sandra shook her head as if to say that she was not quite sure that she had heard him correctly.

"I put it to you, that if a boa constrictor can secret itself aboard without our knowing it, then a killer can do the same thing. I will agree with you on only one point Edward, that all of these deaths so close together could be the work of person that we do not know. If you want me to entertain the idea that all of the deaths aboard *are* the work of someone rather than a series of horrible accidents, then you must also contemplate that there is a chance that I am correct in my assumption that it is not one of us at all". Captain Brigges had been successful in casting the element of doubt into the theory of a murderer amongst them.

There was absolute silence. This gave all of them something completely new to contemplate. And it was frightening. Sandra put it into words.

"The thought that a murderer has had free reign of the ship whilst we have been asleep in our beds.....it's terrifying"

"We should search the ship from top to bottom and leave no trunk, no cargo container unopened." Vaughn proposed the obvious course of action to either prove or disprove the newly formed theory.

"The barrels in the cargo hold are not large enough to fit anybody, But there are other places that may be large enough to secret a man." Hans too was taking the assertion very seriously. Suddenly all of them had a common goal to achieve. If they searched the ship and found a stowaway, then they will have surely found the murderer.

"We should search in pairs Hans you search below with Adrian; Edward you search the galley, the store room, forward companion and Albert's cabin with Vaughn. Sandra and I will search the remainder of the cabins. Arm yourselves with anything that will protect you from attack and shout out if you find anything." Brigges orders were understood by all, they nodded.

The group dissipated and went to carry out their new chore.

***

Edward and Vaughn were in Albert's cabin. There was simply no room in here to hide anything. Both of his chests were opened revealing nothing. His bunk was turned down. Every small cupboard was opened. Nothing out of the ordinary was found.

"Next we check the engine room and the coal room" Vaughn was taking a methodical approach to their task.

***

Adrian was being watched very closely by Hans. Even though Hans did not share Edward's belief that Adrian was the murderer, he thought it better to watch him as closely as he could. They were in the hold and searching for anywhere that could potentially hide a human being. The lanterns that they held barely did the job of lighting the way ahead of them or behind them. The shadows that were thrown onto the wooden surrounds were unnerving.

"Nothing here but the barrels of alcohol" Adrian sounded disappointed. "Nowhere that a man could hide" he looked around. He was about to call the search off because the hold could simply not have hidden a stowaway for such a long period of time. But then he noticed something odd.

"Look at that" he said pointing so that Hans would know what to direct his attention toward. It did little to help Hans figure out exactly what Adrian was referring to.

"What" Hans asked?

"The knot that is tying the very front port-side barrels is a different one to the one that was there originally" Adrian's odd discovery was difficult to grasp at first.

"How do you mean?" queried Hans.

"Andrew was the one that set the very first lot of barrels down and tied them off before we left port. He tied a double overhang to fasten them all together. Now the knot is an Oysterman's" the minor revelation struck a chord with Hans.

"Bill's favourite knot, he used it often." Hans recalled a vital piece of information from his knowledge of Bill.

"Are you sure?" Adrian wanted to be doubly sure that the knot could be attributed to somebody other than Andrew.

"Yah, I am sure" he replied.

"Now that you mention it, I recall that you are correct, Bill did use the Oysterman's knot more than any other, even when it was perhaps not the most suitable. So how did this change from a knot that Andrew tied to one that Bill more than likely tied?' the question did not have an answer. The only two people that could have helped them understand the inconsistency were now deceased.

Hans was looking around the hold as if the answer to their question could somehow be found there. He had a question of his own, one that was more easily solved.

"How many barrels are we carrying?" he said looking evenly at Adrian.

"One hundred and twenty five; you know that" Adrian was a little annoyed at the query. It was not helping solve the knot-dilemma.

"Count them" he said in a tone that sounded like he was being challenged to a task that he would somehow fail. Adrian gave Hans a look as if to ask why. But Hans insisted.

"Count them" he said again, a little more forcefully this time. Adrian shook his head in mild bewilderment and began to count the barrels. Hans, crouching down in the confined space, followed him hobbling around up and down the narrow pathway between the various groupings of barrels. When they had finished their stock-take they looked at each other.

"There are one hundred and thirty" said Adrian confirming the figure that Hans had come up with.

"So what is in the extra five barrels?" Hans' question had an air of menace, which Adrian attempted to dissipate.

"Well certainly not a stowaway, they are too small" he said expecting his reply to bring some sense to the conversation.

"Maybe a stowaway the size of a snake?" Now Hans' thinking was laid bare for examination.

"So you think that there is something other than alcohol in the extra five barrels?" Adrian extrapolated upon Han's idea. "Somebody aboard is smuggling snakes from, wherever they got them, to Italy…why? Who would do such a thing? Are South American snakes worth anything in Italy?" Adrian's string of questions was only serving to make the situation more untenable. They needed answers not more questions.

"How will be find out which barrels are the ones that have been added to our cargo?" Adrian finished off his trail of thinking. But then he just as quickly answered his own question. Adrian looked at the Oysterman's knot and then at Hans.

"We're thinking the same thing" Hans confirmed.

"Quickly help me, let's get that group of barrels untied so we can examine them" Adrian's directive was already in the process of being executed by Hans.

***

Sandra knew her husband better than the men. She queried his reasons for assigning the mid-ships crew's cabins to them.

"Did you want to search the crew's quarters for anything in particular Benjamin?" she asked as he rifled through Edward's, Andrew's and Adrian's possessions.

"Anything that seems suspicious Sandra, I don't really know what I am looking for." He sounded exasperated. Sandra pitched in and began opening draws and cupboards with abandon looking for anything that seemed out of the ordinary.

***

By the time that everyone had gathered back in the galley to report their findings an hour had passed. The Brigges were the first to return from their search. Then Edward and Vaughn entered.

"Did you find anything?" asked Sandra as they entered the galley. Both of their faces showed that they had not discovered anything worth reporting. They shook their heads. Captain Brigges wanted to be sure that they had done a thorough job.

"Did you check the engine room?" he began, but Vaughn's answer pre-empted the Captain from making further inquiries.

"And the coal room, the companion, all of the storage areas, everywhere that a man could possibly hide Captain Brigges; even the row boat on deck, nothing" Vaughn's tone made it clear that he did not want to be second-guessed as to the thoroughness of the search that he and Edward had conducted.

The two men moved to pour themselves a mug of water; Edward holding the mugs and Vaughn pouring from the pitcher that he had taken out of the cupboard. They were quenching their thirsts when Hans and Adrian entered carrying a number of furs.

"What in heaven's name?" Sandra asked as the men tossed them on the galley table for all to inspect more closely. Gathering around and feeling them as they spoke, Captain Brigges wanted to know the facts.

"Where did you find these?" Brigges looked to both of them for a reply. Hans obliged.

"In five barrels in the front grouping, which Adrian noticed were tied with a different knot to the one that Andrew had originally secured it with, an Oysterman's knot; Bill's favourite." They all attempted to digest the information. Sandra was struggling with the inferences.

"Bill? So you think that these belong to him, he smuggled them aboard?"

"No, Andrew set the first grouping of barrels. He did it alone before turning over the next lot to Vaughn for stacking and tying-off. They must have been put there by Andrew originally and somehow Bill found them." Adrian's explanation of the theory that Hans and he had formed was received with amazed looks.

"But why would Andrew smuggle furs to Italy?" Sandra was still confused. Benjamin however put the pieces of the puzzle together very quickly.

"These furs are from Canada, they would fetch a good price in Italy for a clothing atelier to turn them into fine coats. Andrew must have been trying to supplement his income from this voyage? I would never have suspected him of anything like this" Captain Brigges sounded disappointed in himself for not being able to see his Second Mates hidden intentions.

"Is there a connection do you think?" Vaughn asked Hans and Adrian hoping to shed some further light on the death of his younger brother. They all seemed to mull over the possibilities. Then he put together his own probable answer.

"What if Bill found out that Andrew was smuggling furs and Andrew killed him for it. Where was he when Bill….." He stopped when he remembered that Andrew was in the galley with him when Bill died. The theory had no substance. He looked desperately around hoping for something from anyone.

"Maybe…" Edward began and then dismissing his thought simply shook his head.

"At any rate, a few smuggled furs are no reason to murder anyone surely?" Captain Briggs belief was not disputed by anyone. Instead, Edward turned his attention to a more pressing matter.

"Furs, it makes no difference; there was no mysterious stowaway murderer found aboard Captain Brigges, now will you turn back to the Azores." Edward's challenge felt abrasive to Brigges.

"We still have no hard evidence that anyone is murdering anyone aboard Mister Heed. It is still within the realm of possibility that all of these deaths are accidents!" he wanted to reassert his position as Captain. And more than that he did not want to be challenged or questioned by a member of his crew. Edward would not be so easily dissuaded.

"This voyage is a sailing disaster Captain Brigges; turn back to the Azores so that the Spanish authorities can investigate. What else must happen before you will relent? Who will benefit from going onwards to Genoa now?" his tone was malicious. Strangely it was Sandra that answered. The words, disaster and benefit stuck a memory within her.

"We would benefit" she said, and gave her husband a peculiar look.

"How do you mean?" queried Hans.

"No! Sandra, do not say another word!" Benjamin was clearly worried and it showed.

"Be quiet Captain Brigges…..Sandra, what do you mean?" Hans rudely cut across the Captain as he attempted to muzzle his wife. Sandra looked to each of the crew men, they were hungry for her to explain her thinking.

"We took out a substantial insurance policy before leaving home. I remember commenting at the time that if the voyage was struck with disaster we would benefit handsomely from it." She stood up, dropping the fur that she had been holding and backed away from her husband. She had the oddest look on her face as if she was looking at a complete stranger. Eyes turned accusingly upon Captain Brigges.

"Well, what better way to ensure that you collect your *handsome* insurance policy than murdering your crew one by one and making it look like a series of unfortunate accidents." Edward's damning indictment drew no objections from anyone other than the accused.

"Rubbish! Edward Heed, how could you think me such a monster as to murder my own daughter just to collect a financial reward; my family mean more to me than any amount of money. Sandra please, you must believe me." The desperate note in his voice softened Sandra's sudden suspicion. She looked upset with herself for even contemplating it. Looking around she also realised that she had given the crew ample reason to accuse him being behind all of the recent calamities. This upset her even more and she began to cry.

"Oh Benjamin, I am sorry, I don't know how I could have even though such a horrible thing, please forgive me." She said taking his hand. He breathed an audible sigh of relief and patted her hand.

"Thank you my Dear, yes, yes of course I forgive you. This has been absolutely harrowing for you, for us all. But we must not let our fears get the better of us" Captain Brigges plea for rationality fell upon deaf ears. He regarded the crew. They had settled upon the theory that Edward had presented and it seemed that there was nothing that he could say that would change their minds. He knew that if he was to retain leadership he had to concede to the majority in this instance.

"Alright" he said and stood up. "We will turn back to the Azores and get the Spanish authorities to investigate our various accidents. Would that be satisfactory to you all?" he looked around at the hardened faces.

"Yes" said Edward, still giving the Captain an accusatory look.

"Yah" Vaughn added his voice to support the idea.

"Yah" Hans too gave his agreement.

"Yah" Adrian added his vote. They all looked at Sandra as if expecting her to cast a vote in favour of the move as well. She nodded her agreement.

"I will do whatever Benjamin says is best". She was trying to recover some credibility that she felt was lost by originally casting suspicion on him in the first place.

"Then it is settled. I will plot our course back to Vila do Port on Santa Maria. Mister Lorensen, would you please take the wheel. Mister Martins and Mister Gondeschall prepare to raise more sails" Now that the crew were getting what they wanted, they were more than happy to comply. Men left the galley in a hurry to do as they were told. Feeling a little left out, Edward and Sandra decided to follow the others up onto the deck, so they could at least feel like they were participating in the turning around of the Mary Celeste.

The Captain had headed down the corridor for his cabin presumably to go into the wheel house, were the sextant was kept using the connecting stairs from the main cabin. Everyone else went up either the front ladder or the mid-ships ladder-stairs including Sandra. By the time that all of the crew were on deck and Vaughn was half way to the wheelhouse they could see the Captain had arrived at the wheelhouse already. But his actions were the cause for concern, he was frantically lifting and throwing down charts as if he had lost a particular one and could be seen through the glass looking left and right with a good deal of panic on his face.

He had everybody's attention. When Vaughn rounded the wheel house and entered from the door a brief exchange could be seen between them. Vaughn too had a look of surprise and alarm on his face. He ran out and around the wheelhouse to address them.

"The Sextant and the Spyglass are gone!" he shouted and then retraced his way to the wheelhouse, presumably to assist in finding the missing vital pieces of equipment. Edward, Adrian, Hans and Sandra all ran forward to crowd into the wheelhouse to confirm what they had just heard. Captain Brigges had his hand on his forehead and a look of absolute desperation on his features.

"What do you mean *missing*?" hissed Edward at the Captain. Brigges responded by pointing at the wooden box that housed both the spyglass and the sextant, it was open on the chart table, showing the two red velvet recesses that would normally gently house the two instruments.

"They're in your cabin, it was the last place you were re-plotting our course!" Edward sounded convinced that the sextant and spyglass were to be found only a few steps away. Captain Brigges disappeared down the hatchway leading to the main cabin. Edward rudely pushed passed everyone and followed him down. The Captain was busy looking in cupboards and throwing out the contents in a flurry of activity. Edward looked around, by this time Vaughn, Adrian and Sandra had come down the stairs too. Neither of the bright brass devices were anywhere to be seen. They always stood-out as they were highly polished mechanisms.

"I always keep them in the box when they are not in use" the Captain was almost blubbering with apprehension at not being able to identify where the sea-faring tools were to be found.

"You threw them overboard rather than navigate our way back to Santa Maria!" Edwards vitriolic accusation made everybody stop and look at him first then the Captain for his response. Brigges was aghast.

"What? Why would I do such a thing? How could I navigate our way to Genoa without the sextant? Think rationally Edward, you are making a ridiculous assertion. Wherever they are we must find them!" Brigges' retort was difficult to argue with but under the circumstances, the missing contraptions did mean that the Mary Celeste could not turn around and accurately navigate back to the Azores.

"Rubbish!" screamed Edward; he would not so easily be placated. He pointed an accusatory finger at Brigges and added to his allegation.

"You were the one that searched your own Cabin and the wheel house. It was then that you hid them fearing a rebellion from the crew, which you knew wanted you to turn the ship around! You would do anything to avoid the Spanish authorities because you fear what they will do to you....murderer!"

"No, that is simply not true..." Brigges began to defend himself from Edward's verbal onslaught but he was cut off.

"Give back the sextant NOW or we will MUTINY!" Edward's ultimatum could not be ignored; he was shaking with rage. Brigges looked around for support from Vaughn, Adrian and Hans he could see in their faces that there was none to be found. He turned to his wife.

"Sandra, you were with me when we searched the ship, did you see me hide the sextant and the spyglass?" he hoped that they would listen to her. Brigges knew that the inexplicable event had cast further doubt over his veracity; he needed any help that he could get. Almost unbelievably Sandra paused and gave him a far-away look. He was desperate and snapped at her.

"Well?!" he shouted at Sandra. She regarded him and spoke in a feeble voice.

"I did not search the wheelhouse Benjamin, you did that on your own" It was as if his wife's words had convicted him of the crime.

"What, no….wait.." Brigges was now more flustered than ever. He furrowed his brow even further and looked fraught.

"Lock him up and turn out his cabin, we have to find the sextant!" Edward had effectively taken charge of the situation.

"Vaughn, Hans, take *Captain* Brigges to Albert's cabin and lock him in. Sandra help me find that sextant. In the meantime, Adrian, use the compass to steer us a course directly west. It is the best that we can do under the circumstances. When you have secured Brigges, get up on deck to make any sails that we need in order to get us back to the Azores."

"You will be court-martialled for mutiny Mister Heed. All of you will be. Don't listen to him. Don't throw away your honour; I beseech you!" Brigges plea did not garner any support. Brigges was incensed. He could see that there was no reasoning with any of them. He turned to Sandra.

"Sandra, my Dear. Please say that you don't believe this. Without you at my side I will surely go mad." He had his hands outstretched in a pleading manner. Sandra vacillated.

"Benjamin, I want to believe you, but why did you insist on searching the wheelhouse alone. Oh…" Sandra clutched her head in both hands not knowing what to think. Unable to gain support from his own wife absolutely defeated Benjamin. His head fell.

"Do you want to make this easier on yourself, and your wife and just tell us where you've hidden the sextant?" Edward spat the proposition at his former Captain. Benjamin looked at Edward and shook his head offering one last attempt to convince him of otherwise.

"I do not have it Edward; I have not hidden it *anywhere.*"

"Have it your own way then; take him away!" Edward quite dramatically pointed toward the cabin door. Vaughn and Hans moved to flank Benjamin. He looked up at each of them but made no resistance to them as Vaughn indicated that he should accompany them to Albert's cabin. Brigges gave his wife one last pleading look. She could not meet his gaze. He was dejected. The three of them left the cabin in silence.

Chapter 20: Guilty by Circumstance

Vaughn opened the door of Albert's cabin and walked in followed by Benjamin. Hans stood at the door. Vaughn reached around and took the key from the inside lock and looked at the Captain who had moved to sit on the bunk. He looked down at the floor.

"Are you mad?" Vaughn's question caught both Benjamin and Hans by surprise. They looked at him. Brigges indicated that he did either not hear correctly or not understand the question.

"Are you a mad-man? Hell-bent upon murdering all and making it look like accidents, just so that you can collect on an insurance policy?" It seemed to be a genuine question, but one that was so outlandish that under any other circumstances it would not have borne answering.

"No, Vaughn I am not. I have not. I did not. I would…..could not do any of these things" his voice lacked the note of authority that it usually carried. It was as if Benjamin had not even answered the question, but a hollow representation of Brigges had answered instead. Vaughn made a stinging point as he exited.

"How could you have killed your own daughter?" He slammed the door not wanting to hear another denial from the man. The key turned in the lock loudly. Benjamin was alone, a prisoner aboard his own ship.

***

Sandra too was sitting on her bunk. She was lost in thought. The emotion of everything that had happened threatened to overwhelm her, but she fought it off. If she was to be any help to Benjamin she had to think about how they got to this point. Edward was busy looking for the missing instruments. He was talking to Sandra as he did so but she was not listening. This went on for quite some time before Edward realised that Sandra was completely unresponsive. Edward found a box at the very back of the cupboard that he was searching. It was wooden. He pulled it out and opened it. Inside was a single action Colt handgun. In the box were the bullets that could be loaded into the central chamber. He turned it around studying it closely.

"Why would he have a gun aboard?" he asked Sandra, even though he knew the answer. All Captains would have a firearm of some description for emergencies. He wondered why the Captain didn't resort to carrying it during the current crisis.

"Why wasn't he armed during everything that has happened?" he asked Sandra another question that she did not seem to hear. Perhaps it was because being the guilty party he felt that he did not need protection from anything. Convinced that his reasoning was correct, he put the gun back into the box. He would keep hold of it for the rest of the voyage, he thought to himself.

He tucked the box beneath his arm and addressed Sandra loudly hoping to snap her out of her stupor.

"Is there anywhere that he favoured to hide things?" Edward had to ask his question of Sandra three times before she looked up at him.

"What?" she said, not able to offer her usual well-mannered response.

"Favourite hiding place aboard, Sandra, the Captain, did he have one?" Edward was now very annoyed. She shook her head.

"No" she said almost imperceptibly.

"Perhaps it is not something you saw, but something that he mentioned in passing" Edward wanted some clue and hoped that Sandra would be able to provide it. Sandra for her part looked directly at him, but he could tell that she was lost in thought. He gave up and began turning out another cupboard that he had previously searched.

"Not something that you saw" parroted Sandra. This time it was Edward that was not listening properly.

"I'm sorry" he said wanting a repeat of her words. She seemed to light up and become animated.

"Edward, did you not hear what you just said. Not what you saw" she seemed enthused at his words. But he was mystified as to why.

"What are you getting at?' he asked.

"Edward, perhaps we are all looking at what has happened in the wrong light. What if, and please just indulge me, there have been murders on this ship or rather one murder, but also accidents" she was becoming inspired by her own reasoning now. He could feel her mood alter from pensive to one of motivation.

"I'm not quite with you?" he said indicating that Sandra should elaborate.

"What if, Bill *was* murdered by Andrew for discovering his fur smuggling? Thrown overboard entangled in the anchor chain and the latch left half-off and conveniently gave everybody and excuse to not be present when we thought that he was actually murdered; when we all heard the anchor unfurl. But the snake and Albert's choking were indeed horrible accidents. Why do all of the deaths have to be related and attributable to just one person? Could it not be a mixture of murder *and* accidents?"

At first Edward was about to dismiss the very thought as fanciful. But he thought it more polite under the circumstances to humour Missus Brigges. After all, he had just headed a mutiny that had deposed him as the Captain of his ship. And the longer he thought about it the more it felt like there could be a ring of truth to it. But then he spotted an obvious flaw in the odd reasoning.

"What about Andrew, mysteriously catching fire?" he said challenging Sandra's theory behind the recent events.

"Spontaneous human combustion" she said proudly and with such resolve that he was taken aback.

"What in heaven's name did you just say?' he said unable to interpret what had just been offered as a credible explanation for Andrew's death.

"I have read of such things when I was in London with my parents as a young girl. Remember, when I was in the employ of Madam Athalia. Spontaneous human combustion; for no apparent reason and with no scientific explanation a person can simply ignite and burn to death, from the inside outwards." Sandra's explanation was given with such pride that even Edward was reticent to dispute it. But it was such a bizarre thing to say that he couldn't help but seek further clarification.

"I have never heard of such a thing." He sounded more than a little doubtful.

"These are the things normally associated with the other-world, Edward. But they would make the newspapers and be spoken of quite openly. Madam Athalia said that it was a spiritual deficit that was the ultimate cause of such a thing; an evil presence in a person that eats away at the soul until they experience the fires of hell in their living lifetime, one that robs them of their life and condemns them for all eternity". Edward was still struggling, but this clarification somehow made a little more sense, in a peculiar way.

"So what you are saying is that because Andrew murdered Bill for discovering his smuggling operation, his soul burned him in his life to sent him to hell?"

"Exactly!" Sandra confirmed that Edward understood what she was taking about.

"We should tell the others and see what they think!" Sandra was clearly delighted to have solved the riddle of the events plaguing their voyage. She jumped up from the bunk. Edward was still a little incredulous.

"Don't you see what this means Edward? If I am right then Benjamin is innocent and we can release him!" Sandra's ultimate goal was now obvious.

"Hold on just a minute Sandra; we still don't know where the sextant and spyglass are, he simply had to be responsible for those going missing. Who else could have done it?" Edward's stoic refusal to think in her terms annoyed Sandra. She decided that only a majority could help her in this situation.

"That is for all of us to decide now Edward. You have effectively incited mutiny aboard a merchant ship of the United States of America. What I am offering you is an alternative point of view, one that may see you not charged if it turns out to be true, and you release Benjamin. There is yet hope that he will somehow see your actions as in the best interests of all of those aboard " Sandra cleverly offered Edward a way out of his current situation in the hope that it would soften his viewpoint. Edward's eyes narrowed.

"You wouldn't just be saying anything that you can in order to get your husband released…"

"Of course I am Edward, Benjamin is my husband! And it is not just his release that I want but his exoneration from the charge of murder that you have levelled at him!" Sandra's brutal honesty was difficult to argue with. Unknown to Sandra at the time it was a catalyst for Edward to look at his own thinking with renewed eyes.

"Let's tell everybody". Sandra once more made her intentions known and headed up the stairs to the wheelhouse. When she burst open the small doorway leading into the wheelhouse Adrian jumped with fright from his positon the wheel. Realising that it was Sandra he scalded her for her abrupt entrance.

"Steady on Missus Brigges, I am quite jumpy enough without you frightening me like that". But Sandra did not pay any attention to him. She exited through the door to the deck to address Vaughn and Hans who were trimming sails having earlier secured Benjamin in Albert's cabin. She called to them and they looked over at her and she beckoned to them. They looked at each other and began to tie-off the sails that they had been manipulating. Sandra returned to the wheel house and waited for the full complement of crew to join her, Adrian and now Edward who had followed her up from the main cabin. When Vaughn and Hans entered asking what was happening she waved for them to be quiet and listen to her.

"I believe that I have a viable alternative point of view of what has been happening aboard; one that makes sense if you will just give it some consideration." She waited for them to agree verbally to present her theory. She explained it in similar words to the ones that she had used to tell Edward but expanded upon the section about spontaneous human combustion and gave the explanation more gravitas with further thoughts from Madam Athalia, and what she thought of such a thing. When she had finished she waited almost as if waiting for a jury to hand down its findings.

They all pondered by either mumbling words of *maybe*, and *it's possible* or in Vaughn's case complete silence. Vaughn however was the first to offer his support for Sandra's new way of looking at the occurrences.

"I believe that the prospect of Sandra being correct is at least a possibility that we should all consider." His even-handed viewpoint should have been more widely accepted however Hans had his own ideas to bring to the group.

"I think that Sandra is right, up to a point. There may be more than one murderer amongst us. Adrian was on watch when Albert died. I think that he murdered him. Pandemonium erupted and a melee of verbal slings went back and forth before Vaughn took charge of the situation and shouted them all down.

"QUIET!" he screamed, bringing all other shouting to an end. Edward could hardly believe what he was hearing.

"Hans I thought that you were convinced that Brigges was the murderer?"

"Edward I thought that you were convinced that Adrian was the murderer?" they both mimicked each other and made their earlier suspicions know to everyone. Adrian was shocked.

"What, I don't understand, you both thought....what explain yourselves, I am not a murderer!" he was flustered to say the very least. Sandra too was lost now that the revelation was revealed.

"Yes both of you explain yourselves to us what do you mean?" Both Hans and Edward exchanged knowing looks. They had indeed started with the opposing viewpoints but at some time during the explanation to each other had adopted the other's point of view. Vaughn stepped in at this point.

"We met shortly before Bill's funeral service to discuss what had happened. Edward said that he thought Adrian was the killer amongst us because of his family history of insanity and the opportunity he had to commit all of the crimes. However, Hans thought that Captain Brigges was the murderer. Somehow, I don't know exactly when they seem to have swapped their viewpoints with one another." Hans thought it prudent to further rationalise his new outlook on things.

"It does not matter what I thought then, what matters is what I think now. Brigges and Adrian are in it together. They both had more than ample opportunity during each of the deaths to carry them out. They intend to split the insurance money by bringing disaster to this voyage. Who knows what else they could have done before we figured it all out." Although proud of his newly acquired assuredness that he had solved the dilemma that they were in, it did not garner the support that he had anticipated.

"So you still think that Benjamin is a killer!" Sandra was furious. She felt that nobody had actually listened to her at all. "As far as I know Adrian Martins and Benjamin had not even met before this voyage, how could they have planned this whole thing, you are being completely absurd!" she finished her deriding of Han's notion with a cold glare right into his eyes. He could not hold her gaze. Instead he turned once more to Adrian.

"We have to lock up this one as well to ensure our safety" Adrian was incensed once more.

"Hans, I thought that we were friends? How could you even think that I am a killer? It is rubbish all of it. You have lost your mind because of everything that happened." Adrian was shaking with anger at being accused of being a conspirator to Captain Brigges and a murderer. Vaughn was separating them as it looked very much like a fracas would erupt if he did not.

Edward took the opportunity to open the box that he had been nestling beneath his arm. He showed them the contents.

"A gun?" Vaughn stated the very obvious. "Where did you find it?"

"Captain Brigges' cabin. I will load it and keep it close just in case Brigges breaks out of his confinement….and just in case I was correct in the first place and Adrian is involved." His menacing intent was clear. The balance of power had clearly shifted to Edward. Hans tried again to convince the group to lock up Adrian with Brigges.

"We need to protect ourselves, all of us, and unless we can all have the luxury of having a gun to sleep with, then I say that we lock up Adrian as well. It is the only way to ensure that none of us will be the next to mysteriously die!" Hans' plea only served to incite more argument within the group. Again it became a cacophony of accusations and pleas for common sense to prevail. Sandra tried over and over again to push her point of view that Benjamin was innocent of any wrong doing, but it did not garner any support from the men. The missing sextant and spyglass seemed to preclude him from any thoughts of no wrong-doing. They would have gone on arguing for the rest of the day but for the weather. Once more the skies had darkened, and the sound of rolling thunder invoked memories of the storm that they all endured previously during the voyage.

"More bad weather" observed Vaughn. "We need to prepare for another storm. And it looks to be a bad one at that." He pointed the way that they were heading. Lightning could be seen shooting for the thick clouds to the ocean below. The situation facing them served to dissipate the current argument. Nothing had been gained except clarification about what everybody actually believed. With the exception of Adrian who remained at the wheel they all left the wheelhouse to prepare the ship to face the approaching front. Circumstances had given him a stay of judgement on being locked-up with Captain Brigges. That was a thought he did not find appealing in any way.

Chapter 21: The Storm Front Strikes

It was difficult to tell that it was late-afternoon because the sky was so dark. The clouds were thick and obscured the light. Along with the storm came feelings of anxiousness. If this was as bad as the one that they had faced before, they would have their work cut-out for them. Without Albert, Andrew and Bill, it would be more difficult to tend to everything that would need attention. And because of the Captain's confinement they were yet another man short. The situation exacerbated the tensions aboard. Sandra, Edward, Vaughn, Adrian and Hans were genuinely afraid of what lay ahead of them.

In the wheel house Sandra was feeling like a useless cog in a wheel. Adrian could see the others struggling with the Mainsail. It had to be brought down lest the gusting winds tore it.

"Here Sandra, take the wheel, I need to lend a hand to the others". Adrian's unexpected handing over of the duty to steer the ship was exactly the tonic that she needed to stop feeling of little use.

"Certainly" she said; the excitement and nervousness apparent in her voice.

"It will pull to the port and starboard as the ship hits the waves, but steer true to the west and everything will be alright". Adrian's words of both direction and comfort were very welcome indeed. He pointed to the compass as he spoke.

"I shall do my best Adrian, thank you." Sandra let him know that the short tutorial was all that she would need. It was obvious that Edward, Hans and Vaughn needed immediate help. "Go and help with the Mainsail, I shall be able to handle this" she said, giving him the assurance that he needed to leave her to her task. With a nod of approval, Adrian left the wheelhouse. Sandra watched as the four of them struggled with dropping the mainsail. It seemed that each time that they were close another sudden and quite violent gust of wind would either completely defeat them, or at least undo most of the work that they had managed under the difficult conditions. She could hear them shouting to one another. Orders of *one more time*, and *this time for sure* were interspersed with some profanities as the mainsail came down only a bit at a time.

A huge crack of thunder that sounded like it was directly above the main mast made all of them jump with fright. It was quickly followed with multiple forked lightning strikes around the ship.

"We have to get off the deck!" Vaughn bellowed to the others. They needed no more convincing. With renewed effort they heaved and pulled and forced the mainsail down.

"Quickly, tie it down" instructed Hans. Edward and Adrian ran to do so. They worked as quickly as they could, the fear in their blood making the simplest thing like tying a correct knot that much more difficult.

"Yah!" Adrian proclaimed that he had successfully secured his side of the sail to the main boom.

"Yes!" Edward confirmed that he too had completed his chore. Vaughn looked at the rigging and the sails.

"Only the fore topmast shrouds are left. They should be enough to keep us going in the right direction." He summarised the current status of the sails that the Mary Celeste was now being powered by.

"Should we start the engine, like before?" Edward asked

"No need, this time the storm front has swung around and will be pushing us to the west, the last storm we encountered we were heading directly into. No need for the engine unless we lose the two shrouds." Vaughn's experienced observation was backed up by Adrian.

"Vaughn is correct. We only have coal enough for a real emergency now. We should be able to get by without it this time" Another crack of thunder and successive multiple set of lightning strikes nearby put an end to any further discussion.

"I will take the wheel, then send Hans. You take the last watch Adrian. See that everything is secured below" Vaughn's reasonable set of instructions were difficult to argue with. Although Adrian felt that he should be giving the orders as he was the oldest one of the men still on active duty; he could see nothing wrong with Vaughn's plan for rotating the men at the wheel. This way at least there was more than a good chance that the storm would be over by the time that he had to once more take the wheel. He nodded and indicated that he and Edward and Hans were going below via the mid-ship hatch. Vaughn waved his understanding. The wind was so loud in all of their ears that even shouting at each other now may not have been able to be properly heard.

By the time that Vaughn entered the wheel house to relieve Sandra of steering duty she was ready for a rest. The wheel was indeed pulling to the left and right as the ship hit the waves, just as Adrian said that it would. But the force that she needed to exert to keep the ship on-course was greater than she was able to maintain for a long period of time.

"Thank goodness!" she said, sounding relieved to be replaced at the wheel. She moved aside as he took hold of the large wooden apparatus. He was just about to speak when more thunder erupted around them. Sandra inadvertently jumped with fright. A little ashamed at being so fearful in front of Vaughn she apologised.

"Sorry" she said. Vaughn shook his head.

"It is nothing to worry about Sandra, this doesn't seem as bad as the last one." He hoped that his words would calm her at least a little. Sandra then tried to use the current situation to once more obtain the release of her husband.

"Benjamin could help us though this Vaughn. He is a very experienced Captain, he will ensure that no harm comes to us." But the very assertion of not allowing harm to come to a voyage that he would benefit heavily from if it failed did not gain Vaughn's support. He decided to fight her opportunistic ploy with one of his own.

"Missus Brigges, that sextant would really help us right now. If he tells us where it is hidden, along with the spyglass then I will talk with the others to see if we can be lenient and release the Captain." He gave her an even stare hoping to underline his demand. Sandra may not have known as much about sailing as the crew but she was not entirely stupid and retorted.

"Even I know that you need the sun, moon or a bright star to correctly use a sextant Mister Lorensen. All are in short supply in our current predicament." Her unusually terse response did have an effect on Vaughn. He realised that he had been too patronising toward her.

She pointed out the window as if asking if he could see anything other than dark grey clouds and lightning. A little ashamed of his tactic he attempted to justify it to her in some way.

"Sandra, please see it from our point of view. Captain Brigges is the only one that uses the sextant. He was the last one to use it. And just as we need it to correctly plot our way back to Villa do Porto; a destination that he was so adamant that we not return to, suddenly it is gone. That is more than just a little suspicious, don't you agree?" He hoped to force her to at least make that small admission. But Sandra was not going to fall for such a ruse.

"Yes, Vaugh, it is just a coincidence; nothing more. I am certain that when they are found it will clear Benjamin of any suspicion that you all seem so grimly determined to place at his feet." Sandra would have gone on for much longer but for yet another successive round of thunder and lightning. The waves were tossing the ship around much more violently now.

"I am going below." She said announcing her intention to leave Vaughn to his duties. She opened the small doorway leading down to her cabin and crouched down to go through. Just then the ship lurched to one side almost making her lose her balance. She grabbed onto the small door for support. Vaughn reached out to offer her support but she waved him away brusquely, indicating that she had absolutely no need for his help at all. With a loud noise, Sandra slammed the door behind her. Vaughn shrugged with indifference.

***

Sandra decided to not sit and stew in her cabin about her predicament. She was convinced that her explanation of the events was the correct one. Vaughn may not be willing to listen, but someone would. She decided that the best course of action was to visit Benjamin and let him know how she was trying to help him. The ship was lurching in the storm but she navigated the main corridor and stopped outside of Adrian's cabin. She knocked.

"Yes, what? Who is it?" she could hear come from Benjamin inside.

"My dear it is I. How are you?"

"Sandra my love; are the men treating you well?"

"Don't worry about me Benjamin. I have considered the events that have led us all to this point and believe that I have an explanation. But without the sextant and spyglass, nobody will believe me. Tell me Benjamin; did you hide them to prevent us from returning to the Azores?" Sandra looked up and down the corridor hoping that none of the crew would suddenly appear from one of the many doors.

"No, no, no my dear, please believe me. I am as perplexed as anyone as to how they could go missing. I can only think that the real murder aboard has done this for his own ends. Nobody is safe from him as long as I am locked in here. I have a pistol that we can use to defend ourselves…."

"Edward has taken charge of the gun Benjamin."

"Edward!?"

"He found it whilst searching our cabin for the missing instruments."

"But what if he is the murderer? There is nothing to stop him from shooting us one by one!" The very thought sent a shiver through Sandra. It was not something that she had considered. But just as quickly she dismissed it and tried to allay her husband's fears.

"I do not think that Edward is a murderer Benjamin. Let me explain to you what I think has happened." Sandra told him her theory about the accidents followed by a murder and then spiritual retribution via spontaneous human combustion. Benjamin listened with intense silence. When she was done she once more gave him the caveat that was preventing her from winning the support of the men.

"But without the sextant and spyglass, they have no reason to believe me; no reason to believe you. Please, please think Benjamin, when was the last time that you saw them. They simply must have been misplaced. Sandra stared at the locked door. There was silence.

"Benjamin did you hear me?'

"Yes, yes I heard you Sandra. I am pondering everything that you have told me. It is quite a lot to take in." There followed even more silence which began to annoy Sandra.

"Benjamin please, think, the sextant where did you see it last?"

"Sandra, I have no wish to upset you, but I find what you have said quite remarkable. If you are right then there is no murderer aboard at all. But if I am right then there is a murderer and it is he who has stolen the sextant. So you see either way, I still have no idea what became of the instruments. They were in the box the last time that I used them and the box was on the chart table in the wheel-house. Who was in there after me? If we can think about who it was then we have a finger of suspicion to point at someone other than me". Benjamin was being pragmatic. But Sandra was now trying to work out how the missing devices may somehow be woven into her considered explanation.

"Human combustion you say. Madam Athalia knew of this?"

"Yes, Benjamin. I know that neither of us saw Andrew in flames, but all of the others swear by it. And it is the only explanation that makes any sense. Perhaps Andrew removed the instruments in fear of us facing the Spanish authorities back in the Azores. If he did then there is nobody aboard that knows there whereabouts at all. It all fits Benjamin. Don't you see, they must be able to see your innocence now! I shall tell them at once." Sandra's exuberance was dampened by the ship suddenly lurching port and starboard quite violently.

"We must be in the centre of it now!" she proclaimed. "I will be back Benjamin"

"Be careful Sandra, I fear that no amount of sense will be welcomed by the men, they are all frightened, and none of them are thinking properly"

"I will my dear" Sandra kissed her hand and pressed it against the door. Just as she did so the door to the galley opened. Edward came through and stopped dead when he saw Sandra at the door to Albert's cabin.

"What are you doing?" he demanded curtly. To his surprise Sandra did not act in any way like she had been caught doing something wrong. Instead and quite disarmingly, she was glad to see him.

"Edward, excellent, where are the others? I have it all, everything fits perfectly.." she was still speaking with Hans and Adrian came out from the hatch leading to the storage deck below. They were speaking about something and as they climbed up to the mid-level they could see Edward facing off Sandra in the corridor. They both stopped speaking.

"Perfect you are all here, come with me to the wheelhouse I have news and I want you all to hear it at the same time. I will be back my love." She gave a little knock on the door holding Benjamin prisoner aboard his own ship. There was a chorus of *what are you talking about* and *what do you mean* from the three men but she would not divulge anything to them without all four of them being present. She hurried them to the wheel house via her cabin. The thunder reminded then all that there was still a storm raging around them. Additionally the listing of the deck beneath their feet as they tried to navigate the narrow corridor and staircase made the journey longer that it would have normally taken. Sandra continued to wave away the inquiries about what it was that she had to tell them. But then she had a though of her own that needed answering.

"What were you doing below?" her question was so off-subject that it took a moment for Adrian and Hans to register what it was that she was talking about.

"Oh, we heard that some of the barrels had come loose so we went down to tie them up again, and work the bilge pumps to get as much water out of the storage deck as we could". Hans' explanation was perfectly reasonable. Sandra acknowledged it with a simple *Oh.*

Vaughn looked at the troupe filing into the wheelhouse with some concern.

"What is wrong, has something happened below?" He sounded alarmed. Sandra took over the conversation at that point.

"Andrew must have taken the instruments and hidden them, or even worse disposed of them completely. Fearful that we would do exactly as we are now and return to Santa Maria, he wanted to ensure that we did not. Do not look to Benjamin for guilt, he is as perplexed and worried about the safe return of the sextant and spyglass as any of you; as any of us" she said correcting herself. Looking around at their reaction, it was clear to the men that Sandra was immensely proud of her deducing. They looked at each other almost as if trying to decide which of them would speak first in response to Sandra's new assumed substantiation.

"Well?!" she was now quite angry that her reasoning was not immediately adopted as the truth by all of them.

"Perhaps we just need time to mull it over Missus Brigges." Vaughn tried to be the reason in the midst of the doubt that they all felt about the new theory. A cacophony of thunder then drowned out any further attempt to discuss the supposition. A large wave hit the ship from the starboard almost knocking all of them from their feet. The wheel spun and Vaughn lost control of it momentarily. He cursed loudly and with Hans' help managed to get it back in hand.

Even from the wheel house they could hear that once more some barrels had broken loose in the cargo hold.

"Quick go below and get those barrels secured!" Vaughn instructed the men. There would be no further discussion about Sandra's new belief now, the safety of the ship took precedence and she knew that.

"Yes of course" she managed to say in support of Vaughn's orders. She stood aside and allowed the other three men to pass. They disappeared down the hatch to attend to the urgent task.

"I can at least help you with the wheel Vaughn" she offered. Not wanting to offend her any more than he already had, he nodded and smiled allowing her to take one site of it. Keeping the ship on course took more effort now that the storm had intensified.

***

Various emergencies had to be attended to during the storm. Rigging that broke under the strain of the wind. The cover to the row boat came loose and had to be refastened. Various cupboards in the galley regardless of how securely they were fastened managed to spill tin crockery and cutlery over the floor. The bilge pumps needed to be worked more during this storm than the fierce one that they had encountered approaching the Azores the first time. But eventually the storm subsided and the men were able to hoist the main sail once more. Vaughn retired from his steering duties and without even taking any dinner, went straight to his bunk to sleep the deep sleep of a very weary man. Hans was nodding off by the time that Adrian relieved him at four o'clock in the morning. It was very cold and Adrian had brought with him a large pea-coat and a very large scarf. He insisted wrapping it around his head as if he were an artic explorer. Hans would have made more fun of the sight but like Vaughn before him, all he wanted to do was retire and sleep in his comfortable and warm bunk.

Chapter 22: Thursday November 23rd, 1871

The morning was a stark contrast to the evening prior. The sun was shining there was not a cloud in the sky. Vaughn looked through the porthole. He was yawning and stretching in his bunk taking it all in. His belly rumbled notifying him that he should have probably eaten before going to bed. His thoughts turned to breakfast and what he would soon be eating. But there was something niggling in the back of his mind. At first he thought that it was just more thoughts of Bill, and how lonely he felt without his younger brother. How was he going to explain to their parents back in Germany what had happened to him? He knew exactly what his mother would say, of all the careers that they both could have had on land why did they choose the sea? He recalled a similar objection from her when Bill decided to follow in his elder brother's footsteps and become a merchant seaman. He also remembered Bill's answer to their mother '*Because I want to work in the sun and see other countries'*. Vaughn smiled at the memory. Just as quickly as it had brought him pleasure the thought brought him back to reality.

"Hans ! The Sun! The Sun it is on the wrong side of the ship, we are heading in the wrong direction!" Vaughn scrambled to get out of his bunk and pull on some daywear. Hans sat up in his bunk and tried to ascertain exactly that Vaughn was shouting about.

"What?" he asked rubbing his bleary eyes.

"The sun is on the wrong side of the boat, we are heading directly east! AWAY from the Azores!" he simplified his message so that

Hans would not have to interpret what he was trying to communicate to him. This got Hans' attention who similarly jumped out of his bunk and looked around for some appropriate clothing. They both pulled on their boots and tried to lace them up whilst exiting the cabin.

"What's all the noise?" Edward had stuck his head out of his cabin door.

"We're sailing east instead of west. What is Adrian doing?'" Hans was more than a little accusatory with his tone. This had an immediate effect upon Edward who visibly stiffened.

"Why would he not want us to get to the Azores!" Edward began a rant but Vaughn and Hans were more eager to get up on deck and confront Adrian than discuss it below. They clambered up the mid-ship ladder-stairs and onto the deck with Edward, without shoes on, following closely behind. They could see that Adrian was still at the wheel. The three of them strode purposefully toward him and as they got closer they could see that his eyes were closed.

"He is asleep at the wheel" Edward snarled. Vaughn was the first to reach the wheel house door which he flung open.

"Wake up Adrain, why are we heading due east?" Vaughn waited for a response. Hans and Edward either side of him. There was no response from Adrian. Vaughn got a sick feeling in his stomach. He stepped into the wheel house.

"Adrian?" he said more gently. Adrian stood motionless gripping the wheel, his feet parted to give him better balance and leverage.

"Look" Hans pointed to the white canvas pants that Adrian was wearing. They were absolutely soaked with red. Vaughn approached Adrian from the right and Hans from the left. They both took in what they saw. Each of them was shaking with nervousness. All three were getting a sinking feeling in their stomachs. The scarf covering Adrian's neck was soaked through with blood. They guessed that the black pea coat that he was wearing was similarly drenched. It was almost as if an unspoken moment passed between them acknowledging that this must be the case. Adrian's blood had found its way to his pants. But not a drop was to be seen in the deck anywhere. His clothing had managed to soak all of it up. Adrian was pale. He was not breathing.

"He's dead" said Hans almost imperceptibly. Vaughn and Edward did nothing to argue. It was clear that Adrian was dead. He had somehow managed to bleed to death holding the wheel.

"How?' asked Edward looking at Adrian's face first from one side then the other. Vaughn took a chance and reached forward and pushed the blood-soaked scarf down from his neck with his unsteady hand, revealing a gash that circled the base of Adrian's throat. They all let out a gasp and corresponding stifled cry. There was silence that seemed to linger in the air of the wheel house for an eternity. Then;

"Brigges killed him!" accused Edward.

"How? He is locked up below" Hans retorted.

"He must have another key, he has been playing us for fools all along!" Edward would not hear any logic that exonerated Brigges from this murder.

"Be sensible Edward. Brigges let himself out and somehow managed to slit Adrian's throat and turn the ship around without any of us noticing!" Vaughn was once more the voice of reason in the trio,

"I'm going to check that he is still there." Edward was about to leave when the door to Sandra's cabin opened and she began to enter the wheelhouse. Alerted by the shouting she wanted to investigate what was happening. From where she was Sandra could see Adrian and the bloodied mess that he was. The deep cut in his throat that must have surely bled him dry. She screamed and fell backwards down the stairs onto the floor of her cabin. Vaughn and Hans rushed to her assistance. Edward looked down the stairs too, but then back at Adrian's standing corpse. He tried to remove one of Adrian's hands from the wheel. He was unable to do so. Acting on a hunch he reached gingerly over to Adrian's head with both hands and tried to tilt it either back or forward. He could not.

"Look at this quickly, the both of you!" he shouted down the stairs. Only Hans appeared in answer to his call.

"Look at what?" he asked

"Adrian, he is as stiff as a board. Rigor mortis has set in" he said. Hans shook his head at the absurd notion.

"Are you mad, he couldn't have been dead for long enough for rigor mortis to have set in…" Hans was in no mood for stupidity.

"Look. I cannot move his head; I cannot release his grip from the wheel." Edward's insistence captured Hans' attention. He tried to push Adrian's head a little. It was exactly as Edward had said. Adrian's body was incredibly stiff.

"But that is impossible. Even if he was murdered at the beginning of his shift it has only been four hours. Rigor mortis takes at least twelve hours to set in?" Hans was incredulous.

"It must have been Brigges" said Edward once more indicting the Captain "It had to have been him, there is nobody else that could have done it!" Even after he finished his sentence Edward realised that it was a ridiculous assertion.

"You could have done it! There is nobody else in your cabin. You could have crept out whilst we were sleeping and cut him with one of your oversized knives. Adrian could have been asleep at the wheel, He wouldn't have known what hit him." Hans' counter accusation enraged Edward.

"How dare you! I am not …" Edward's tirade in his own defence would have continued but for Vaughn shouting out from below.

"She is coming around." Hans and Edward went down to see if they could be of any assistance. Sandra's eyes were open now. Vaughn lifted her into a sitting-up position.

"Do you need some water?" he looked around for a pitcher. She shook her head.

"No……….Oh poor Adrian; how; who?" Sandra struggled with the obvious questions before bursting into tears. Vaughn looked up at Hans and Edward.

"Get Adrian's body out of the wheel-house. And above all, turn us around to head due west."

***

It took both Edward and Hans, still growling at each other, to remove Adrian's body from the wheelhouse. Pushing his body into a shape of repose was not easy. His limbs threatened to snap rather than give way; but after much pushing it was done. He was laid on the plank and wrapped in a blanket which turned red as it too soaked up the blood from its surroundings.

***

The remaining passenger and crewmembers of the Mary Celeste gathered in the galley. Captain Brigges had been brought in. The situation surrounding Adrian's death had been explained to him in detail by Vaughn. Edward stood ominously with the gun in his hand letting Brigges know that he would only need the flimsiest of excuses to use it. Brigges listened to the accusation from Edward.

"You must have another key. You let us all believe that you were our captive and you waited until we were all asleep before murdering Adrian." Brigges was more than a little flustered.

"Yes I have a spare key, but it is in my cabin, not on my person. I could not have done this horrible thing!" Then trying to calm himself, he took a risk and gave his thoughts on what had happened. If he did not Edward would have Vaughn and Hans and God-forbid, Sandra believing his rantings. And foremost in Brigges mind was disarming Edward.

"You are the one that has done this Edward. You think that I am the murderer so I am locked-up. But you also think that Adrian could be the murderer and you, seeking to protect yourself from him, used one of your knives and your butcher's training received in an abattoir to slit Adrian's throat. Search me. Search the cabin, the key that you think that I have used to help me perpetrate this crime in the cover of darkness is not to be found. It is on a chain that hangs beneath my table in my cabin." Brigges could see from the doubt on Vaughn and Hans' faces that he was beginning to win them over.

Brigges strode over to the place where Edward kept his unusually large and varied collection of knives. The leather case that contained them was exactly where it should have been.

"We all know that this is where you keep your knives Edward." Brigges took the case over to the table and unfurled it revealing all of the knives. He lifted out one, the one with the largest handle. It gleamed in the light. He did so with another large one, this time a clever. It too, like all of Edward's knives, was pristine. He chanced with a third and held it up. Blood was evident on the sharp edge.

Brigges spun around and triumphantly showed everyone.

"See!" he said with venom. He pointed the knife at Edward who was pointing the gun at Brigges.

"Murderer! You may have only killed Adrian because you thought that he was guilty, and you wanted to protect yourself from him, but no matter what the reasons, you are still guilty of murder Edward!" Brigges sounded so confident that he had unravelled the circumstances surrounding Adrian's death that when Edward looked to each of them for support he found none.

"I don't know how that blood got on my knife. But you said yourself, we all knew where to find them. Anyone could have used it and put it back to cast suspicion on me. You are a desperate man that hopes to deflect suspicion from himself but it is not working." He looked to Vaughn and Hans and then Sandra. He could tell that they did not believe him. If they looked nervous about him holding a loaded gun before they were positively alarmed now.

"Perhaps you had better give me the gun." Vaughn tried to sound calm, but wanted nothing more than to get the gun away from Edward as soon as possible.

"No! I need it to protect myself; protect us all…from him!"He once more scarily waved the gun at Brigges.

"I will go to the main cabin and locate the spare key. If it is there and it fits the lock then Captain Brigges could not possibly have been the murderer. I have the only other key to Albert's cabin. If I do this will you give me the gun Edward?" Vaughn hoped that his conciliatory plan would meet with success. Edward was not enamoured with the thought of giving up the only firearm on the ship. He looked again to Hans and Sandra. They appeared frightened of him.

"Don't look so afraid. I want to protect you" he said trying to regain their confidence.

"You can help us Edward by surrendering the gun; unless there is truth in what Benjamin says." Sandra' support for the disarmament was not what Edward wanted to hear. He was about to object again when Hans joined in.

"What have you got to worry about Edward? The more you insist on holding on to the gun the guiltier it makes you look. Don't you see that?"

Brigges felt a little relieved. His plan had paid dividends; now they all wanted to see Edward surrender the firearm. Edward clutched the gun to him. He tried to weigh up the pros and cons in his mind, but the situation made it difficult to think properly. He could not come up with a valid excuse now to keep it. If the very people that he said that he wanted to protect with it, were afraid of him, and thought him blameworthy because of it, then damn the gun.

"Who should hold it then?" he asked.

"Vaughn" Sandra replied. She sought support for her idea. Hans agreed and so did Captain Brigges. Edward very reluctantly handed over the weapon. There was an audible sigh of relief from Sandra and Benjamin.

"Good. Now let me go to the main cabin and find those keys." Vaughn took charge of the pistol and left the galley. Edward glared at Brigges. The silence that enveloped the two of them was thick with malice. Vaughn seemed to be away from the galley for longer than he would have needed to complete such a task. At the point where Hans was about to point that out, the door opened and Vaughn appeared holding up the chain with the spare keys to the entire set of locks on the ship.

"It took me a while to locate, but Captain Brigges was correct. The spare key to Albert's cabin is indeed on this chain. He could not have set himself free overnight and killed Adrian."

A new crisis began to build from this point. It was clear now that Benjamin could not have been the murderer. All eyes turned to Edward.

"It was not me I tell you! I was asleep in my cabin all night" he said trying desperately to free himself from the burden of accusation.

"Without a single witness to corroborate your story" Hans said.

"I don't know how that blood got on my knife? It couldn't have been me. I am always so careful to clean my knives after their use." His tone increased in urgency. Once more Hans countered.

"We all know that Edward. You are obsessively clean with your precious knives. What better way to cast doubt than to not clean it after murdering Adrian. Which of us would ever believe that you would put away a knife with blood on it? Well you weren't smart enough this time Edward." Hans was more than smug with his retort, he was absolutely gloating. Edward was fuming with rage.

"I tell you I am not a murderer. I did not kill Adrian…!" Vaughn sought to diffuse the situation by reminding Edward that he was now in control of the gun. He pointed it at Edward.

"If Captain Brigges is correct you are the murderer. If you are correct he is the murderer. Either way we cannot have either of you at liberty aboard this ship. The both of you will be confined. There is no more to it." Vaughn was in no mood to pander to Edward's hysterical cry of innocence.

"I am not going to be locked up with that killer!" Edward sounded terrified at the prospect.

"Nor I with that murderer!" Captain Brigges snapped back.

"You will both be locked in your cabins. I will hold all of the keys. Now if you are both finished with your childish antics? We have a burial at sea to perform. Who will say the words?" The surprise change of subject was exactly what was needed to diffuse the situation. What was more surprising though was the reply.

"I will." Sandra stood up. "It should be me. If you insist upon locking up Benjamin during the service then I shall take his place and perform the rites". It was unprecedented; a woman performing a service normally associated with clergymen and ranking officers. Somehow, though, it seemed correct that the Captain's wife now take on that role. Vaughn and Hans, although a little taken aback nevertheless agreed.

"We shall meet on deck in five minutes. Enough time for me to lock up these two" Again Vaughn waved the gun indicating that he was not prepared to argue the point. Neither Benjamin or Edward objected.

"At least under lock and key I will be safe from you!" Edward had to have the last word no matter what.

"Come along" Vaughn ushered them with the gun barrel to the galley door.

***

Sandra acquitted herself of the religious service duties with aplomb. She had regained her composure and for all intents and purposes had carried off the duties of ship's Chaplin. Hans and Vaughn listened in stoic silence to her readings and reminders from the scriptures that man was made from ashes and dust and would soon enough return to that state. The wind fluttered the sails above them as they both lifted the plank and watched as Adrian's bod slide off and plunge into the Atlantic Ocean. A small trail of blood had been left on the plank. All of them noticed it, and with an off-hand remark to clean it, from Sandra, Vaughn tipped a bucket of water over it. Having been so previously well oiled, the blood too washed away without a trace.

The three of them stood looking at the waves undulating below. Other than the waves lapping at the sides of the ship and the wind catching in the sails there was silence. What else was there to say under the circumstances? Each was left to his or her own thoughts. One of Sandra's spilled from her mind into the real world.

"Not a trace" she said to nobody in particular.

"I'm sorry" asked Vaughn, thinking that Sandra had meant to say the words aloud. Realising that she had uttered at least a part of her trail of thinking she felt that she should illuminate the men.

"Oh, I was just thinking. There is now not a trace that anything had happened to Adrian. Not a drop of blood in the wheelhouse, or on the plank. It is like......." She hesitated trying to find the right words to complete her thinking.

"It's like he was never here" offered Hans.

"Yes, that's it; like he was never here at all" Sandra realised what a dreadful thing it was to even think such a thought. But after all that they had been through, she could not find it in her heart to apologise for being so dower. A longer silence followed broken once more by Sandra.

"What now?' she asked of Hans and Vaughn. It would have been easy to read too much in her question and begin to suppose what could or would possibly happen to the remaining people aboard the Mary Celeste, but Vaughn elected to take the question on face-value.

"We continue sailing west in the hope that we come across at least one of the islands in the Azores. Without that sextant we cannot be accurate about our course." He finished and without a further word went toward the wheelhouse obviously to untie the wheel and take it in hand himself. Hans looked up and realised that the conditions called for more sail. He skilfully picked which of them that he would hoist and went about his business. Sandra stood where she was and looked out to see for a few more moments; then deciding that she could be of no help to the men made her way to the nearest hatch to return below.

***

It was early in the afternoon when Hans entered the wheelhouse to talk to Vaughn. He gingerly opened the door leading down to the Captain's cabin. Satisfied that Sandra was not inside and could not overhear what he was saying he put into words what he had been thinking about all day.

"I have a new idea Vaughn. How things could have happened that left us where we are now." He had Vaughn's full attention.

"Go on"

"What if Sandra has come up with the right idea, but the wrong outcomes. What I mean is what if there is really more than one murderer aboard. Edward creeps into the wheel house fearful that Adrian is the murderer and kills him in self-defence. Andrew somehow managed to get some of the ship's alcohol on him and accidentally lit a match that was in his pocket. He went up in flames, but not before he had murdered Bill so that he could keep his smuggling a secret. You don't believe all of that rubbish about human's bursting into flames because of the spirit-world do you? Utter nonsense. But here is the part that I want you to think about really carefully. Where was Sandra when Sara was strangled by the snake? Where was she when Albert choked to death? What if she has been working in collusion with Captain Brigges all along the both of them in it together to collect the insurance money that is covering the failure of this voyage?" Hans finished his proposal.

Vaughn was not accepting it at all.

"Kill her own daughter? Don't be so ridiculous Hans. Where was she when Albert choked to death; with us in the galley…I think. And as for Edward killing Adrian; he had the gun at the time, why not just shoot him if he felt so threatened?" It was difficult to remember even though it was only a few days ago. The sudden rash of deaths was overpowering it played tricks with their minds. But Vaughn thought that he was right in defending Sandra. Hans was angry that his idea was so easily dismissed.

"Edward couldn't use the gun to kill Adrian because then we would have known it was him. By using one of the knives he gets to cast suspicion on anyone that knew where they were, which was everybody aboard. He is clever I tell you. We need to watch him every minute of the day!"

"Well there is not much murdering he can do from where he is. And Captain Brigges too, both locked up, the gun safely here." He indicated where he had it positioned in his belt for safekeeping. "There will be no more unexplained deaths from now on." Even as Hans heard Vaughn say those words he felt uncertain. He did not feel safe with Brigges and Edward under lock and key. He did not feel safe now that Vaughn had the only firearm on the ship. Trying to overcome his feeling of uneasiness Hans offered yet another alternative in a droll tone.

"Maybe the voyage really is just cursed?" Vaugh gave Hans a disapproving look but did not otherwise respond.

Chapter 23: Saturday November 25th, 1871

Hans, Vaughn and Sandra said very little to each other over the day following Adrian's burial. They ate individually in the galley without the company of the others. They all slept very little. The rigours of having only three people running the entire ship were beginning to show on all of them. They were tired. Vaughn insisted that the wheel not be tied-off at any stage, so each of them had to take turns in holding it and ensuring that they remained heading west back toward the Azores. Sandra would not take no for an answer, she too had her turn at the wheel. The day was divided up into shifts of eight hours. Vaughn took the first shift, Sandra the second and Hans the night-shift. They got through Friday the 24th of November without incident other than Sandra insisting still, that Benjamin be released from captivity. The morning came, it was now Saturday.

***

Hans arrived just prior to Sandra taking over from Vaughn for the afternoon shift at the wheel and reported to Vaughn.

"Brigges and Heed are insisting on being able to wash and for a change of clothes and to use the companion. Also Brigges is insisting on talking to Sandra. She has not been to speak with him this morning." He yawned his way through the briefing.

"Very well; I will take Captain Brigges to his cabin for a change of clothes and so that he may wash. He can speak to Sandra before she takes over the wheel. Here take it for a few minutes until she is ready." Hans took the wheel from Vaughn. Vaughn went below via the mid-ship hatch and arriving at the door to Albert's cabin. He produced the key and opened the door. Captain Brigges had been looking out the port-hole he turned with a look of anticipation on his face. Clearly he had been expecting his wife and disappointed to find that it was Vaughn opening the door.

"I wish to use the companion…" he began but Vaughn waved his had motioning for him to stop.

"Yes Captain Brigges. Companion, food, wash, new clothes and you want to talk with your wife. Come along you can do all of those things in your cabin. I will fetch you something to eat whilst you perform your daily ablutions." Vaughn was offering exactly what Brigges wanted. He gave a gruff harrumph and nodded his appreciation.

"Thank you Vaughn. I assure you that I will not cause any trouble. I give you my word as a gentleman." Vaughn indicated that Brigges should go to his cabin, and motioned that he would be in the galley.

"I won't be far away" he said lifting his shirt to reveal the gun. Brigges was incensed that Vaughn had not simply taken him at his word but was so eager to clean himself up and see Sandra that he did not bother pointing out how disappointed he was in his crewman. He made his way toward his cabin. Vaughn watched him go in and then went to the galley door. He paused wondering if he should let out Edward to have something to eat now, or wait until Brigges was safely locked up and then allow Edward some small liberty. Then he head Captain Brigges calling from within his cabin, loudly and urgently.

"Sandra, wake up!, Sandra !" Vaughn knew immediately that something was wrong. He ran down the corridor and flung open the door to the Captain's cabin Brigges was leaning over the bunk. He had Sandra's shoulders in his arm and was shaking her.

"Sandra wake up please wake up!" his tone was beginning to be frantic. Hans appeared from the steps to the wheel house.

"What's wrong?" he said climbing down the stairs. Vaughn ran to be beside Brigges. Sandra was motionless unresponsive. Brigges was beginning to cry.

"Sandra why won't you wake up pleeeeease! Sandra please! Wake UP!' he shook her more violently. Vaughn and Hans interceded, preventing him from a repeat of that action. It was almost unconceivable. Sandra was dead.

"She is not breathing" said Vaughn his voice choking as he spoke. Brigges put his ear to her chest.

"Heart?" asked Hans. Brigges did not respond.

"Is her heart beating?" he asked more angrily. Brigges lifted his head from Sandra's chest and shook his head.

"Nothing" he said so faintly that they almost didn't hear him. There was a moment of silence and then an uncharacteristic explosion of emotion from Captain Brigges he sucked in a lungful of air and cried out in agony. It was a long and painful cry, difficult to listen to because it was awash with torment. His cry petered out only to begin again with another lungful of air sobbed in and let out in anguish. Brigges clutched his deceased wife to him and continued to cry.

Hans and Vaughn could not believe what they were seeing. It did not make any sense at all.

"But I saw her only last night when she took over from me" Hans said "she was fine; looking forward to a good night's sleep. There is no blood, no sign that she has been….." He paused unwilling to say the word murdered, it had been spoken too much on this voyage already. It took some time but Captain Brigges eventually control his crying, but it subsided into a low sobbing. Vaughn put his hand on Brigges shoulder in a display of comfort for the man.

Wanting to investigate more, Vaughn pulled the blankets down revealing Sandra in her sleeping gown in its entirety. There was no sign of blood. She had not been cut like Andrew. He looked around the cabin. Everything was in its place, no signs of a struggle. Whatever happened it was not the result of violence. Vaughn looked at Sandra's neck thinking that maybe, somehow, she had been strangled in her sleep. The frilly nightgown was in the way. He reached over and gently pulled the frills down revealing her neck. No sign of violence. Brigges reacted to what Vaughn was doing. He gave the seaman a glare of anger. Vaughn removed his hand from Sandra's night-dress.

"Perhaps it was her heart Captain Brigges; with everything that we have been through, it was too much and she had heart-failure." Benjamin looked at Vaughn but could not say anything; he was still to overcome with emotion. He looked back at his wife lying motionless in his arms. Very gently he laid her back into their bunk. He tidied up her hair and straightened out the crumples in her nightgown. Then as if she were an infant being put to bed he pulled the blankets up to her chest and folded the top of the sheet over the blanket neatly. He finished tucking her up safely and leant forward and kissed her gently on the forehead. Then he began to cry again.

The ship lurched suddenly as the wind caught the sales. Hans realised that he had not tied the wheel and they were at the mercy of the wind and waves. Vaughn motioned for him to return to the wheelhouse. Hans, almost grateful to get away from the situation, retreated up the stairs and out of sight. Vaughn was left to try and deal with Captain Brigges.

"Perhaps it was a stroke Captain. Whatever it was, it looks very much like she died peacefully in her sleep". Vaughn hoped that his words would somehow offer Benjamin some solace. From his observation of Sandra lying in her bunk, she did not look to have been in pain. In fact quite the opposite, her expression was one of quiet repose.

"We should prepare her for burial." Vaughn said after a while had passed. This seemed to jolt the Captain back to reality.

"No!" he said sharply.

"But Captain, if we leave her….."

"No Vaughn; No!" Brigges raised his voice, he was irate at the very suggestion, no matter how realistic it was, he simply could not face parting with his wife. Vaughn considered for a while. The weather had not exactly been hot. It was lucky that they were travelling in the November. Had it been one of the summer months, there would be no question of disposing of the body as quickly as possible. Vaughn guessed that it would take some time for Benjamin to come to the conclusion that Sandra must be buried at sea like all of the rest. Perhaps he just needed a little more time. He was still pondering this thought when Benjamin interrupted him.

"If we bury her at sea, it is as if she has died like all the others. No Vaughn. Let me keep Sandra from that fate for just a little while, please." The torture was evident in Captain Brigges' tone. It was impossible for Vaughn to resist. He could not see the logic in what Brigges was asking, but could not bring himself to argue the point either.

"Yes Sir" he said. He left the Captain to be alone with his wife and went up the stairs to the wheel house shutting the door behind him.

Hans was predictably at the wheel. What Vaughn was not expecting though were the tears rolling down his face. Hans wiped them away and shook his head.

"It is too much Vaughn. Too many deaths to bear; this truly is a cursed voyage; a cursed ship." He looked over the deck of the Mary Celeste as he spoke. Vaughn was prone to agree, but did not want to fuel the fire of superstition in his compatriot. He tried to think of something to say that would take Hans' mind off the thought that they were at the mercy of a curse.

"One thing is for certain Hans, neither Edward nor Captain Brigges could have had anything to do with Sandra's death. They were both safely locked up for the night. It must have been from natural causes. No marks from strangulation, no blood, no sign that there was a struggle in the cabin. There is nothing cursed about a poor woman who has died of natural causes more than likely from the strain of losing her daughter and everything else that has happened aboard since we left the Santa Maria." Vaughn hoped that his attempt to rationalise the situation would take Hans' mind off the very thought of a curse hanging over them all.

"What if……" Hans was clearly about to argue the point but then realised that Vaughn had pre-empted any theory that he could readily come up with about Brigges or Edward escaping from their confinement and killing Sandra in her sleep.

"Accidents, murder and death by natural causes; that is what you believe is it?" Hans sounded like he was challenging Vaughn.

"Yah" said Vaughn confidently. Hans shook his head but did not reply.

"Brigges wants time to be with Sandra. I have left him alone. I will try to convince him to bury her tomorrow." Vaughn could see that Hans was about to protest and then added "He has lost his daughter, his command and four of his crew as well as his wife Hans, we can do this much for him surely." When Vaughn illustrated what it must be like from the Captain's point of view, he found it difficult to argue.

"Yah" he said, capitulating through gritted teeth.

"Alright then, it is now all up to us." Vaughn stated what he thought was the very obvious but Hans missed the point completely.

"What do you mean" he said blinking at his friend innocently.

"Sailing the ship, Hans; it is now up to us. Unless you wish to release Edward to help us and give Captain Brigges back his command?" Vaughn knew the answer to both of those questions before he asked.

"Nein!" said Hans quite vehemently.

"Then it will be twelve hour shifts each until we make the Azores." Even the thought of it made Hans tired. But there was no other viable alternative. The idea of having Edward and Brigges loose whilst he tried to catch some sleep filled Hans with dread. He was still secretly sure that one or the other killed Sandra, even if he did not know how or even why. But all that mattered now was reaching port and getting off this ship before he became the next victim of either a murderer or the curse that was the Mary Celeste.

"How much more time will you give Brigges before you lock him up again?" Hans wanted to reassure himself that Brigges would indeed be secured again. Vaughn looked at the closed door leading down to the main cabin.

"Let's give him some more time, and then I will take him to the galley for some food and back to Albert's cabin". This pleased Hans.

"Good" he said satisfied with the plan.

***

Captain Brigges had been remarkably compliant when Vaughn collected him. He seemed to have been drained of all will. He offered no resistance. He did not want to eat anything, but made use of the companion and then returned to confinement without any argument.

Vaughn then dutifully released Edward who had to be filled-in on the recent events. Edward was incredulous.

"You are sure that it couldn't have been murder. Brigges may have had another key..."

"There is no other key than the two that I have Edward. It was not murder. Try to be rational, I know that this is upsetting, but please think before you accuse Captain Brigges of killing his own wife. He was locked up all night." Strangely this had the exact opposite effect that Vaughn hoped. Edward became very defensive.

"You think that I did it don't you!" he was more than a little angry. The assertion caught Vaughn off-guard.

"What? No! Nobody thinks that you did it Edward. Sandra must have died of natural causes; there is nothing strange here..." He said trying to inject a little common-sense into the man.

"Then release me. If you don't think that I am a murderer, why and I locked up?" It was clear now that Edward wanted to turn the situation around to aide him.

"There is still the matter of blood on your cleaver Edward. Have you got an explanation for that?" Vaughn countered with the evidence that was being held against the Steward.

"I told you I don't know how that got there. We don't even know that it is Adrian's blood. Maybe it was left there when I slaughtered the pig whilst docked at Villa do Porto". The plea sounded too desperate for Vaughn's liking. Edward realised from the expression on Vaughn's face that his argument was not helping prove his innocence. He was about to change tact when he thought the better of it.

"What is the use in trying to convince you? Providing you have Brigges locked up I feel safe."

"Come along, let's get something to eat in the galley and then I can lock you up again so that I can feel safe." Vaughn made fun of Edward who failed to see the humour in the ribbing at all.

The day and night passed slowly for everyone aboard. Benjamin felt like an empty vessel. He had been robbed of his daughter and now his wife. What more was there left now? Edward brooded in his cabin. Hans did his twelve-hour shift and was replaced with a bleary-eyed Vaughn. Hans guessed correctly that Vaughn had not managed to get much, if any, sleep.

Chapter 24: Sunday November 26th, 1871

Vaughn felt that it would be best if Brigges prepared Sandra for burial. In complete contrast to the previous day, he offered no resistance to the idea. He sewed a canvas shroud for his wife's burial. It took him the best part of the morning. By the time that Sandra had been wrapped up and sewn in to her burial covering it was almost noon. The sun was shining. The day itself was in total contrast to the way that they were all feeling. Edward had been let out of his cabin to attend the service. Captain Brigges could not bring himself to say the words for this particular service so it was incumbent upon Vaughn to do so.

At the conclusion Vaughn closed the small black bible and moved toward the plank upon which Sandra lay. But Benjamin stopped him.

"No. I will do it." He said. He leant down and placed his hands on either side of Sandra's head and pressed his forehead to hers through the cloak. Then beginning to sob once more he lifted the plank and Sandra's body slid off plunging into the water below. Captain Brigges cried quietly. Even the otherwise suspicious Edward could not help but be moved by what he saw. Hans and Vaughn both wiped tears from their eyes. Nobody spoke for a very long time. The silence was eventually broken by Edward.

"How much longer before we make port?"

"It's difficult to say" Hans responded. "If we had the sextant it would be easy, but without it, all we can do is sail west and hope that we are not so far off course that we miss them completely". It was not the cheeriest of thoughts; marooned at sea without the ability to accurately navigate to any destination.

"It is not something that you will need to worry about Edward. Back to your cabin Hans and I have work to do." Vaughn interjected hoping to scuttle any dour comeback that Edward may have been planning to Hans' assessment of their situation. For a moment it looked as if Edward was about to argue once more, but he must have thought the better of it and simply acceded instead.

Captain Brigges looked out to sea. Vaughn was about to ask for him to return to his temporary Brigg, but could not bring himself to be so callous. To his surprise Brigges turned around and noticing that Edward was being herded toward the hatch he said

"Back to our Cabins? I could do with some solitude". He moved to accompany them without any resistance. They all went below deck, Brigges, Edward and then Vaughn.

***

The day passed uneventfully. Hans and Vaughn did their best to keep the sails in trim with the favourable winds. The wheel was constantly attended by one or the other. Although it was exhausting work, they were driven by the thought of reaching a safe port. Vaughn knew that Hans was convinced that they were all cursed. The very though turned Vaughn cold too. But he did not want to give in to such seafaring superstition. And besides, it was too grim a thought if there was any truth in it. Eventually the evening light came and along with it a voracious appetite. Nobody aboard had eaten very much because of the circumstances. Vaughn told Hans that he would feed Edward and Brigges and then replace him at the wheel so that he could sate his own hunger as well. But Hans offered to take on that chore. Vaughn did not have the energy or any reason to object so he allowed Hans to do so.

Hans busied himself preparing a hot stew. The results were quite good, or so he thought. He dished it out in three bowls and then left the galley to fetch Edward and Brigges. When he returned with them he handed one of the bowls to each and took one for himself and they all began to eat. Not a word was spoken between any of them. Brigges for his part still looked like he was a hundred miles away. Edward was grateful of the food but had a perplexed look upon his face as he ate it. He looked at Brigges and then at Hans. Both were eating without hesitation. Edward looked into the stew as if it would tell him why he was finding it so unpalatable whilst his silent dining companions were not. Then out of nowhere Captain Brigges spoke.

"I have lost my daughter and my wife within one week." Hans looked at Edward who then looked at Brigges. They weren't sure if he was expecting an answer or not. What sort of response could you give to him? Brigges went back to eating quietly. Both Hans and Edward were quietly relieved that they did not have to engage in this particular conversation with the Captain. The three of them went on eating. Edward again began to focus upon how awful his meal tasted.

He struggled through more spoonfuls simply because he was so hungry. But eventually it became too much for him and he felt compelled to speak.

"Who made this?" the sudden and quite curt question startled both Hans and Benjamin.

"I did" responded Hans.

"It tastes......odd" he said brusquely. The inference that the fine stew that he had made not being to the liking of the Steward did not sit well with Hans. He was more than just a little offended.

"Then perhaps you could do us the honour of making our next meal then your majesty." He said in a mocking tone. Edward was incensed at being made fun of simply because he thought the stew was dreadful.

"How can you both sit there eating it like it is pleasant?" he further insisted. This prompted Captain Brigges to come into the conversation.

"I don't know what you are complaining about Edward. How often do you get somebody else cooking for you as the ship's Steward? You should be more grateful. It is a fine stew Hans take no notice of Mister Heed, he is being petty and belligerent for no reason." It was the first glimmer of the Captain that he used to be that Hans had seen in a long time.

Edward would not be silenced he was getting angrier by the second at being so flippantly brushed-off. He could feel his blood pressure rising in his head. It got harder to breathe. The blood was rushing through his head so quickly and with such force that he could hear it in his ears. Suddenly he realised that he could hardly breathe at all. He had to fight to draw air into his lungs.

"Careful Captain Brigges, I fear that Mister Heed is about to lose his temper". Hans observed how angry Edward was looking and how red he was turning. But to their surprise he did not explode with a vehement diatribe. He dropped the bowl that he was holding, the remaining stew spilled out onto the wooden flooring. He stood up clutching his throat. This prompted both Hans and Benjamin to stand up too. Something was clearly very wrong with Edward.

"What is it man, tell us, what is wrong with you!?" Brigges command went unheeded. Edward's eyes began to bulge and he looked desperately around the galley as if in search of something, anything that could help him. He gasped and fell to his knees. He wanted to get out of the galley and get up on deck. Maybe he could catch his breath there.

"He can't breathe?" shouted Hans.

"Give him room. Loosen his collar" Brigges tried to be practical, but Edward wasn't wearing a stiff collar. His shirt already had its top button undone.

"What do we do?" Hans was panicking, he felt completely powerless. With a stifled cry and final gasp Edward collapsed forward lay motionless at their feet.

"Edward?" Hans and Brigges leant down and turned him over between them. Edward's eyes were partially open, staring.

"Heart, listen for his heart" prompted Brigges. Hans put his ear to Edward's chest. He looked up at Benjamin.

"Nothing" he said.

"Are you sure, let me listen" they changed places. Sure enough Captain Brigges listened for a heartbeat and found none. He looked at Hans in disbelief.

"What could have happened? If I didn't know better, I would say that he had been poisoned!" Brigges startling realisation shocked Hans. He looked at the bowl that he had hastily set down. It was all but finished, perhaps only one large spoonful left. Brigges too looked to his bowl, similarly placed aside in a hurry during the crisis. It was in a similar state of near emptiness.

"How do you feel?" Brigges asked Hans. He responded by holding his chest and feeling his own heart. It was pounding in his chest.

"My heart is beating very fast" he said beginning to panic.

"Don't be alarmed Hans, that is only to be expected. Mine is too. Can you breathe properly?" The words were both comforting and anxiety causing at the same time. Hans drew in and let out a few breaths. He realised that there was nothing wrong with his breathing whatsoever.

"I'm fine he said." This had the effect of noticeably calming his pounding heartbeat. He said it again louder this time as if trying to convince himself as much as he was telling Captain Brigges.

"I am fine, no trouble breathing, my heart is returning to normal". He breathed a sigh of relief.

"What about you?" he asked nervously.

"Nothing wrong with me." He looked again at the prone body of Edward. His mind was racing. What could have done this? For just a moment he thought that Hans had something to do with it. Hans was the one that handed them their meals. But he resisted the idea. It did not bear contemplating; it had to be something else.

"Maybe one piece of bad meat that Edward did not cure properly?" It was a faint hope of offering a plausible explanation to yet another death. Hans caught on to the idea.

"Do you think that is what it was? Imagine that; the ship's cook, responsible for his own death. Poor bastard!" Hans sounded absolutely convinced that that's what it was that caused Edward's untimely and dramatic death. Brigges was amazed at how readily Hans accepted the flimsy explanation. But perhaps after everything that had happened, he needed any explanations to believe in; something that made sense and could be reckoned with. Anything that did not involve the supernatural or a lunatic murderer that was amongst them picking them off one by one.

"We have to let Vaughn know." Said Hans

"We should both go." Offered Benjamin. Hans was glad of the idea; the thought of getting out of the galley right now seemed somehow very appealing.

***

When they climbed up the forward hatch they could see that there was nobody at the wheel. Giving each other an alarmed look they approached the wheelhouse together. Brigges opened the door and they both surveyed the empty room. The wheel had been tied off. Suddenly the cabin door opened and Vaughn appeared he looked at both of the men in confusion.

"Where is Edward?" Vaughn demanded to know of Hans, he was conspicuous by his absence.

"Where have you been?" he countered.

"In the companion" he replied giving Hans a look as if to say, where else would I have been?'

"Edward is dead" said Brigges succinctly. Vaughn visibly reacted as if he had been punched.

"How!" he shouted at them.

"We think that he was poisoned by some meat that he did not cure properly." Hans was anxious to give Vaughn the plausible explanation. But then he shook his head as if no longer believing the words he had just spoken. Instead he turned back to Brigges

"No! You killed him didn't you? I know you did. Don't try to deny it!" Hans was enraged. Brigges actually backed away he was so taken aback by the unreasoning accusation. Hans was pointing his finger directly at Brigges face. He was shaking with anger. Vaughn knew that he had to intervene now to prevent Hans from going any further with his angry tirade. Thinking as quickly as he could, even though still shocked by what he had heard, he managed to put together an argument that he hoped would settle Hans down a little.

"Hans, listen to me. How could Brigges have poisoned Edward? He was locked up whist you were making the evening meal. It is insanity to think that he snuck out of his confinement and somehow managed to poison the bowl that Edward was about to eat. Who handed them their meals Hans? You I would wager and not Captain Brigges. The next thing you will be accusing me of killing him. Be sensible. Now is not the time to lose your head. We are sure to sight the Azores soon and this nightmare of a voyage will be over once and for all. We can both catch a cruise ship back to civilisation. But for now I need you to keep calm and stay reasonable. Can you do that

Hans?" Vaughn's plea was designed to offer Hans a glimpse of how they could soon escape the traumatic situation that was this journey. He hoped that it would resonate with him and bring him back to reality. He was correct.

"Yes" he said visibly trying to calm himself. "You are right Vaughn; of course. Yes. I can." The myriad of affirmations helped to ease the tension in the wheelhouse.

"But I won't sleep unless he is locked up again!" He again pointed to Brigges, who responded by rolling his eyes.

"You are incredible Hans. You still believe that I am somehow guilty of murdering....who, all of the men that have died my daughter, my wife? No amount of insurance money will ever be able to replace them Hans. Or do you think that I am just opportunistic and have capitalised upon the unfortunate accidents that have happened on our crossing of the Atlantic? You sir are an imbecile!" Brigges uncharacteristic insult shut Hans up completely. He was so gobsmacked that he couldn't think of anything to say in response. Instead he grumbled and reiterated his stance.

"He gets locked up or I stay awake until we see land!" Hans remained resolute in his demand. Brigges threw his hands up in the air in exasperation.

"Fine; I will return to my confinement!" Captain Briggs concession to being locked up again went a long way toward diffusing the tension that was filling the air of the wheel house. He resigned himself to another night locked in Albert's cabin.

Chapter 25: Monday November 27th, 1871

The following day began with a brilliant sunrise. Nobody aboard noticed it however as they were all so deep in thought about the plague of deaths that had visited their ship. It was difficult to keep a positive attitude. You would have had to be superhuman to do so. The only thing that was holding them together, such as it was, was the thought of reaching land soon. There had been so many deaths, so many burials at sea and yet another one to add to the list.

Vaughn had taken it upon himself to prepare Edward's body. Like the others it was shrouded and sewn closed. Even though Hans objected, Vaughn wanted Captain Brigges present for the service. The three of them stood over Edward's body almost unable to believe that death had touched the Mary Celeste once more. Hans read from the bible and when he was done, Brigges and Vaughn lifted the plank sending Edward's body to the sea.

There was a feeling of déjà vu. They had stood here so often doing exactly the same thing with various members of the crew or passengers. Again, there was silence after the burial. Nobody could think of anything appropriate to say. The fluttering of the sails above distracted them all from their introspective thoughts.

"The sails need trimming Mister Lorensen." Observed Captain Brigges. "And by the look of it there is more inclement weather ahead." He pointed out to see. Sure enough there were grey clouds gathering. It certainly did not look as serious as either of the major storms that they had encountered previously, but it test their mettle with only the two of them to run the entire ship.

"Hans…" Vaughn was about to ask if it would be alright to leave the Captain free during the storm so that they at least had three people to manage the vessel. Guessing correctly exactly what he was going to ask Hans objected immediately.

"No Vaughn! We can handle the ship ourselves. We don't need *his* help!" Han's vitriolic tone left in no doubt that he would not entertain the thought of allowing Brigges to help them.

"But…" began Vaughn in a vain hope to change Hans' mind. Again he was cut off before finishing his sentence.

"I said No! Lock him up again. I don't feel safe with him on the loose." Hans made no pretence to hide his feelings or lower his voice so that Captain Brigges would not hear. Quite the opposite he directed his responses toward Brigges even though he was responding to Vaughn.

"Alright, alright! Keep your shirt on!" he said trying to calm down his fellow crewman. "We will just have to work harder to manage everything ourselves." Vaughn was angry at Hans' inflexibility.

"Please come along Captain Brigges" said Vaughn. Brigges did not even bother to argue. He too felt that he could be useful given the coming situation. However he could see that there was no reasoning with Hans. It would be better to quietly accept his fate for the time being and put his trust in the two able seamen that they would see the ship through this next tribulation.

***

The storm was mostly wind this time rather than lightning and rain. The ferocity of the sudden gusts was making it difficult to decide which of the sails would be best left up to handle the flurries. Sometimes it was a blast of wind and other times it was merely windy. Hans and Vaughn were kept busy at the wheel and then hoisting and dropping sails according to the prevailing conditions, which seemed to change often, almost as if to hamper their best efforts.

It was during one of the sudden squalls that Vaughn was outside attempting to bring down the main shroud when he signalled to Hans to give him a hand. Hans waved his acknowledgement and dutifully tying off the wheel came outside to help. The wind was cold. He shivered as he ran to help Vaughn bring the shroud down and together they were tying it up when another sudden gust caught them off-guard. The Main shroud threatened to capture the wind and inflate the sail again.

"Bring it down quickly!" shouted Vaughn. Hans did not need to be prompted he was very much aware of what needed to be done. They pulled and pulled. It took a mighty effort from them both but they managed to get the main shroud down once more.

"Now tie it down" instructed Vaughn. Hans couldn't help but think that Vaughn was stating the very obvious and was tempted to respond in a smarmy way. However the situation was too precarious for sarcasm. The sail had to be made secure. Hans had not noticed, but the small pouch that he kept around his neck had come out of hiding beneath his shirt during the recent struggle. He pushed past Vaughn to get to the appropriate ropes that would secure the sale. Vaughn could feel something rub against him and caught out of the corner of his eye the pouch. It fell to the deck unnoticed by Hans as he busied himself to tie the ropes.

Vaughn could now let go of the rope that he was holding he bent down to pick up whatever it was that Hans had dropped, and froze. The pouch had fallen to the deck and three rings had spilled out onto the deck. Each had the largest diamond that Vaughn had ever seen.

Having finished securing the sail, Hans now turned to see Vaughn leaning down looking at something on the deck. He saw then the rings that he had secreted on his person for the entire journey splayed out on the deck, with Vaughn reaching for them.

"Leave them alone!" Hans screamed but it was too late, Vaughn had scooped them up and was inspecting them in utter amazement. He knew these rings somehow. Vaughn's mind worked furiously. It was not that he had seen them before exactly, but he knew them because they had been described. That was it! The newspaper article that was read out in the tavern that he and Bill and Hans and Adrian had visited prior to leaving New York Harbour.

He turned on Hans.

"These are the rings stolen from the museum in New York! The rings from the Dame Victoria Madison collection!" He turned them over in his hand and recalled the description that was read to him.

"Seven carat diamonds, one circled by emeralds, one sapphires and one smaller diamonds." There was absolutely no doubt that these were the rings that the Police were looking for from the museum in Winthrop street.

"From the French jewellery house of Chaumet! I remember clearly when Adrian read it out to us in the tavern!" Vaughn was incensed.

"You are a thief Hans. You stole these rings. They must be worth more than this ship and cargo combined!" Vaughn's mood was darkening with each passing second. He instinctively reached for the gun that he had been in his belt. He pointed it at Hans. Hans instinctively took one step backwards.

"They are mine Vaughn give them back!" Hans looked panicked.

"It was you all along wasn't it?" Vaughn was now shaking with a mixture of the cold wind blasting them and the anger welling up inside of him.

"No, NO!" insisted Hans, but Vaughn would not listen to him.

"You have killed almost everyone aboard to protect your secret haven't you!?" Vaughn advance on Hans with the gun. Hans retreated. He was shaking his head.

"Nobody knew about the rings Vaughn, I had no reason to kill anybody. I wanted to sell them on the black market in Italy and then leave the employ of Brigges there. I was going to return to Germany with my money and live the life of a rich man. No more low-paid jobs aboard merchant ships for me. I want to live life Vaughn. You cannot blame me for that. The museum won't miss the rings. I only took what I needed." Hans was almost blubbering trying to justify what he had done.

"I don't believe you. If you are capable of robbing a museum then you are capable of anything. How could I have trusted you all of this time? What a fool I have been!" Vaughn raised the gun and pointed it directly at Han's face. Hans flinched and held up his hands in front of his face in an instinctive but feeble attempt to protect himsef. "You were the one that handed Edward his meal, you said so yourself. You must has slipped a poison into it. You have been killing everybody aboard one by one so that nobody finds out about your devious plan!" Vaughn was becoming increasingly angry now, Hans could see that Vaughn's anger was escalating beyond anything he had displayed before. And Vaughn was holding a loaded gun right in his face.

"No, please Vaughn, I may be a thief but I have not killed anybody, please believe me."

"You will trade places with Captain Brigges until I figure out what to do with you. Get below!" he pointed at the mid ship hatch with the gun. Hans was so scared by this point of Vaughn's anger that he did not offer any resistance.

"Yes, I will go. Please don't shoot me Vaughn". He hurried to comply with Vaughn's direction. He clambered down the ladder-stairs and stood back waiting for Vaughn to join him. Vaughn did his best to come down the steep decline whilst continuing to point the loaded gun at Hans. When he got to the bottom of the stairs, still keeping Hans in his unblinking sight, he took the accumulated set of keys from his pocket and threw them at Hans. They hit him in the chest and fell to the floor.

"Pick them up. Unlock the door!" barked Vaughn. Hans did so and fumbled with the keys trying to find the exact one that unlocked the door to Albert's cabin. His hand was shaking as he did so. Eventually he managed and pushed the door open. Brigges was standing there looking at them both, clearly wondering what was going on.

"Captain Brigges, Hans will be replacing you in confinement" explained Vaughn and Hans moved to do just that. Unable to comprehend the sudden turn of events Brigges felt compelled to ask the obvious.

"What has happened Vaughn. What has Hans done?" Vaughn reached into his pocket and produced the pouch, handing it to Brigges. He took it and looked inside.

"Rings?" he said, none the wiser.

"Stolen from a museum in New York from a private collection; worth a fortune." Vaughn gave a brief summation of the origin of the rings. Brigges looked at Hans now standing where he had been only moments earlier.

"Hans stole them? Are you sure?" Brigges almost couldn't believe what he was hearing.

"We read a newspaper article about them the night before we left dock. The police will no doubt be very happy to have them back and the perpetrator behind bars".

"No Vaughn please don't turn me in. We can split the rings; one each. Yes, that would be perfect. We can sell them on the black market......."

"Be quiet man. Do you think that Vaughn and I would agree to such an underhanded deal?" Brigges spoke for what he believed was both himself and Vaughn. Reaching for the door he slammed it shut. Turning the key and pulling it out he turned to face Vaughn.

"We will leave him to the Spanish authorities. But for now I can feel that the ship is listing to one side. We both need to get back on deck and get us through this wind-storm."

"Yes Captain Brigges. You can depend on me". Vaughn put the gun back into his belt and made his way up the stair-ladder once more. Brigges followed. Surveying the situation the Captain checked the rigging, the sails and said.

"You take the wheel; I will stay out here and see to the trimming of the sails. Together we can get through this Vaughn. I know that we can".

"Aye Captain." Vaughn somehow felt like saluting the Captain but managed to resist and simply went to carry out his orders.

The two of them battled the storm together with aplomb. Sails were hoisted when needed and dropped when they became a liability. It just felt somehow that the ship itself was back on course in more ways than one. The subterfuge that was Hans' hidden persona of a big-time thief hidden amongst them all had, now that it was exposed, given relief to the situation. There was no logic to it, but it felt right. Hans was now exposed; Brigges freed from confinement and the ship was heading, hopefully, safely, back to the Azores and the end of this nightmare.

Eventually the storm subsided. Evening was falling and Vaughn and Benjamin were in the wheel house discussing what to do with Hans.

"If he was able to break into a museum and steal rings worth goodness knows how much money, then I cannot see that piddling lock holding him throughout the night. He will pick it for sure and slit the throat of whichever one of us is trying to sleep." It was apparently now incumbent upon Vaughn to fantasise about the worst-case scenario now that Hans was excluded from such conversations. Brigges hadn't thought of it in those terms, but was clearly alarmed at the very idea.

"Maybe we should tie him up so overnight?' Brigges offered a pragmatic solution to the perceived problem.

"Broke into a museum Captain Brigges, a lock and ropes are not going to hold him. I want him off this boat. I say we give him clothing and blankets enough to keep him warm, put him in the rowboat and tow him along so that he can do us both no harm." Vaughn's solution for confining Hans in a way that could not easily be overcome was inventive to say the least. Brigges considered it carefully.

"He could not possibly pull himself back to the ship if we continue to get these favourable winds." Benjamin stroked his chin. "Yes Vaughn that is a splendid idea. That way whoever is steering can easily keep a watch on the row boat trailing behind us. The one that is not on duty at the time can sleep easily. It is a good plan Vaughn. It is unusual, but this is a very unusual situation, so I say that we do it. He can help lower the boat over the side. Go and fetch him and have him provision himself with whatever he thinks that he will need for the night." Brigges was now enthusiastic about the idea. It solved a problem and would perceptibly make the Mary Celeste more secure to be aboard. Anything that improved their situation welcome.

Invigorated that the Captain approved so completely of his proposal, Vaughn went to make the arrangements.

***

When Vaughn arrived back on deck with a fully-laden Hans, the captain tied-off the wheel and joined them at the rowboat. Vaughn partially removed the cover and told Hans to drop his blankets, food and extra clothing inside.

"I will not completely remove the cover, you may like to reattach it from the inside to prevent yourself from getting wet from the spray". Vaughn had given his plan more thought and had injected it with a sliver of consideration for the now disgraced crewman. Hans was incensed.

"You just want to keep the rings to cover your gambling debts! Admit it Vaughn that is what you are thinking isn't it?" Hans was clearly not happy at what was about to happen to him and was lashing out at Vaughn.

"Gambling debts?" Brigges looked at Vaughn hoping that he would clarify the situation. Vaughn turned noticeably red with embarrassment. He stumbled through a few words that did not mean anything. Brigges thought that he may have been answering in German at first. But then he clarified his defence for the both of them.

"I may have succumbed to my gambling daemon Hans, but I have never stolen anything from anyone to cover those debts. I have always worked hard and paid them off. This will be no different." He was ashamed but defiant that Hans' accusation would not sully his good character. Hans was not convinced.

"The sale of just one of those rings would more than pay off every gambling debt that you have ever had many times over and still leave you with money enough to live a very comfortable life Vaughn. I say that we split the proceeds from the sale of the rings........"

"Stop it Hans. Nobody is selling the rings. They are being returned to the collection that you stole them from and you are going to an American jail for their theft and that is that!" Captain Brigges was adamant in deflecting any temptation that Hans placed in their way. Happy that Hans now seemed visibly defeated, Vaughn added salt to the wound.

"Now help me lift the boat over the side."

Hans looked at both of them steadily. He could see the determination in their faces. There would be no deal that he could strike with them, he knew that now. He begrudgingly helped Vaughn hoist the rowboat on its miniature boom and swing it over the side.

"Now get in!" demanded Vaughn. Hans clambered aboard the small boat. He checked everything that he had deposited previously into it. He had enough provisions to see the night out in a measure of comfort. He was already planning to re-attach the cover so that he would not get wet whilst being towed by the Mary Celeste.

"Lowering away!" he heard Vaughn announcing that the boat was being lowered. Hans checked the knot of the rope that was tied to the front of the small craft. It was a good job, nothing to worry about there. Nevertheless, the thought of being towed throughout the night was not a cheery one. But he had some confidence that both Vaughn and Brigges were able seamen and knew how to accomplish such a task without incident.

The boat hit the water and immediately Hans began to tie up the cover so that he wouldn't be sprayed with water for the entire time that he was in it. He huddled underneath the cover. It was quite roomy with just him aboard. The boat was jostled up and down side to side. He was an experienced seaman but this could easily result in sea-sickness if it continued for the entire night. He hoped that it would be more smooth when the boat made it safely to the back of the Mary Celeste and was being towed in its wake.

Brigges and Vaughn had by this time attached the lengthy rope to the back of the ship and were waiting for the coiled rope to exhaust itself. The rope unwound and soon the slack was taken up. Hans was again jolted in his small craft, guessing that the rope was now towing him behind the main ship. He grumbled but settled in for the night knowing that he had the cold comfort of looking forward to being back on board the ship tomorrow morning. The night came. There was no moon. Taking turns in the wheelhouse neither the Captain nor Vaughn could actually see the rowboat, but they knew that it was there because of the tension in the rope tied to the rear of the ship.

Chapter 26: Tuesday November 28th, 1871

Vaughn woke up in his cabin. It was barely the beginning of sunrise. The light in the sky was dark-blue. Soon that would change to lighter and lighter shades until that beautiful colour of pre-sunrise would spread across the sky. It was Vaughn's favourite time of day. If he was on land, this would be the time of day just prior to all of the birds waking up and beginning their twittering. He felt rested. It had worked. Having Hans off the ship whilst he had the opportunity to sleep had paid the dividends that he had intended. He had slept soundly. Yawning and stretching he found a fresh set of clothes and pulled them on. Then after a quick visit to the galley to grab some stale bread and make himself a hot cup of tea he made his way through the corridor to the main cabin so that he would enter the wheelhouse from within.

Opening the door he could see that Captain Brigges had fallen asleep at the wheel. The sound of the door opening alerted Brigges to his own shortcoming and he jolted himself awake.

"Good morning." He said trying to be cheery. Vaughn knew better and managed to give him a wry smile and countered with his own jibe.

"Yah, Good morning Captain, did you sleep well?" He asked with a smile. Knowing that he had been caught sleeping on the job, Benjamin did not try to cover it up anymore.

"Ah, yes, sorry about that, it simply overtook me I am afraid to say." He was genuinely apologetic.

"How is our outcast this morning?" asked Vaughn. The sky was bright enough now that they would easily be able to see the boat in tow. Both of them looked to the back but could not see the boat from where they were. They would need to be outside of the wheel house for it to be in view. But the rope that was towing it was plainly visible. It was slack.

"What the!" Vaughn opened the door and ran out to the rear of the ship. Brigges, not bothering to tie off the wheel followed him. The row boat was nowhere to be seen. Vaughn grabbed the rope and began to pull it in. He had not taken in very much at all when he came to the end of it. It was frayed; broken.

"Hans!" exclaimed Vaughn now sorry that he had ever relegated his former friend to the rowboat. It was nowhere to be seen.

"We have to go back for him!" he shouted. Brigges looked at Vaughn.

"Go back?" he said incredulously. "The row boat could have been gone for hours, I don’t know how long since I have been asleep."

"When did you last check it?" he shouted

"Around four o'clock in the morning, it was still attached, I am certain of it." Brigges responded.

"So about an hour then" Vaughn was contemplating how to best turn the ship around and search for the wayward rowboat. There was a growing feeling of unease in him.

"Turn the ship around Captain Brigges, we have to find Hans, we have to!" He exclaimed. Brigges for his part was more thoughtful about the tragedy that had revealed itself with the morning light.

"Be rational Vaughn. It could have drifted way off course. And without a spyglass, how could we ever have a hope of finding it." Brigges was being far too logical for Vaugh.

"You did this on purpose!" he screamed his face only inches from Brigges. "You wanted to keep the rings for yourself and claim the insurance money from this doomed voyage!" His accusation did not have the effect that he thought that it would on the Captain.

"You're wrong Vaughn; you did this! You crept up on deck and seeing that I had fallen asleep cut the rope so that you could keep all of the rings and pay off your gambling debts and still live like a rich man from the proceeds!" Benjamin's counter accusation stung Vaughn.

"You're mad!" he said trying to defend himself from the logic of Benjamin's thinking. Vaughn drew the gun that he had been keeping in his belt and aimed it at the Captain. Any truce that had existed between them was now dissolved.

"I will see that the Spanish authorities try you for the crimes that you have committed aboard this ship *Captain* Brigges!" Vaughn had a mad look in his eyes. Brigges could see that he was almost unhinged with desperation from everything that had happened.

"You are correct of course." Brigges sudden demure admission was his attempt to diffuse the situation. But instead it simply added more fuel to Vaughn's anger.

"RIGHT! About you being a cold-blooded murderer that would stop at nothing to claim an insurance policy?" Vaughn was almost laughing with manic angst at the Captain's words. But Brigges held up his hands in a gesturing motion for Vaughn to calm himself.

"You are right about turning the ship around. Even if it is a small hope of finding Hans in the row boat in the midst of the Atlantic; it is still a hope. We have to at least try. I'm sorry that I even implied that we should do otherwise. Prepare to turn us about Mister Lorensen." The affirmative action was more of a soothing remedy for the situation that was escalating. Vaughn looked as if he had been slapped in the face. He took a moment to register that he was getting his way and then acknowledged it.

"Turn about it is!" The response lacked the usual warmth that Vaughn would imbue it with. And Brigges noticed that there was no use of his title in the response. But he had galvanised Vaughn back into action and away from the pointlessness of arguing which of them was guilty of the row boat's separation from the Mary Celeste. Right now all that Brigges was thinking about was how to manage the precariousness of his uneasy treaty with Vaughn. Vaughn did still possess the only firearm on the ship. That was something that Brigges was keenly focussed upon right now.

***

It took a lot of effort on the parts of both men, but the ship was turned around. Now it was heading directly back upon its former course; or at least as accurately as could be described by simply following the compass bearing. The pair took turns at the wheel and the other at the very front of the boat looking out over the rolling blue of the waves in the vain hope that they would spot the row-boat with Hans inside. The first hour flew past and the supposed point where the smaller craft was separated from the larger was reached. Vaughn insisted on taking over watch-duty forward. He clung on to the railing and looked desperately right, left and straight ahead. The minutes ticked by with excruciating slowness. Nothing, as far as he could see; Vaughn could feel his heart sinking.

Captain Brigges joined him, much to Vaughn's surprise. He must have tied-off the wheel, assumed Vaughn correctly.

"I thought that two sets of eyes would be better than one eh Vaughn?" Brigges' offer would under normal circumstances have been welcomed. But facing the despair of losing yet another crewmate clouded Vaughn's ability to see it for what it was. Even if Hans may very well have been behind at least some of the deaths, thinking of him abandoned in the middle of the ocean brought a human aspect to the man. Vaughn could barely carry the burden of how Hans must be feeling now adrift, alone, without any hope. Instead of thanking Brigges for his assistance, he lashed out at him.

"This would have stood a much greater chance of success if we still had the spyglass!" He practically hissed the sentence to Benjamin. Brigges actually flinched at the words as if they had physically hit him.

"Vaughn........" he began to defend himself and realised that it was a hopeless battle, one that he could never win.

"Keep your wits about you Vaughn. We may yet spot him and have to alter course at a moment's notice." Brigges words went unacknowledged by Vaughn. Both men stood there looking out to sea. The minutes turned into a quarter of an hour, which in turn became half an hour.

"There is still hope." Vaughn said out of nowhere, breaking the frosty silence that had been endured by them both.

"Yes Vaughn, there is still hope." Brigges agreed. Vaughn chanced a quick glance at the Captain. He tried to measure the sincerity of what he had heard with what he was seeing. He involuntarily shook his head and returned his focus to the Atlantic Ocean.

An hour past with no real sighting; the concentration of their eyes on the undulating surface made for the occasional false-sighting. Both men were guilty of this and when in turn they had raised the hope of the other, only to dash it with further investigation, it became a kind of torture that they inflicted upon each other every now and again.

Two hours past and the vestiges of hope that had grown in Vaughn when he heard the order to turn the ship about began to fade. Nevertheless, he tried to convince himself that there was still a faint hope of finding the row boat. The prevailing current may have dragged it further away than he first thought. Time dragged on and on. Brigges left him to survey the ocean alone and returned to steering the ship. Vaughn eventually succumbed to fatigue.

"Why are you trying so hard to find Hans? He was the one who poisoned me!" Edward's stinging words struck Vaughn awake. He had fallen asleep and collapsed to his knees. It was a nightmare, albeit a brief one. The thought of the recently deceased Edward accusing Hans of his own murder sent a shiver though Vaughn. He stood up and tried to shake off the image that had pushed itself into his mind's eye. Guilt enveloped him. He had fallen asleep on the job and with renewed vigour he looked out to sea again. Still nothing, the conditions were perfect. He couldn't have wished for better, but still the ocean refused to give up the place that it was hiding Hans.

Guilt was replaced with anger at failing to spot the row boat. First it was anger with himself for not succeeding in recovering his crewmate. Then it was anger with Brigges for ever employing him on this voyage of the damned. Yes, that was it. He now truly believed, just as Hans had said, that the voyage was cursed from the very beginning and this was only the latest spiteful offering from that curse.

Vaughn gave one last look over the waves. He turned, frustrated and marched to the wheelhouse.

"I'll take over here!" he said gruffly. Brigges did not object or offer any other response. He could see from Vaughn's expression that he was in a foul mood. Brigges nodded and left to assume his position at the front of the boat to search for Hans.

***

Vaughn had been steering the boat for hours now. Brigges had not offered to swap their positions. The majority of the day was gone, soon it would be sunset. There would be no point in continuing the search by moonlight even though it would be a full moon tonight. It simply did not cast enough light to spot a row boat in the choppy conditions around them.

Benjamin was tired and thirsty and could see no point in continuing the search, but he did not want to say that to Vaughn. He heard footsteps behind him.

"Vaughn; would you like me to take over steering?" he asked as Vaughn approached him. "There will still be light for another half an hour or so. Hope springs eternal as the saying goes..." Brigges was interrupted by Vaughn.

"Was this a part of your plan Brigges?" Vaughn sounded strange, strained.

"Plan?" asked the Captain innocently.

"Yes; plan to have us turn-about and head away from the Azores." Vaughn looked right into Brigges' eyes. Benjamin could not believe what he was hearing.

"This was not my plan Vaughn, it was yours." He said trying to reason with the man.

"You created the entire situation by setting Hans adrift knowing that I would want to do the humane thing and try to recover him. Get rid of yet another crewman and it should be easy to finish off only one more. That is what you thought isn't it? But it isn't working Brigges. I say we turn about so that I can get you into the hands of the Spanish authorities as quickly as possible!" Vaughn had a slightly manic look in his eyes.

"You wanted us to head back and look for...." Brigges once again tried to make him see reason.

"We have sailed in the wrong direction for nearly an entire day. What a complete fool I have been to fall for your wicked deception. No more! Turn us about *Mister* Brigges and make all sails necessary to get us to the Azores as quickly as this damned ship will travel across the sea!" Vaughn's order was not to be reckoned with, Brigges could see that. He hoped that acquiescence would help calm Vaughn.

"Straight away Mister Lorensen; the sooner we make port the better." Brigges agreement with the command had the opposite effect of the one he had assumed.

"You would like that wouldn't you? For us to turn about and completely abandon Hans. Well he had provisions enough to see him through. I say that we drop all sails, drop anchor for the night and begin our search again at morning's first light". Vaughn contradicted his own previous order. Brigges shook his head unable to fathom the sudden and seemingly irrational change of plan.

"What?" Brigges was becoming desperate to find some way to comply with Vaughn, who was becoming increasingly distressed. He thought for a moment to once again agree with Vaughn, but then second-guessed himself. What if agreement brought with it another accusation of wicket intention? But he could not think of anything else on the spur of the moment. He chanced it.

"An excellent plan Mister Lorensen; we may yet spot Hans and rescue him. Or overnight, with the full-moon due, he may spot us. He has oars in the row-boat; he will be able to return to us safely." He finished his promise to conform to Vaughn's will and tensed wondering what sort of response he would receive.

"That's more like it Mister Brigges. We have to think of the welfare of all of those of us that have survived this journey through hell. Make it so." Vaughn's almost unnatural calm did nothing to dissipate Brigges own unease.

"Yes Mister Lorensen, straight away" Brigges was grateful to get away from Vaughn and begin to drop all of the sails one by one. It would take some time and from the look of it, Vaughn was not going to assist him. Watched closely by Vaughn, Brigges made good the order and soon the sails were all down and secured and the anchor was released. The sound of it unfurling reminded Vaughn of finding his younger brother dead, entangled in it when it was raised. He could be seen reliving the moment. Brigges spoke breaking into the unpleasant memory.

"I'm going below to get something to eat" He did not wait for permission from Vaughn but instead mad his way to the nearest hatch to go below. Vaughn's eyes followed him.

Chapter 27: Nightfall

The two men sat in the galley together eating and drinking in silence. Each regarded the other when the other was not looking. Each if, the other had seen would have recognised an expression of deep suspicion. Brigges knew that if Vaughn wanted to lock him up again, he would be powerless to prevent it. It was unlikely because it would be impossible to run the ship with just one man. This gave Brigges a little bargaining power, but not much. Vaughn after all, had the gun; if there was only some way to get it off him? Perhaps as he slept tonight?

As if reading his mind Vaughn spoke breaking the stony silence.

"You'll be sleeping in Albert's cabin again tonight Brigges; safely locked up so that I can get some sleep." Benjamin's hopes fell when he heard what Vaughn was planning. The Captain pondered the situation a little further and responded in a calming manner.

"Yes, of course Vaughn, as you think best." He hoped that acquiescing would start to ease the tension between them. Vaughn looked up from his meal and gave Brigges a cold regarding stare. For just a moment Benjamin thought that he may have inadvertently sparked an irate reaction from Vaughn. But no adverse reaction was forthcoming; Vaughn continued to stare at him for a while more before returning to his meal. Benjamin breathed a silent sigh of relief to have Vaughn's eyes off him for the time being. He wasn't sure if it was disgust that he could see in Vaughn's eyes or contempt; but whatever the feelings he did not want them directed at his person anymore.

***

Retiring for the evening couldn't come soon enough for Benjamin. He was grateful to be escorted to Albert's cabin and locked in once more. However when he tried to settle on the bunk Benjamin realised that having Vaughn out of site was somehow more unsettling than having him close by. He could hardly sleep his mind was whirring with so many thoughts about what was happening. It would be a long night.

***

Vaughn took his bunk and mumbled to himself as he tried to settle down.

"He did it for sure, all of it." Sleep would not come easily, but he was so fatigued that he knew that it would come eventually. He clasped the gun closer to his chest for comfort.

Chapter 28: Wednesday November 29th, 1871

At sunrise Benjamin surprisingly found himself woken by the sound of the unlocking of the cabin door. He had slept for longer than he would have thought. He stirred himself quickly not wanting to be in the least bit compromised while in the presence of Vaughn. He tried to judge Vaughn's mood as he entered the cabin. Vaughn was again pointing the gun directly at Benjamin.

"Good morning" said Brigges sardonically. The tone was completely lost on Vaughn who answered gruffly.

"It will be a good morning if we find our lost shipmate. And it will improve your chances of not being executed at sea for the murder of the passengers and crew of the Mary Celeste." Brigges was shocked. He drew breath to object in the strongest terms to the accusation, but thought the better of it under the circumstances. He did not want to engage Vaughn in a heated exchange. Instead he swallowed his need to immediately defend himself from the words and instead supported Vaughn's earlier reference.

"It looks to be a fine day Mister Lorensen; plenty of visibility to spot our missing boat and reclaim it." Brigges even managed a small smile to underline his optimistic outlook.

"Hoist the sails and bring up the anchor; we need to find Hans." Vaughn did nothing to disguise the revulsion in his voice. Benjamin tried his best to not react to the unmasked insult.

"Straight away Mister Lorensen." he straightened himself up and pulled on his boots tying them up as quickly as he could. Then with

Vaughn in tow he marched out of the cabin and up the ladder-stairs to and onto the deck of the ship. Surveying the situation he judged the prevailing winds and decided on the fore-shrouds and the fore and main topmast shrouds and of course the mainsail. He went about hoisting the various sails under the watchful eye of Vaughn. Then when he had finished he moved over to the anchor and began to wind it up. It was noisy and hard work on his own but he dare not ask Vaughn for assistance for fear of the response.

When he had managed to get it to the surface and locked into place he looked at Vaughn as if waiting for further instructions.

"Take the wheel and steer us due east. I will keep look-out for the row-boat." Vaughn's tone had not improved. Brigges nodded and made his way to the wheel house to do as he was instructed.

And that is how the entire morning passed. Vaughn looking out to sea hoping against all hope that he would spot the missing row-boat, and Brigges steering the ship directly east as instructed, further away from the Azores.

***

At midday, there was a crashing sound. The mainsail began to flap about unrestrained and no longer performing its function as main propulsion for the brigantine. Brigges tied off the wheel and came running out to the main mast. He was met by Vaughn. They could both see as clear as anything that the ropes that tied the mainsail to the main boom had broken.

"They will have to be replaced" Brigges made the statement as if asking for Vaughn's permission to jump into action. Vaughn looked around. The only ropes available on deck would not be good enough to do the job.

"Get some proper ropes from the stores below. The job has to be done correctly." It was insulting for Vaughn to even suggest that Captain Brigges would even contemplate anything less than a perfect repair job. But just as with all of the other insults that he had been forced to bear, Benjamin did not react. Instead he agreed with Vaughn.

"I'll go" he said and went to the mid-ships hatch to go below deck. He hurried to the stores compartment and sorted through the various spare ropes that were there. He located the two that he would need in order to affect repairs and then returned the others to the cupboard. Even under these circumstances, Brigges was neat and tidy.

When he made it back on deck he threw the ropes down in front of him before completing his climb though the mid-ship hatch.

Vaughn was nowhere to be seen. He looked around him puzzled. Had he gone below through the wheel house access? The thought of his half-crazed and armed crewman out of sight was very unsettling indeed.

"Vaughn" he shouted, hoping that he would see Vaughn's head pop up from inside the wheelhouse. Nothing; he shouted back down the hatchway from which he had just emerged.

"Vaughn! I have the ropes I am back on deck now!" there was no response. There was no other explaination, he must have gone below. With another quick survey of the empty deck around him he scampered back down the ladder. The corridor was equally as empty as the scene up on deck that he had just left. He walked over to the galley and opened the door. There was nobody inside. Then one by one, calling as he did so, he opened every door and large storage cupboard door as he made his way down the length of the corridor. Each cabin and cupboard served to raise the anxiousness in Benjamin. One of the storage cupboards that he opened spayed forth a mixture of cans and other spare bits and bobs. He jumped back with alarm frightened by the scattering objects.

He held his heart; it was pounding hard in his chest. There was only the engine room and coal storage room and his cabin left. Other than that, he would have to search in the cargo hold below.

Opening the door to the engine room he called out once more.

"Vaugh; are you there?" the engine room glimmered in the light that was cast into it. He moved over to the coal room and opened the door. There was only coal. Returning to the main corridor he looked at the door to his cabin. Never had it seemed so ominous as it did now. Steeling himself he took hold of the handle and gripped it tightly. Turning it he swung the door open and looked inside; it was empty. The door to the companion was closed. Why was Vaughn not responding to him? Why would he have gone below anyway? If he was in the companion why not simply say so?

"Vaughn are you in there?" he asked firmly. There was silence. With mounting alarm he walked over to the door and flung it open. Empty.

"Where could he be?" Brigges said to himself aloud. He looked at the stairs to the wheelhouse. There was nothing to it he would do a circumference of the deck and check the rigging. Perhaps Vaughn was up one of the masts and somehow the sails had obscured him. That must have been it, he told himself. But he couldn't escape the feeling that Vaughn was somehow taunting him. He was the one that had the gun. What reason could he have for acting this way? Perhaps he had gone completely mad and had decided to stalk him like a hunter stalking its prey. He knew so little about Vaughn. The thought of him lurking somewhere aboard waiting to pounce set the Captain's nerves on edge.

He began to walk up the steps to the wheel house with all of these thoughts going around and around his head. He paused unable or unwilling to open the small door that would take him into the wheelhouse. He was at a complete disadvantage. If Vaughn really had gone completely mad, he would have little chance of reasoning with him, and even less of somehow getting the gun away from him. He turned and surveyed the room for something that he could secret upon himself to use against his assumed assailant.

Brigges eyes settled on a brass rod that helped keep the books in their shelf. He descended the stairs and regarded it more closely. A blow to the head with something like this would be more than enough to incapacitate him. He hurriedly unscrewed the mountings that held the rod in place. It was thin, but strong. He felt the weight of it in his hand. Then looking again up the stairs to the closed hatch, he slid it down his belt and covered it with his coat.

Brigges opened the door to the wheel house expecting to see Vaughn for some reason. It was as empty as all of the other parts of the ship that he had just visited. A cursory look at the compass reassured him that they were still sailing, albeit with a detached mainsail, eastwards. He looked up and down the masts and the rigging. There was nobody there. The deck was empty. Turning he opened the door to exit the wheelhouse.

Vaughn's body lay there. His neck was clearly broken; his head was at the strangest angle to the rest of his body that there was absolutely no doubt in Brigges mind, Vaughn was dead. His eyes were open staring at nothing. As Benjamin stood there unable to comprehend how this could have happened, the main boom whizzed past the top of the wheelhouse. Brigges eyes followed it.

That must have been it. Vaughn got battered by the main boom which was now lurching to the left and right uncontrollably because of the loose mainsail. He tried to kneel down and realised that he couldn't because of the brass rod that he had secreted upon himself. He withdrew it and threw it to the side of the wheel house floor. It clambered into a corner. Then kneeling down he inspected Vaughn's head more closely.

Although the neck was clearly broken, there was no sign of trauma to the head. If the main boom had struck Vaughn, it would have pulverised one side of his face for sure. He reached down and lifted Vaughn's head. It moved with unnatural ease now that the spine was detached from it. Turning the head he expected to see that the side on the deck was the one that had been struck by the boom. It was not. There was no blood anywhere. He replaced Vaughn's head on the deck.

For a long time Brigges sat there with the corpse of Vaughn wondering how he could have died. He could not have put a timeframe upon his numb musings, but by the time he managed to snap himself out of it, the sun was going down.

"The gun" he said aloud. The sound of his own voice was jarring in the silence. He opened Vaughn's jacket. It was not there. He looked around frantically. Nothing; it was inconceivable. He found the small bag that contained the stolen rings but no gun. He emptied the rings out into his hand and looked at them without really seeing them. He returned them to their pouch and absent-mindedly put them into this pocket.

Once more looking for the gun he walked around the wheelhouse and even looked on top of it. Vaughn must have dropped it when the boom struck him, he thought. But it was nowhere to be seen. Again he addressed himself as there was nobody else to hear him.

"He must have dropped it overboard?" he said. Then a thought struck him. Now that Vaughn was dead he did not need to get the gun away from him. In fact he did not need the gun at all now, but the disappearance of the only firearm aboard the vessel was unnerving.

He had to give himself something to do. Vaughn would have to be prepared for burial. But the lurching of the boat mercifully directed his attentions elsewhere. The sails still needed to be repaired. That would take the rest of the day at least, and judging by the light and the position of the sun, he would have to hurry.

The mission gave him focus. He went about repairing the mainsail rigging. Doing the best job that he possibly could somehow became of paramount importance. Benjamin cut away the ropes that had broken and scaled the main mast in order to attach the replacements. He did so and threw the lengths downward to the deck.

They could now be attached to the main boom. It would no longer be swaying from side to side.

After he had done this, he stood back and observed his handiwork.

"A splendid job Benjamin" said Sandra pleased at her husband's obvious skill. Benjamin jumped backwards from the apparition. There was nobody on deck but him. The vision was brought from fatigue and stress. He shook his head in a vain attempt to clear it. Perhaps if he had something to eat he would feel better. He went back to the wheelhouse only to once more encounter Vaughn's corpse.

Benjamin looked down at the body. Somehow he could not bear to prepare it for burial. The thought of another service to lay to rest the dead aboard his ship made him want to be sick. In a second he made a decision. He reached down and picked up Vaughn in a fireman's grip and lugged him to the back of the boat, pushing him up and over the railing he disposed of Vaughn's body into the ocean. He knelt down suddenly exhausted by everything that he had done that day. He looked at the waves that had claimed the last of his crewmen.

"No more" he said to nobody. The sun set behind him. It was dusk. The Mary Celeste continued to sail directly east.

Chapter 29: Thursday November 30th, 1871

Captain Benjamin Brigges woke up startled. He was confused at first. There was something important that he had to do; but at that moment he could not for the like of him remember what it was. He rubbed his eyes and looked out of the porthole. It was daylight. He could not bring himself to appreciate what a fine day it was. There was that lingering feeling that he should be doing something other than what he was. He wanted to get out of the bunk and take care of it, whatever it was, straight away. It would be better than pondering the situation that he found himself in and how he came to be in it. Besides it was nice to wake up in his bunk in his cabin again. The time that he had spent in Albert's cabin was an unwelcome memory now. He was once more Captain Benjamin Brigges of the Mary Celeste. In complete charge of every decision that needed to be made in order to ensure the ships safe arrival at her destination.

Taking a breath he proceeded to do exactly that; even if the actual deed that needed such urgent attention was eluding him just at the moment. Struggling with his boots he grumbled a little beneath his breath. Reaching for some clothes he found the cleanest shirt and trousers and pulled them on, fastening both with equal care. A flash of a memory opened up before him like a vista. In an instant he remembered what it was that had so occupied his thinking. The ship was still heading toward Genoa.

"I should turn us around and head back to......." He was speaking aloud. It felt comforting somehow. It made his cabin, and indeed the entire ship seem not so completely devoid of life. But then an alternative though found voice.

"Why? It wasn't my idea to head back to the Azores?" in that instant of reasoning he made up his mind to continue on his original course toward Genoa.

"With luck I'll spot Gibraltar and then be able to chart an accurate course to Genoa". With his newfound plan cemented in his will, he set about making it become reality.

"I shall start with a hearty breakfast, like all good seafaring men do". With that thought too now made vocal, he moved to the stairs that led to the wheelhouse.

"First though, I must check that all is well". He walked up the short staircase and through the small door into the wheelhouse. Everything was as he left it the day before. The wheel was tied off. He leant over and checked the compass. The ship was heading east, just as he wished to do so.

"Good; good" he said looking through the window at the sails billowing in the wind. Everything was as it should be. It was now time for breakfast. But perhaps a quick look around the horizon. He exited the wheelhouse to the deck. The sun was shining, the wind blowing favourably. It was a good day for sailing. The sea was a little choppy, but nothing that the Mary Celeste couldn't handle with aplomb. Something drew the Captain to the very rear of the boat. He waked over to the rear bannister and looked down. There clinging to the bottom of the wooden balustrades was Vaughn hanging on for dear life. He looked up at the Captain with an anguished look on his face, his mouth opening surely to cry out for help. Benjamin jumped back in terror crying out loudly as he did so. He looked at where Vaughn's fingers should be holding onto the point where the deck met the balustrades that held up the bannister. There was nothing.

Shaking his head to clear it he stepped forward fearfully, gingerly and looked down at the scene below. The water was rushing past the rear of the boat. There was no sign of anyone. With his heart beating faster and short of breath Benjamin closed his eyes and opened them. Luckily, there was still nothing but the water swirling around the rudder. Everything was exactly as it should be. He stood there looking down at the water for a long time. He then looked at the horizon and after a while, convinced that he had calmed down, walked the circumference of the deck inspecting everything as he was prone to do as the Captain. When he was satisfied that everything was ship-shape he decided that he should eat something.

***

When Captain Brigges entered the cabin Edward was standing there leaning over the stove just as he had been so many times before. Brigges jumped with fright. He looked at the stove. There was nobody there. Again his heart was jumping with the shock of seeing the deceased man back at his post.

"Edward is dead, as is Vaughn" he said aloud. The tone was strange. It was almost as if he was trying to convince himself, but sounded uncertain of his facts. There was nobody to agree with him, nor contradict him. He moved over to the cupboard and opened it. He would make some porridge; that would be a good breakfast. Taking out the oats and selecting an appropriately sized pan from those hanging nearby he set about making his morning meal. It took some time to boil properly on the stove, on low heat. This gave him time to visit the companion in his cabin and generally clean himself up for the coming day. By the time he returned to the galley his porridge was well and truly thick and creamy. He found the milk powder and made a small amount enough for his porridge and for a hot cup of tea. He put the kettle on the stove and removed his porridge. Taking a spoon he mixed some of the milk into it and stirred it around. He looked through the provisions for the sugar and located it. Adding a spoonful he mixed it well in with the porridge and then found a suitable bowl to pour it all into. The result was exactly what he imagined when he set out to make it. His breakfast smelt wonderful. He took it over to the table and sitting down began to eat it whilst he waited for the kettle to boil. Already the day was looking better. He was heading toward his destination. There was nothing to stop him.

***

The rest of the day passed routinely. He began to feel more secure about himself and his situation. He trimmed the sails when he needed to. At one point he had to take down the flag flying from the rear main gaff, and untangle it. But this and all of the chores that he did around the boat made him feel better. Raising the flag again filled him with purpose. He would see out this journey and make port in Genoa and then Venice, and then...... Pausing, he caught himself feeling like he was walking down a dead-end street. What was he going to do when he reached port? The thought threatened to overwhelm him. It suddenly felt like a monumental problem with no solution. He panicked and couldn't breathe properly. Falling to the deck he clutched his heart as if that was the cause of this lungs suddenly not being able to take in enough air. He was choking with something, was it poison?

"No!" he managed to say even though it was stifled. But the act of giving voice to his objection somehow helped. He could breathe a little easier now. He said it again with a more resolute tone.

"No!" Again he felt a little better. If he denied this huge problem then it helped him gain his breath. That is exactly what had to be done then. He would not think about this excruciating dilemma now. He would face it when the time came. That was it. That was the solution to easing his terror. He would fix himself some dinner and retire for the evening. Tomorrow was another day.

Chapter 30: Friday December 1st, 1871

Captain Brigges had a restless night. The images of the dead people that he had seen during the day intruded into his dreams. He woke up in a sweat three times that he remembered. It was probably more, but any further instances were lost in the twilight of that state in-between dreams. When he woke up it was barely dawn. He decided that it would be best to keep himself busy today, just as he had the previous day. He readied himself and in a repeat of the day before, fixed himself porridge and tea for breakfast, after inspecting that all was well with the ship. The day was overcast but not unpleasant.

After his breakfast he went on deck and looked around him. The empty sea stretched as far as he could see in all directions. He was completely alone. Try as he might to keep an optimistic outlook, he found it harder to do so with each passing moment. The sea gave away nothing. He had been at sea for more years than he cared to remember. But now he desperately wanted to be on firm dry land. Thoughts of how he was going to explain all of the missing passengers and crew to the authorities in Genoa began to fill his head making it feel like it was going to explode. He became short of breath.

He looked down at the deck. It felt easier to look at the beautifully crafted planks that made up the deck than look out to the endless rolling ocean. He tried to calm himself. He thought that he had succeeded when he noticed that there was fog around his feet. He looked up and could barely see ten foot in front of him. The fog came out of nowhere. He backed up scared of how it could have enveloped the ship so suddenly. He did not see any signs that the weather was going to change and so dramatically. It was unprecedented in all of his years. He stepped backwards a couple of times and brushed a rigging rope.

Turning to see it he came face to face with the dead body of Albert, entangled in the rigging just as he had been found. Face purple and tongue swollen protruding from his mouth. Eyes half rolled into the back of their sockets. Benjamin screamed and jumped backwards.

The fog was gone. There was no sign of Albert's body. Everything was as it should be. The overcast day was cool and windy, but unchanged from when he first arrived on deck. He clasped his head with both of his hands.

"I am not going mad!" he said and then as if he did not believe it the first time, said it again with more conviction.

"I am not going mad!" he looked around him. There was nobody to reply; no-one to confirm his affirmation. Benjamin let out a slight whimper. Then as if the sound of it jolted him back to defiance, he straightened his posture and marched to the mast eager to hoist the mainsail. It was a good wind and he needed to make full use of it.

***

The Captain had managed to keep himself busy for the entire morning. He had a break for lunch. He made himself a sandwich, the bread was stale but he didn't mind. It was not the first time a sailor had had to eat a meal made with stale bread. He wondered if he should bake a new loaf. Standing in front of the wheel house looking out to the vista all around, he chewed on his sandwich and pondered it for a short time. That was it he thought, that would keep him busy for a part of the afternoon. There were more than enough supplies to see his new little project through. He finished his lunch and noticed something about half way up the deck.

At first he couldn't determine what it was. It was a shape in blue. As he looked at it some more it began to make sense. It was a little girl sitting on the deck of the boat facing away from him. She was wearing a navy-blue dress and matching bonnet. Sara had a dress just like it. A haze descended upon him. He walked forward and called out to his daughter.

"Sara - is that you?" There was no response to his question; however the girl did start to sing. He knew the song. Sandra had taught it to Sara on the first part of the voyage. He walked closer and bent down putting his hand on her shoulder. She turned to face him. Her face was that of a skeleton. A boa constrictor emerged from her mouth. Benjamin jumped away and screamed loudly shutting his eyes so tightly that it hurt. But he needed that pain; it brought him back to reality. There was no sound but the lapping of the waves and the sails flapping in the wind.

Carefully he opened his eyes. He was alone on the deck of the ship. He started to cry. Falling to his knees he began to question everything about himself. Why he was even on this ship? How he came to be here? What would he do when he reached port? How would he explain the missing crew and passengers? He beat his face with his clenched fists. After a while the energy drained from him. He couldn't face being here any longer. He stood up and walked to the edge of the deck. The railing would be easy to jump over he thought to himself. For a long time he stared at the ocean rolling around him. It would be quick. He would not try to stay afloat. He had lived a good deal of his life on the water, why then should it not be the ocean that ends his life?

The minutes became hours. The hours became the remainder of the day. It was sunset when, shaking his head at his own inability to throw himself into the Atlantic, he made his way to his cabin, completely and utterly dejected.

Chapter 31: Saturday December 2nd, 1871

Captain Benjamin Brigges woke to the sound of somebody crying. He could hear it in the realm between awake and asleep. It was quite pronounced. He wondered as he came to full consciousness whom it could be? Then the realisation struck him as he managed to pull himself to alertness that it was he. He stifled himself and tried to stop manifesting the obvious signs of stress that he was exhibiting. Suddenly feeling ashamed for being so emotional he did his best to set it to one side and face the day as best as he could. Taking in a deep breath he righted himself and looked out of the porthole. It was just another generic day like the last. He did not even notice if it was sunny or overcast. Brigges was just going through the motions because they offered some comfort and routine. That was what he wanted right now more than anything else.

Climbing out of his bunk he moved to the table and poured some water from a pitcher into a bowl and using a cake of soap began to clean himself up ready for the day ahead.

***

Brigges looked the part of a very stoic proud Captain. He wandered the ship righting rigging and sails when they looked like they needed attention. He did not speak; he did not smile. Everything that he did, was for the good of the ship and the voyage toward Genoa and then Venice. The morning passed by without him even noticing.

Before he knew it, the sun was directly overhead. It was noon. He would have some lunch and then set to work scrubbing the deck. It did not look as if it needed attention. All was ship-shape indeed. But it would help pass the afternoon.

When he went below he tried to occupy his thinking with what he was going to do the following morning. He needed to keep busy. That was the key to making this voyage pass by more quickly.

Entering the galley he set about preparing a meal that he would satisfy his hunger. Somehow he had actually managed to convince himself that all was well and that he would be able to survive the adversity that had beset the Mary Celeste. He had in hand a bowl of broth that he had prepared that morning. It would suffice. Moving to the table he set it down and placing his spoon on the table beside the bowl took his seat.

Looking up he saw that Hans was sitting directly opposite him. Benjamin jumped up and nearly screamed aloud, it took all of his might to stop it. Opening his eyes he expected his frightening vision to be gone, just as they had each time before. Hans remained sitting resolutely where he had been, looking at Brigges with an odd expression on his face.

Brigges closed his eyes again and opened them. Hans was still there; silent.

"You are not real!" he said in a loud voice. Again he closed and opened his eyes. Hans was no longer sitting at the table instead he was a hair's-breadth from Benjamin's face. Brigges jumped backwards in alarm.

"What do you want!" he screamed at Hans. Horrifyingly Hans answered him.

"I warned you Brigges, that this was a voyage of the damned and you did not believe me. But you believe me now don't you?" Hans extended his hand to touch Brigges' face pointing an accusatory finger. Benjamin jumped backwards and crouched down calling out loudly.

"Yes, Yes YES, I BELIEVE YOU; this is a voyage of the damned" he burst into tears, which flowed freely down his face and into his beard. He drew breath only to holler all the more loudly. He sounded like he was choking whenever he drew more breath only to renew his bawling once more. This went on for a considerable amount of time. Unable to tell for himself, how long he had been wallowing in tears his extraordinary show of emotion began to subside. He managed to look up and around him. He was alone in the Galley.

This did not have the calming effect that a logical person may have expected. Instead it renewed his emotional turmoil all the more. He clenched both fists and banged them on the deck over and over again. The tenuous hold upon reality, that he had fooled himself into believing was strong, was broken. His life seemed to crumble down around him as if it were a poorly built structure unable to withstand the force of the assault that it had undergone over the last few weeks.

"I am not going mad; I am not going mad; I am not going mad" he repeated it over and over as if he was trying to convince himself that it was a fact. Or perhaps the more that he said it the more likely it would be to be true. Whatever the reasons the darkness of depression had taken hold of him. He was drained of all of his energy.

Collapsing on the floor, partially from relief that the nightmarish vision of Hans was gone and partly because he was exhausted from his tantrum, Brigges sobbed some more before falling into a deep sleep.

Chapter 32: Sunday December 3rd, 1871

At some point throughout the night, Brigges had aroused himself from his unintended sleep on the floor of the galley. It was pitch black. He had no clear idea of what time in the night it was. It was so dark he could not see the face of the pocket watch that he took out to check the time. Feeling his way forward, he managed to make it back to his cabin and climb into his bunk before once more sleep overtook him.

***

When he awoke on Sunday the third of December in the year eighteen seventy one Benjamin Brigges was a desolate soul. The entire world seemed to press in on him. He felt sick; a sickness that would never be cured. He felt unimaginably tired as if all of the sleep that he had just had, had done little to relieve his fatigue. Another day and night of sleep may just begin to be enough to assist him. Benjamin felt as if the very core of his being was hollow. He was an empty vessel with nothing but a huge dark void within him, bottomless and unfathomable. He wanted to curl up beneath the blankets and try to forget who he was, where he was and what he was attempting to do.

He gathered bit by bit, every last vestige of willpower that he could muster and managed to get out of the bunk. He was still fully clothed from the following day. He looked down at his attire, it seemed shabby to him. But he could not find the strength to wash and change. Something external to his introspection began to intrude into his consciousness. It was a sound that he should recognise, but did not. Shaking his head, aware that something needed his attention he looked around the cabin hoping that sighting something would help him in his quandary. Nothing did. The sound continued, and like a bolt of lightning it suddenly revealed itself to him. It was the sound of footsteps on the deck above his cabin.

Boot heel and sole in perfect pairing dropping down on the wooden deck above. Step after step was loud and clear to him now. He froze. A chill moved from the top of his head down through his face and neck into his shoulders and sank into his stomach making his nausea all the more pronounced. He looked up at where the sound emanated, following it he traced the footsteps around the back of the wheel-house and to where the door to the small room would be. He stopped breathing.

Without a shadow of doubt he heard the familiar squeak of the wheel-house door open. The footsteps moved inside and the door shut with a deliberate slam. Brigges` heart was pounding not only in his chest but in his head. It was so loud now as to threaten drowning-out his ability to hear anything else. He fixed his eyes upon the stairs that led to the wheel-house. He could not see from where he was, but he knew that the small door was shut at the top of that short flight of stairs.

For a moment there was no more auditory sign that somebody had entered the wheelhouse. Then the small door opened allowing in light from the room above it. Brigges had to stifle a scream. A footstep landed with terrifying menace on the first step. Brigges felt like his heart was going to break through his ribcage and explode outwards. A second step down the short stairs toward him rang through the air like a roll of thunder. Brigges gulped down a breath of air and again held his breath. Another step and he could see the boot and trousers of the person descending the stairs. Another step and he could see clearly the legs of the man intruding into his cabin. Brigges felt feint. He had to breathe, he had held his breath for too long. He let out a puff of air accompanied by a groan. The sound although made by him, increased his feeling of dread and terror all the more. Two more steps down and he could see the torso of the man. He was dressed in clothes that were familiar. But that thought was lost in the abject panic that gripped every inch of his mind and body. Two more steps and Brigges saw who it was; a dead-man entered his cabin.

Brigges ran for the door of his cabin and flung it open so hard that it crashed against the wall. It bounced back and would have cut off Brigges escape but Benjamin was already through the doorway and into the main corridor. He bolted down it in an instant and reaching the galley door flung it open with equal force. Jumping through it, it too bounced off the wall and then slammed shut behind him.

Brigges ran to the counter and looked for the incredible set of knives that Edward had kept there. They were gone. He started to open draws and cupboards with manic speed. Nothing; the knives were no longer there. Turning around he could hear the footsteps in the corridor. They stopped at the door of the galley. It opened slowly and the man stepped through and regarded Brigges with a cold stare.

Chapter 33: Returned

Time stood still. Benjamin looked at the man standing in the galley. His look was returned with a manic smile. Benjamin closed his eyes and opened them several times, each time hoping more than the last that the vision would disappear; it did not.

"No; no!" he somehow managed to say aloud in spite of his throat feeling like it was constricting on him. He knew in his heart that this was different to the visions that he had been experiencing over the last few days. Although not quite sure how he knew this, all he did know was that this was not a figment of his tortured imagination.

"Not going to greet me Captain Brigges? How disappointing, after all we have known each other for so many years!" It took Brigges all of the effort he could to say his next word.

"Albert!?"

"Yes, it is I, your trusted right-hand man and first mate. I wasn't sure that you would recognise me in your current, shall-we-say, fragile condition."

"You couldn't be real? I saw you choked to death, tangled in the rigging. I buried you at sea?" Benjamin's voice was weak, a former shell of its once confident tones.

"Are you sure? I don't feel dead" Albert's tone was mocking. "Come and touch me convince yourself that I am real." Benjamin almost imperceptibly shook his head.

"Come along now Captain, it is important to me that you believe that I am really here and not one of these imagined visitations that you seem to have been experiencing recently." Again, his tone was disdainful, scorning the Captain's weakened hold upon reality. Brigges again refused.

"Well there is nothing to it then, I shall just have to come to you" Albert took two steps toward Brigges. Benjamin let out a loud scream.

"No, God please no; stop!" Benjamin had crouched down and was hiding behind his arms trying to block out the sight of Albert. It had little effect. Albert took two more deliberate steps toward Benjamin and then stopped. Brigges didn't know which was worse, the dead-man encroaching upon him or not advancing. Both felt equally chilling under the circumstances. He whimpered making a sound like a small dog.

"I've been watching you. You have seen things that aren't really there haven't you?" Albert's question did nothing to alleviate the rising terror within Benjamin. He made some more noises and remained cowering behind his hands.

A hand clasped Benjamin's forearm the feeling of which made him scream out and jump so high with terror that he hit his head on the ceiling of the galley and fell in a mess to the ground. Shaking his head, Benjamin tried to clear the ringing in his ears. The pain in his skull somehow managed to help Brigges come almost to his senses again. He looked at his arm where Albert had touched him. He looked at Albert in disbelief.

"You are here! You are real?" Brigges was incredulous. Mercifully keeping a respectable distance Albert nodded affirming the Captain's realisation.

"Oh yes I am definitely real Captain Brigges, as real as you. Surprised to see me?" Albert's tone had a ring of malice in it, lost on Benjamin who was now struggling to make sense of this bizarre situation.

"Yes....yes....but.. how? I buried you at sea, I am sure of it." It was an effort to find the words to begin to question Albert on his sudden appearance.

"You came across my poor dead brother on deck and buried him at sea Captain Brigges not me. We do look alike even though there is about one year between us. Oh yes poor old Finnius his end was quite ironic. He never liked the sea, he was a land lover through and through; now he has been buried at sea. Isn't that funny?" Albert's almost dismissiveness concerning his dead sibling renewed the feeling of dread in Benjamin again.

"What kind of man could be so casual about the death of a family member?" Brigges was horrified, but Albert completely ignored his question. He shook his head and tut tutted.

"No, no no Benjamin; you have to walk before you can run." The quixotic rebuff left Brigges scratching for understanding. He could see that Albert was expecting another question. That was it he suddenly realised; he had to ask a question that Albert wanted to answer. Brigges scrambled for the next most urgent thing that he wanted to know.

"How did you secret your brother aboard for all of this time without any of us seeing him?" Brigges searched Albert's face for some kind of sign that he had now asked a *correct* question. He had. Albert's face almost lit up with glee.

"That's more like it Benjamin. Well, Finnius and I had lunch on the day of departure and I used a poison on him that I came across in Haiti whilst attending the Voodoo practice of raising the dead. It is the poison from a local blow-fish. It causes a state known as a catatonic trance. It looks to the average person like death. Heartbeat and respiration are slowed down to such an extent as to be virtually undetectable. He didn't even see it coming. I blew some of it in his face and the next thing he was effectively dead to the world. I bundled him into my chest and carried him aboard. Simple." Albert looked pleased with himself. Benjamin's mind had picked up on something that Albert had said.

"Carried him aboard in your large chest?" he repeated hoping that whatever distant memory that the scene touched would reveal itself.

"Yes; I am sure that it wasn't very comfortable, but he was hardly in a position to complain now was he?" Albert was amused at the thought of Finnius doubled over in a macabre imitation of a foetus. Benjamin was remembering how what they thought was Albert had been found tangled in the rigging on deck. Then he remembered something that Sandra had said to him.

"How could you have possibly carried him in that chest, he must weigh at least as much as you?" Again Brigges had asked a question that Albert was not disposed to answer. He looked disappointed and shook his head signifying that he had no intention to provide a solution to the vexing problem. Brigges was dismayed, what to do; what to ask?

"That is why your chest had air holes in it. So that Finnius could still breathe?" Brigges realisation pleased Albert, he nodded. But now

Brigges mind was racing to bring more sense to the situation that Albert had described.

"We left port on the eighth of November and reached Santa Maria on the twenty-sixth of November. He would have starved to death even if he was in a *catatonic* trance." Brigges offered his logical conclusion. Albert was nonchalant.

"The effects of the powder wear-off after a few days. I would allow him back to consciousness just enough to feed him some milk or porridge and then put him back to sleep again. After all, I needed to keep him alive if I was going to kill him." Albert waited for another prompt from Benjamin.

"Why..?" he started and immediately realised that it was not a question that would be answered. He altered his line of questioning.

"How did you do it?"

"Ahh that's more like it Captain Brigges! I had always planned to create the illusion of my death after we visited the Azores. This is the longest part of our voyage. What better way than to spend it dead in everybody's eyes so that I could have the run of the ship and get up to all sorts of mischief without any of you suspecting. The fog was just coincidental and a very happy one at that. When you were all at lunch, I tied off the wheel and crept back to my cabin carrying Finnius up on deck. Fortunately he had started to revive from the effects of the poison, but not enough sadly, to stop me from wrapping the rigging rope around his neck and watching him strangle to death. It was quite exhilarating."

Benjamin could scarcely believe his ears. Albert was a friend of his that he had known for years, but this man before him seemed like a complete stranger.

"How can you be so cruel, so..." he had to stop this question mid-way recognising that it was not one that Albert had any intention of answering. Try as he might Benjamin could not think of anything else except how callous Albert was.

"Did you like my pet? I smuggled her aboard as well" he looked malevolently at Brigges sending him cold with fear.

"Pet?" asked Brigges, his voice shaking.

"The boa-constrictor; it was in my other smaller chest, also with air holes so that the poor dear could breathe; also kept fed with milk and the odd mouse that I found in the hold." Benjamin listened with increasing dread.

"You brought that snake aboard?" he said angrily.

"Oh yes, specifically so that your lovely daughter could play with it; sweet little Sara. May she rest in peace" Albert's revelation was bereft of compassion or sympathy for the toddler's demise. Benjamin's anger gave him strength. He lifted himself off the floor and stood up to face Albert.

"You put that thing on my sleeping daughter?" his rage was building.

"And it crushed her like a twig" he replied and started to laugh. Benjamin snapped he bolted forward swinging his fist with all of the might that he could muster. He struck Albert in the face. Albert took the blow and looked at Brigges with bemusement. Brigges called upon his schooling boxing lessons to jab Albert in the stomach and then a right hook again to the face. But none of the blows were having any effect whatsoever. Brigges stepped back suddenly panicked that he was unable to make Albert even flinch.

"Are you quite finished?" Albert asked with distain.

"What are you!?" Brigges screamed at him. He was responded too, with the usual shaking of Albert's head.

"Why did you race in here when you saw me in your cabin Captain? What is it that you hoped to find, something to protect you from a walking dead-man? Perhaps Edward's knives?" he regarded Brigges with contempt. It was clear from his tone that he knew the answers to all of his questions before asking them. This was some kind of charade. Brigges knew that he had no other choice than to continue asking questions that Albert wanted to answer.

"Yes, I wanted to find Edward's knives. What have you done with them?"

"I threw them overboard. Too many knives what was Edward thinking carrying all of them onto such a small ship? I used the same poison on him that I used on Finnius you know." Albert had started to malevolently smile again. It took a while for Brigges to comprehend what he was saying. But the realisation was coming and it felt like a dark cloud threatening to envelope him.

"Sandara too. It wasn't a heart attack; just a catatonic trance." Albert's words stung Benjamin. It felt like he was going to throw up as the comprehension of what Albert was saying gripped him.

"You mean…" he said.

"Oh yes, I assure you Captain Brigges that both Edward and Sandra were very much alive when you buried them both at sea. If only you had waited long enough they would have recovered." Albert started to laugh maniacally. He only broke up his laughing with further taunting.

"So you see. I was not really responsible for their deaths Captain, you were. You may as well have put your gun to their heads and pulled the trigger. Captain Benjamin Brigges: murderer!" He continued to laugh. Benjamin's world fell apart around him. He had prematurely buried his wife at sea. The thought of her trying to breathe whilst she sunk below the water was too much for him. Brigges fainted.

***

When he awoke Albert was standing over him.

"This will never do Captain, get up there is still so much for you to learn." Albert reached down and picked up Benjamin as if he were a rag-doll. Plonking him on his feet he slapped him around the face lightly. It brought Benjamin back to the present.

"How could you let that happen? Why didn't I wait before burying them?" Benjamin could not forgive himself for what he had done. Even now knowing that he had fallen into a trap that Albert had planted for him, did not matter. He felt responsible for Sandra's death and Edward's death. He started to cry, which angered Albert.

"None of that Captain Brigges" he gave Benjamin another slap across his face this one had real strength behind it, it hurt.

"We have to continue our little journey towards the reason that I have done all of this to you. Aren't you interested?"

"Yes" Benjamin heard his own answer, but it sounded like it came from somebody else. However it was true, in spite of the uncanny circumstance in which he found himself. He simply had to know why Albert had planned such an elaborate set of murders on his ship.

Chapter 34: Murders Revealed

"Whom shall we deal with next Captain? I wonder." Albert began to stroll around the confined space of the Galley. This made Brigges more uneasy than having him close at hand. Benjamin looked around furiously for anything that could help defend himself from this maniac. Albert turned swiftly facing Brigges. For a horrible moment Benjamin thought that he had figured out what he was attempting to do. To his relief Albert held up a finger and with a smile said.

"Andrew!"

Brigges curiosity was piqued.

"Yes, Andrew suddenly catching fire like that. How did you do it?" Benjamin was curious now, but continued to dart his attention to anywhere else in the room in the hope of finding aide, whenever he knew that Albert was not looking at him. Albert continued his diatribe of murder.

"One of the oldest school-boy pranks invented Captain. A cup of liquid balanced on the top of a partially opened door, in this case to the forward companion. Albert fell for it completely. Or should I say, it fell on him completely. Although in my inventive improvement of the joke, it was filled with some of our cargo. The alcohol soaked his torso. I was secreted in my cabin at the time. He was furious, let me tell you. He thought that it was one of the others and believe me was not amused in the slightest. I followed him as he went on deck and threw a lit match before he had the chance to say anything to anyone. He went up like a roman candle it was quite a sight even if I do say so myself." Albert finished off his casual description of a hideous murder with a resounding laugh. It made Brigges sick to hear it. He could only imagine the terror of Andrew's last seconds, spent in agonising pain.

"The sharks that attacked him when he flung himself overboard were a welcome surprise even to me. I wager that it was the first time that they had cooked flesh to feast upon." Again Albert roared with laughter. Brigges could barely stand anymore. He closed his eyes and for a brief moment prayed that everything that he had heard and seen were the imagined daemons of a deluded mind. He actually hoped that he had gone insane and that he was imagining Albert and his gruesome explanations.

When he opened his eyes Albert was standing very close to him. Benjamin jumped backwards in alarm.

"Something the matter Captain?" Albert asked with mock concern. Brigges did not dare say what he was thinking. Instead he tried to direct a question at Albert that would meet with approval. He had a good idea of what that question should be.

"Adrian was clearly murdered. His throat cut. There was no hope to explain it away as an accident. Why?" Brigges tried to sound as if he was still in command of the ship and his first mate even though he knew it to be false. His question did have the desired effect; Adrian smiled and nodded.

"Ah yes, Adrian, that would be the next easiest of my murders to explain to you Captain. Let's just say that he fell asleep and I cut him in a way that I knew would bleed him to death. I thought that it was very good of me to wrap him back up in that scarf to soak up all of the blood. Think of the mess that he could have made." He gave Brigges a look of expectation, as if he was waiting for gratitude for the courtesy that had been extended. Brigges was horrified and had no intention of doing so.

"Fell asleep!? He must have noticed you slitting his throat the way that you did?" Again Brigges tried his best to sound forceful. Just for a split-second Brigges thought that he had angered Albert with his question. He steeled himself for a reprisal.

"Let us just say that the clever way that I disposed of Bill has some relevance to why Adrian did not wake up as I was making my slowly lethal cuts." The statement only served to cloud the issue.

"What do you mean?" asked Brigges perplexed at the reference to Bill's death. How could they be connected except for the person whose hand they died at?

"I take it that he did not somehow become entangled in the anchor just before it released itself?" Brigges waited for an answer. Albert met his question with silence. He was not shaking his head, so he knew that the question had not been rejected but he was not gleefully answering it either.

Albert took a step backwards. His face was sullen. Then the strangest thing that Brigges had seen in all of his days happened. Right before his eyes, just like a bullfrog, Albert's throat swelled up to be twice, no more than that, three times its normal size. Brigges instinctively stepped backwards in horror and tripped on something that was behind him, he did not see what, and fell on his backside to the deck.

With a loud whooping swooshing sound Albert expelled the air that had swollen his neck and spat out a small thing that landed directly between Brigges outstretched legs. He jumped a little out of fright, then looked closer at the thing that was in-between his legs. It was a small black sea urchin, round, black with spike tendrils protruding from it in every direction. He was appalled. He looked at Albert incredulously.

"You regurgitated that? You ate it? And spat it out? How? What?" he fumbled for the words to convey what he was thinking. It was almost unbelievable, but there it was there in front of him. Albert was making no further attempt to talk to him at the moment. Shaking his head in disbelief and disgust he reached forward to pick up the thing just to prove to himself that it was real.

"I wouldn't touch that if I were you Captain!" Albert's overly loud warning startled Brigges. He snatched his hand backwards like he had just touched a naked flame.

"Why?" he asked.

"It secretes a poison that makes the recipient very susceptible to suggestion." The explanation from Albert did absolutely nothing to enlighten Brigges.

"What? How? How did you get it in your stomach? Why aren't you affected by it?" Brigges could see that Albert was not prepared to answer his queries. He had to find a question that Albert would answer.

"Bill, had one of these in the back of his neck when we pulled him up."

"Yes, he was only too glad to wrap himself in the anchor chain when I asked him to. I do believe that he was smiling as I released it plunging him into the ocean. The most pleasing thing about Bill's death was that the water would have snapped him out of his little trance. He would have been very aware of what was happening to him the moment he hit the water." Again the proud announcement of another successful murder drew a raucous round of laughter from Albert. When he managed to settle himself it was only to ask ghastly rhetorical questions.

"Do you think that he tried to hold his breath? Or struggle with the chain? He would have been in an absolute frenzy as he was dragged below the waves." Albert's amusement at the grisly deaths that he had masterminded was gut-wrenching. Brigges own thoughts turned to his own death. Surely Albert had something equally as hideous in store for him. Without realising it he had begun to shake.

"Captain!" Albert's loud call snapped Brigges attention back on to the murderer standing before him.

"You look cold. I can see that you are shaking. And you look pale. Come up on deck and get some fresh air. It is a beautiful day."

The offer filled Brigges with dread. Was this where Albert intended to kill him? By his reckoning he only had to hear how Hans and Vaughn were killed by the maniac before he ran out of people to question Albert about. Then for sure it would be his turn. Brigges shook his head.

"Come along now Captain Brigges, I will not take no for an answer". Albert stepped forward and appeared to be reaching down to aid Brigges to his feet. He was mistaken. Instead Albert plucked the small black sea urchin from the deck and opened his mouth, wider than any one he had seen before. Albert deposited it in his mouth and swallowed. Brigges could actually see the lump travel down Albert's throat and disappear into his torso. Albert smiled at Brigges and offered him his hand.

Brigges scrambled to his feet eschewing the offer of help. He pointed at the door leading to the main corridor and said.

"After you Mister Richards" This garnered a look of surprise from Albert.

"No Captain, surely after you" he retorted.

"Really, now it is my turn to insist. I have nowhere to run Albert. What do you think that I am going to do? I have already failed to overpower you once. I shall not make that mistake a second time." Brigges tried with all of his might to give Albert a pleasant look. He did not know if he succeeded or not, but Albert did acquiesce.

"As you wish Captain" he marched over to the door and opened it widely and looked back at Brigges expectantly. Benjamin nodded.

"Right behind you" he followed Albert out of the galley and into the corridor. They reached the mid-ship without Albert looking back to check upon Brigges whereabouts. Brigges looked around furiously and his eyes saw something that he may be able to use. Albert turned to face him.

"Your turn" he said politely indicating that Brigges should climb the steeply arched staircase-ladder. Brigges of course refused. He would need Albert to climb up first if he was to enable his hastily created plan.

"No Albert, please, after you" he said as politely as he could muster. Giving a small dismissive snort, Albert turned and began climbing up the ladder. Brigges reached over for the oil lamp that was hanging in the corridor and hastily followed Albert making his steps on the wooden step-rungs louder than he would normally to assure Albert that he was indeed following.

The brass and glass oil lamp was lit. He could feel that it still had oil in it. He recalled filling it at some point over the last day or so but could not for the like of him now remember exactly when that was.

Albert disappeared through the hatchway and as Brigges neared the top rung with his hand he gingerly placed the lamp on the top run of the step. It would still be below the final step up to the deck so would be out of Albert's sight. Brigges navigated around the carefully placed lamp and scurried on deck so that he would not raise the suspicions of Albert. It took all of his will power to not look backwards down the steep stairs to ensure that the lamp was still safely there. Instead he looked right into the eyes of Albert who was waiting for him.

"You are correct Mister Richards, it is a fine day indeed". He looked around him. It was a true statement. There was a good wind blowing. The sails were billowing. A few beautiful white clouds were scattered in the perfect blue sky. The sun was shining.

Brigges could not believe the irony. This could very well be the last day of his life. He was surely soon to be killed at the hands of a maniacal murderer. How could it be such a perfect day on the day that he was about to die.

Chapter 35: Siphonophore

"I think that it is time that I asked you about Vaughn" Brigges took the initiative and set the agenda for the continuance of their conversation. This pleased Albert immensely and it showed on his face. Brigges remained strategically near to the access way. He stood his ground as if he had made a decision that that is where he wanted to be to hear about how Albert had surreptitiously murdered his crewman.

Albert scratched his chin as if weighing up what he was about to say. The response was not what Benjamin was expecting.

"I will tell you if you tell me why you threw him overboard?" Albert seemed genuinely interested in the odd behaviour from the Captain. This made Brigges very self-conscious and he shifted in his spot uneasily. He looked down as if ashamed of what he was about to day.

"I couldn't bear the thought of conducting another service for the departed." The answer was brief but it explained Benjamin's mental state at the time. Albert was surprisingly empathetic.

"I understand Captain Brigges; I really do. So many deaths in such a short period of time; it must have been very difficult for you?" Albert's question had the ring of being rhetorical, but Benjamin wasn't sure. He elected to not even try to answer such an obvious conclusion.

"For my own part, Vaughn's death had a certain lack of finesse to it compared to the others. I swung the boom around on him when he wasn't looking. It snapped his neck like a piece of straw." Albert smiled broadly at the memory of Vaughn's last seconds of life.

"And of course I had to throw that nasty gun overboard. I couldn't risk it falling into your hands now could I? That weapon may have actually have had some hope of hurting me". Upon hearing Albert admit this, Benjamin wished more than anything that he was holding that gun in his hands right now.

"But you have yet to ask me about Hans, Captain Brigges?" The sentence cut through Benjamin like a knife. Seeing that it had an unsettling effect on Brigges Albert mocked him.

"You surely don't think that he is still alive out there somewhere floating around in the row boat? Come now Captain Brigges what kind of murderous mastermind would I be if I had let him escape my clutches. I assure you that he is quite dead."

"How?" Brigges asked. His heart began to beat faster filling his neck with blood that he could feel pumping through his veins. This was it, the final murder revealed. Next would be his own.

"I boarded him at night when he was asleep. But just before I tell you exactly how I killed him, perhaps you would now ask me some of the more urgent questions that you have on your mind. Don't be shy, I won't stop you anymore".

This was unexpected. Brigges froze for a moment.

"How did you spit that sea urchin from your mouth? Was this another trick that you learned in Haiti at the hands of your Voodoo magicians?" Brigges did his best to try and prepare himself for whatever the answer would be. He in fact dreaded it. He had led Albert toward an answer that he hoped would explain what he had seen. Some way for him to rationalise what had happened. Albert looked offended.

"You disappoint me Captain Brigges. An educated man like you thinking that it is all about Voodoo practices. I assure you the reality is far removed from anything that you could possibly imagine." Albert began to pace in a circle whilst he divulged to Brigges the truth about himself.

"I am not a human being Captain Brigges. I thought that would have been obvious to you. I am a Siphonophore. At least that is what your learned naturalist Charles Darwin would call me." He paused awaiting a reaction from Brigges. Benjamin's mind raced. He had heard the word before, but where? Somewhere back in his days of being schooled. And the reference to Charles Darwin the naturalist had something to do with his knowing the word. Siphonophore? He said it to himself over and over in his mind. Then there was a flash of realisation.

"A Portuguese man-o-war!? A jellyfish!?" Brigges produced the explanation of the word in an eruption of remembrance.

"Exactly Captain. That is precisely what I am. Oh not the kind that you have ever come across before, but essentially an evolved jellyfish." Albert stopped pacing long enough to applaud Brigges for his elucidation. He started to walk in a small circle again looking up at the sky, out to see and back at Brigges as he continued his account.

"I became self-aware about five years ago. I existed off the coast of Portugal as a sea creature, an organism that is made up of other living creatures, and together we form one being. You call our species Siphonophore. Imagine my surprise when we stung a man that was swimming off shore and realised that we could attach ourselves to him and absorb the information that was stored in his brain. We became immediately imbued with all of the knowledge that he had ever learned. It was exhilarating. Suddenly we knew that we were a sea-creature and that there was an entire world of land-dwelling creatures that we had never known before. We simply had to know more. Another hapless swimmer provided more information. But this time not just about humanity, but about ourselves too. You see this time instead of just sucking out all of the information stored in his brain, we were able to change our own form. We took on the shape of the human that we had gleaned knowledge from.

It took a lot of effort, make no mistake Captain. And in order to nurture our strength for the transformation, it was necessary to digest most of his body." Albert stopped walking and looked directly at Benjamin.

"You are not Albert Richards, you just look like him." Brigges summation was validated.

"Yes! He stupidly went swimming before attending that Voodoo ceremony that he had arranged to go to. We had been on the island disguised as a human and had become fascinated with him. His curiosity, his zest for learning about other-worldly things, Albert was quite an adventurous fellow. We followed him into the water, and absorbed him. In an instant we knew everything that he knew and became an exact replica of Albert. It was we who attended the ceremony to raise the dead. We who convinced the Voodoo witch-doctor to part with some of that precious powdered blow-fish poison." Albert paused again. Brigges mind seemed to be telling him something. There was a point that Albert had made that now seemed very important. What was it? Albert was leading him to a conclusion. The image of Hans appeared in Benjamin's mind. Albert had not told him what had happened to Hans.

"Hans. You said that you crept aboard the row-boat whilst he slept" Brigges said nervously.

"To digest him Captain; we were hungry and tired of waiting for the one meal that we really wanted. You commented during the voyage about how Albert did not have the appetite that you recalled. That is because our need is for living flesh, blood, muscle, sinew and bone. We can live for a long time between meals. But now the time has come for us to eat again." Captain Benjamin Brigges world stood still for an eternity within a second. He was to be the meal that this thing would now eat.

"And now you see Captain, everything that has led to this moment. We want to increase our knowledge more and have chosen you to be that conduit. We want to live for a time in polite society and mingle with your kind; none of them suspecting that we are what we are." Albert looked like he had finished telling Brigges everything that he was going to tell him.

"But I still don't know why you did all of this?

"All of this Captain Brigges? The skilfully planned murders? Watching your mind deteriorate beneath the burden of death after death. That is the reason that we did it all Benjamin. All of it was simply amusing for us, nothing more; a way to pass the time of this tedious voyage.

You know something? I had planned to murder Sandra whilst we were in port at Santa Maria. I followed you up to the fort and waited for an opportunity to separate you and Sara from her. But I thought the better of it. It would be more amusing to have you be responsible for her death. And besides, I couldn't take the chance that upon her untimely death, you may cancel the rest of the voyage and return to New York."

Benjamin could scarcely believe his ears. The Siphonophore was completely bereft of care for human life. He knew that it would be pointless to plead for his life. There was nothing resembling mercy in the envelope that housed these creatures living together as one. Brigges began to crouch down. He hoped that Albert, or the creatures that looked like Albert would misinterpret it as a signal of complete and utter defeat.

He twisted his body around to face away from the thing, thus shielding what he was really doing. Reaching down he grabbed the lamp and brought it to his chest clutching it for dear life.

"I see that you are intelligent enough to accept your fate Benjamin. We are much stronger than your species. That was how I managed to carry Finnius aboard in my chest with such apparent ease. Come; let me end your suffering." Albert praised the Captain's lack of resistance to the inevitable.

"I would like to say that this won't hurt a bit, but I am certain that it will be excruciating." Albert laughed at his cruel jibe. Brigges summoned every bit of willpower that he could. He focussed upon Sandra and Sara. He would avenge their deaths as well as the deaths of everybody else that had died at the hands of this monster.

Straightening up but still facing away from Albert he listened. He wanted Albert to be a little closer before he attacked.

Becoming impatient, the Siphonophore took a step forward. Brigges turned up the flame on the lamp so that it sprung into a tall flickering column of fire. Spinning around he took aim and hurled the lamp with all of the force that he could muster at Albert. It shattered and immediately exploded with flame covering Albert. The Siphonophore screamed aloud in a shrill that was incapable of coming from a human's throat.

Rushing forward Benjamin threw himself at the creature engulfed in flames feet first. He landed two feet directly mid-torso and kicked with the soles of his shoes as he made contact. The Siphonophore fell backwards overboard and Brigges fell onto the deck.

Gathering himself up he ran to the side and looked over. There was no sign of the thing anywhere. The waves lapped against the side of the boat. There was nothing else. He raced down the side of the ship thinking that he may simply be looking in the wrong place. Perhaps the ship was moving faster than he thought and it was further behind than where he had anticipated to see the body. He was still looking overboard when he heard two loud steps behind him.

He spun around in fright. The creature was standing there staring malevolently at him. It must have swum beneath the ship and climbed aboard on the other side. Brigges heart skipped a beat. There was nothing to help him. He turned to run.

"There is nowhere to run Captain Brigges; nowhere to hide!" The creature hissed venomously at him. In an instant Brigges thought to use the boom to try and do to the Siphonophore what it had done to

Vaughn. He ran to the back of the boat. Turning he saw that Albert was following slowly.

There was no hope. If that thing really was stronger than him then he would need more than a swinging boom to tackle it. He concocted a plan in an instant of time. He would untie the wheel and steer into the wind making it easier for him to catch a favourable wind that would hopefully provide strength enough to whack this thing back to the ocean from which it came. The insanely impossible odds of achieving this miracle did not have time to occur to Brigges. He ran to the wheel house and slammed the door shut locking it behind him.

Albert had a malevolent smile on his face and looked to be simply strolling upon the deck, in no particular hurry to get anywhere. Brigges looked up at the sails billowing with wind. He spun the wheel to alter the direction of the Ship. Stage one of his plan was done.

"Open the door Captain Brigges" Benjamin looked through the porthole of the door to the wheel house. The thing was there looking at him.

"Come now Benjamin, you want to open the door for me don't you?" For some inexplicable reason, he did. There was a burning sensation in the back of his neck. Brigges absent-mindedly reached around to find out what was causing it. He felt the points of what must surely be one of those small black sea-urchins embedded in his skin. But it did not matter. All that he wanted to do was comply with what Albert wanted. It would make him very happy to do so. He took a step toward the door.

"That's it Benjamin, open the door for me. I don't want to break it down, even though I am more than capable of doing so. I would rather that you open the door for me."

"Yes" responded Brigges in a small weak voice. He reached out and unlatched the lock. Albert opened the door and entered the small room.

"Excellent. Now turn around." Benjamin complied. Unseen the Siphonophore began to lose its cohesive shape; the form that looked exactly like Albert Richards. It became gelatinous and covered the head of Captain Brigges. The jelly like substance penetrated his ears and his nose pushing upwards and inwards. The jelly penetrating him was cold, it jolted him out of his trance and he realised exactly what was happening to him. Opening his mouth he screamed the longest loudest most anguished scream of his life.

The Siphonophore sent even more jelly down Brigges throat stifling the scream. Soon the head of Captain Brigges was completely enveloped. Next his, torso and the remainder of his body were covered with the creature. Captain Brigges was eaten alive by the thing and raped of every bit of knowledge that he had ever learned in the process.

Chapter 36: The Dei Gratias

Captain Moorebank strained to see more detail through his spyglass. He turned to his first mate.

"It is definitely the Mary Celeste, but I cannot see anyone on deck. This is very peculiar indeed. Prepare a boarding party Mister Deveaux, they may be below and in need of assistance" His first mate jumped into action.

"Prepare the row-boat!" he followed this by shouting three names of the people that would accompany him over to the wayward ship. Captain Moorebank went back to looking at the Mary Celeste through his spyglass.

"Benjamin. What has happened?" he said to nobody. His second mate however was standing close enough to hear his words.

"Captain?" he inquired. Realising that he had been wondering about his friends fate aloud Moorebank used the opportunity to bark some more orders.

"See if you can hail them. Do your best Mister Webb" his voice was laden with concern and it was clearly affecting his general demeanour. The second mate scurried away to do as he was told.

***

Captain Moorebank had skilfully piloted the De Gratias as close to the Mary Celeste as he dared. The conditions were good, but the Mary Celeste was not being steered and could easily veer into his ship. The row boat was sent over and they boarded the stricken ship. Oliver Deveaux and his three men searched the boat. There was no sign of anybody. They moved together from the wheel-house and then down into the Captain's cabin. Huddled together they later described a feeling of dread pervaded the ship and it caused them enough anxiety to not want to separate during the search of the ship. Finding cabin after cabin completely empty only served to heighten their feeling of fear.

The search of the lower deck was fear-provoking enough, but then the need to descend into the cargo hold was positively scary. The men all decided that it was best to go together. They tenuously did an inspection of the cargo. One of the men still had enough presence of mind to do a barrel count so that it could be included in their report back to the Captain.

***

Oliver Deveaux reported back to Captain Moorebank who perplexed at the whereabouts of his old friend and his friend's wife.

"Nothing? No sign of where they could be?" he asked incredulously.

"The row boat is missing Captain, they must have abandoned ship?" offered Oliver.

"But why? By your own description the Mary Celeste is still seaworthy. What could have possibly made them leave it and take to the sea in their rowboat?" Oliver did not answer, unsure of whether or not the question was rhetorical. Moorebank was facing a mountain of questions and absolutely no answers.

"The Sextant and spyglass are missing too Captain" offered Oliver in an attempt to support his assertion that the crew for no good reason abandoned their ship. There was another awkward pause whilst Moorebank tried to fathom what he was hearing.

"What shall we do with it Sir?" asked Oliver. The ship's disposition was the last thing on Moorebank's mind. The safely of the disappeared crew and passengers however were. He tried to clear his head. This was important and had to be dealt with right now. Bizarrely it helped to ease Moorebank's puzzlement about the disappearance of the Captain, Passengers and crew.

"Under international salvage laws we will take it over. Prepare a crew. We will furnish you with the necessary navigational equipment. You will take command in my name and make for Gibraltar. When you make port there, report to the authorities. Do you understand?" Moorebank did the only logical thing that he could think of.

"Yes Captain" replied Deveaux and hurried away to make himself ready to take command of the Mary Celeste.

Moorebank looked out to see lost in thought about Sandra, Sara and Benjamin. "What could have happened to them?" he said aloud to nobody. He began to fret about how he was going to write up this peculiar event in his log.

He did not see it, nobody aboard the Dei Gratias did, but a shape was lurking below the water where Captain Moorebank stood. Had he seen it, he would have then noticed it drifting away; almost as if were deliberately leaving the two ships to their own devices. Without realising it Captain Moorebank and his crew were being spared by the Siphonophore. It amused the twisted sense of humour of the creature, to leave behind it a mystery that people would ponder, talk about and argue over for many years to come. The creature decided to swim in the direction of the British Isles. That is where it would take its newly acquired knowledge. It would live amongst the citizens of a grand city there and blend into the crowd. Already it was planning to murder more people in the grizzliest ways possible that it could imagine.

The End

Connect with Aenghus Chisholme

Visit my website on www.aenghuschisholme.com

Works by Aenghus Chisholme

Merlin the Sorcerer AD 491

King Arthur is facing a war with the murderous Saxon Lord Aelle over the artisan land of Anderidae. Unknown to him magical forces have conspired with Aelle to ensure Arthur's defeat.

Guinevere the Queen AD 494

Queen Gwenhwyvar and Sorceress Morgan Le Fay pursue the stolen Excalibur to a magical labyrinth where it is guarded by powerful Minotaur.

Sir Gawain and the Green Knight AD 499

An animated corpse has Sir Guaen in its sights. How can you kill something that is already dead?

Arthur the King AD 517

Caught in an untenable situation King Arthur is manoeuvred into a battle he cannot possibly win.

Murder on the Mary Celeste

One by one, the passengers and crew aboard the merchant ship Mary Celeste are being picked-off by an unseen assassin.

Jack the Ripper: The murder of Madam Athalia

A clever young detective thinks that he can outwit the most cunning killer in the history of London.

The Best Things in Life Begin with the Letter B

Consumerism can lead to happiness, providing you know exactly what it is that will make you happy. Enjoy a tour of the material and immaterial world of the exclusive and the everyday.

Commissioned works

I am available to write something for you; fiction or non-fiction. Contact me through my website and tell me what you have in mind.

www.ingramcontent.com/pod-product-compliance
Lightning Source LLC
LaVergne TN
LVHW091020080826
845145LV00002B/303